THERE WAS SILVER IN THE HILLS . . .
AND BLOOD ON THE LAND.

Mike Wakefield—The big, burly stage driver, he was a man with dreams linked to a lovely woman . . . and nightmares tied to memories of the Orient.

Ku Xuan—The mysterious half-Chinese beauty, she was on a quest for her father, but her heritage was the reason someone had decided she must die.

Cole Granger—A no-account highwayman, he was a dangerous low-down cur who would kill anyone for two bits . . . or Mike Wakefield for just the pleasure of it.

James Beckett—A former sea captain, he had been a missing person for nearly twenty years, now he'd come back to face his past . . . and die if he must.

Li Chen—A trained assassin, he was master of every deadly skill of murder . . . and his mission was to eliminate Ku Xuan and the man she loved.

The Stagecoach Series
Ask your bookseller for the books you have missed

STAGECOACH STATION 40:

SILVERADO

Hank Mitchum

Created by the producers of
**Wagons West, The Badge,
Abilene,** and **Faraday.**

Book Creations Inc., Canaan, NY · Lyle Kenyon Engel, Founder

BANTAM BOOKS
TORONTO · NEW YORK · LONDON · SYDNEY · AUCKLAND

SILVERADO

A Bantam Book / published by arrangement with
Book Creations, Inc.

Bantam edition / March 1989

Produced by Book Creations, Inc.
Lyle Kenyon Engel, Founder

ISBN 0-553-27766-9

Published simultaneously in the United States and Canada

Bantam Books are published by Bantam Books, a division of Bantam
Doubleday Dell Publishing Group, Inc. Its trademark, consisting of
the words "Bantam Books" and the portrayal of a rooster, is
Registered in U.S. Patent and Trademark Office and in other
countries. Marca Registrada. Bantam Books, 666 Fifth Avenue,
New York, New York 10103.

PRINTED IN THE UNITED STATES OF AMERICA

O   0 9 8 7 6 5 4 3 2 1

STAGECOACH STATION 40:

SILVERADO

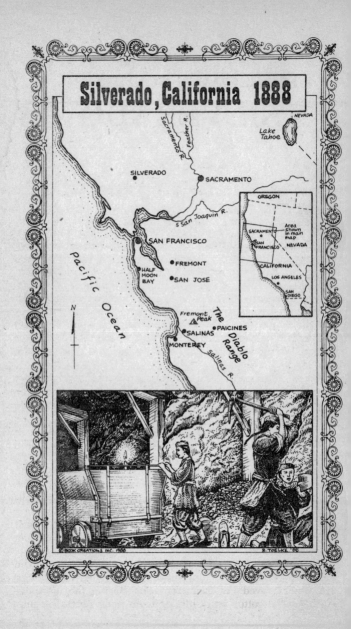

Silverado, California 1888

Chapter One

The late spring sun beat down directly overhead as a large wagon pulled by a team of four powerful dray horses wended its way up the dusty mountain road toward the field office of the Silverado Mining Company. Lying in the bed of the heavy, slow-moving wagon was a cargo of steel bracing for shoring up tunnels at the mine, and sitting on the front seat was the driver, thirty-two-year-old Mike Wakefield. The steel was being delivered at the personal order of the mine's owner, Walter St. John, who had also insisted that Mike be the one to deliver it.

Although normally found behind a six-hitch team, on the driver's box of a Concord coach belonging to the California Stage and Freight Company, Mike was not being derelict in his duty, for St. John also owned the stage company. Mike was St. John's top driver on either conveyance, and when critical equipment had to be delivered promptly, the mine owner frequently used him for the task.

Reaching the mine site, Mike pulled his team over to the place where his cargo would be unloaded. He set the brake on the wagon and hopped down from the driver's seat, stretching his six-foot frame to work out the aches acquired during the long trip from San Francisco. He had started out just after dawn, first taking a ferry across the bay and then driving north to the mine.

The sun, just beginning its descent, reminded him of the appetite he had built up during the hot, grueling trip. He had removed his buckskin jacket during the morning, and the blue cotton workshirt he wore underneath was now

1

sweat stained, clinging to his powerfully built chest and broad shoulders. A handsome, dark-haired man, Mike had a strong chin and a mouth that seemed always to be on the verge of a smile, as if he were perpetually amused by some private joke—although his penetrating blue eyes could turn cold in an instant.

The driver had been coming to the Silverado mine for years, but the mining operation still fascinated him, and he looked around eagerly at the sights, sounds, and smells of the place. Zigzagging wooden trestles supporting the tracks for the ore cars made a filligree on the face of Mount Diablo. White wisps of steam feathered out of the vents of the press mill, and its cylinder steam pipe boomed loudly, as though the place were under a cannonading. Boiling out of the high smokestack was a large plume of black smoke, its sulfurous odor blending with the more pleasing smells from the dozens of makeshift kitchens of the Chinese and American cooks serving their respective workers. And from those workers came a constant stream of talk, an occasional laugh, and frequent oaths.

While Mike was removing the heavy brown tarpaulin covering his cargo, two Chinese coolies passed the wagon, moving in the peculiar shuffling gait that looked odd to most Americans. Putting their palms together, the coolies bowed their heads slightly toward Mike, in a gesture of respect. As he mirrored their gestures, Mike knew that his understanding and appreciation of the Chinese were the reasons that St. John liked to send him on trips to the mine, where so many Chinese workers were employed. Indeed, one of the reasons St. John had hired him in the first place was that Mike had spent time in China in his youth, where he had learned the Mandarin language (the primary dialect of that vast country) and gained respect for the Chinese culture and work ethic.

When he had finished uncovering the steel beams, Mike crossed to the mine office, a roughly built wooden shack that was halfway between the press mill and the main mine entrance. Pausing on the porch, glad to be out of the hot sun, he knocked once on the door and entered.

Lon Dumey, the mine manager, was sitting at his desk, his face hidden behind the latest edition of the *San Francisco Chronicle,* dated May 28, 1888. The front page was facing Mike, and he could clearly read the headlines:

WALTER ST. JOHN ENLARGES OPERATIONS
AT SILVERADO MINING COMPANY
Tunnels to Be Lengthened
New Shafts to Be Dug

Putting down the paper, Dumey said, "Afternoon, Wakefield. What have you got for me today?"

"Steel bracing for the shoring in number three shaft," Mike answered.

Dumey stared at Mike and leaned back in his chair. "I didn't order nothin' like that."

"I know. Mr. St. John did—after he took a look at the shaft last week. He said to tell you he wants the bracing in place before there's any more blasting."

Sniffing derisively, Dumey declared, "He's a little late for that." He stood up and walked past Mike to the doorway, then stepped out onto the porch.

"What do you mean?" Mike asked, following him outside.

Dumey pointed toward the mine entrance, fifty yards away. "Hell, we've been blastin' in there all mornin', and nothin's happened. You go back and tell Mr. St. John to save his money." Then he laughed and added, "Or better yet, give me and my men an increase in wages instead."

Mike shook his head. "Look, I don't want to have to stand here and argue with you, but—"

"Fire in the hole!"

"Fire in the hole!"

"Fire in the hole!"

The standard warning of blasting about to begin was being carried from man to man.

"We're ready to set off another charge," Dumey said with a shrug. "Ain't no way I can stop 'em now."

There was a muffled, hollow thump, and Mike could feel the ground shake. Smoke and dust poured out of the mouth of the shaft, and when the dust settled, Dumey grinned smugly.

"See what I mean? Nothin' to worry about. Now, why don't you take your bracin' back to St. John and tell him we don't need it. I get paid by the yard of material I take out of that mine, and I ain't gonna waste any of my valuable time shorin' up a shaft that don't need shorin'."

Mike made no move to leave. "Dumey, whether you put

the bracing in or not is between you and Mr. St. John—but my bet is you'll either put it in or you'll be working somewhere else. And speaking of wasting valuable time, I've got better things to do than stand here and argue with you. My instructions are to deliver this steel to you, and that's just what I intend to do."

With the manager trailing behind him, Mike walked over to the wagon. He had just started loosening the cargo tie-down ropes when he heard the first faint shouts. As the words were repeated, he strained to hear what the miners were saying.

"Missed shot!" a miner just inside the shaft entrance yelled, and everyone outside stopped what they were doing and looked toward the mine with apprehension.

The driver, too, knew what it meant, and his blood ran cold. When placing charges in a tunnel wall, the miners generally used a pattern of seven holes and charges. In the center of the face to be blasted, they drilled three holes about two feet apart, arranging them in a triangle. Then they drilled a "reliever" hole at the top of the face, "edger" holes at each side, and a "lifter" at the bottom. The explosions had to be timed so that the center charges would go off first, creating a cavity into which the slightly delayed blasts on the top and sides could squeeze the surrounding rock. Finally, the lifter blew the rubble out into the tunnel, where it would be accessible for loading into hopper cars.

Occasionally one of the sticks of dynamite would fail to detonate, creating a dangerous situation. The unexploded charge could be located easily, since it would be in a mound of rock protruding from the face, but it had to be removed with great care by someone who knew exactly what he was doing. Mike, feeling greatly relieved that he was out in the open air and not down in the mine shaft, wondered how the miners could so casually work in the bowels of the earth, with all the attendant dangers.

Suddenly there was a low rumble and another cloud of dust gushed up from the shaft.

"A cave-in!" one of the miners shouted. "My God, there's been a cave-in!"

Mike's heart started to race, and he suddenly felt clammy all over.

The shout started a panic, and all the other miners, both Chinese and American—even those not working near the stricken tunnel—started running out of the shaft, for a collapse was the most terrifying danger facing a miner.

It was not a total collapse, Mike knew, for there wasn't enough dirt for that. Also, a total collapse would have sent a much larger gust of air whooshing out, as though it had been blasted by a giant bellows. But a partial collapse was just as dangerous for those miners laboring in the tunnel that was affected.

"I . . . I don't see how that could have happened," Dumey stammered, staring in shock at the mine entrance.

The driver looked sharply at the mine manager and growled, "Well, it looks like Mr. St. John knew what he was talking about."

Realizing that the collapse was restricted to the deepest part of the shaft, the workers who had run out in panic began drifting back toward the entrance of the mine in twos and threes.

"We've got to get 'em out!" one of the men shouted.

Walking over to stand with them, Mike stared as they did into the gaping black maw of the shaft. "How many men are left inside?" he asked.

One of the miners, his eyes gleaming from a face blackened with coal dust, looked over at Mike. "Maybe four or five white men."

"How many all told?"

"I don't know. Countin' coolies . . . probably around twenty."

"Twenty? You mean there are twenty men trapped in there?" Barely able to control his anger, Mike looked over at Dumey and called incredulously, "You sent twenty men into an unshored tunnel?"

"Like the man said, they're mostly Chinese," Dumey replied.

"Dumey, you have to organize a rescue party to go down there," Mike demanded of the callous manager.

"Who's he gonna get?" one of the miners asked. "You sure ain't gonna catch *me* goin' down there, so long as that missed shot's still alive."

"Me neither," another added. "I ain't gonna risk my life to save no chinks."

Coming up beside Mike, Dumey shrugged. "You hear what they're sayin'. Seems to me like the best thing to do would be to blow up the offshoot tunnel and relieve the pressure so's no more of the shaft collapses. That'll keep anyone else from gettin' hurt."

"What about the men who are in there now?"

"There's only five white men, and like as not they're already dead. I say there's no sense in riskin' the lives of any more men just to try and bring out their bodies so's they can be buried all over again."

"You don't know that they're dead," Mike challenged.

"If they ain't yet, they soon will be. The pressure's gonna cause that missed shot to go any minute, and that's gonna bring down the rest of the shaft."

"You're not even going to *try* to get the men out?"

"I know it sounds bad, but I'm just lookin' out for the livin'," Dumey said defensively.

"Sure . . . as long as the living are white men." Mike stared disbelievingly at the man for a moment. Then without a second thought he took a carbide lamp from one of the miners and, grabbing a pickax, started toward the shaft.

"Mister, you got any idea what the hell you're doin'?" one of the miners called. "It's damn near suicide to go down in there with a missed shot! That stick goes off, the rest of the shaft'll be comin' down on top of you!"

"Let him go," Mike heard Dumey growl. "If he wants to be a hero, I ain't gonna stop him."

Mike would not have called himself heroic; he simply considered all human life precious, whether the person was white, black, red, or yellow. He knew that this sentiment put him in a minority, for most Americans—like these mine workers—considered the Chinese a lower race. The irony, he reflected as he made his way into the shaft, was that most Chinese felt the same way about non-Orientals. Any Chinese who made friends with an American felt that he was being very magnanimous in accepting a Westerner as his equal.

The offshoot tunnel was at a right angle to the main shaft, so that within a few yards all light from the entrance was gone. Holding up the carbide lamp, Mike flipped the friction wheel a couple of times with the palm of his hand. The wick popped, and then the lamp came on, hissing loudly. It sent out a narrow beam that lit up the area of the tunnel directly ahead but left the recesses on either side in utter blackness.

With the carbide lamp showing the way, Mike continued down into the tunnel, moving through the rubble and broken shoring. He found the offshoot tunnel to be considerably smaller than the main shaft, and if he had put his arms out, he could have touched the walls on either side. The roof was also lower, although he could still walk upright, and the tunnel descended into the mountain at a much steeper angle than did the main shaft. The farther he walked, the deeper he got, until he began to feel as if he were descending to the very core of the earth.

"Damn, does this tunnel go all the way to hell?" Mike asked aloud. Although not in the habit of talking to himself, he found that the closeness of the mine troubled him far more than he had thought it would. He felt a sense of foreboding beyond anything attributable to the immediate danger of another collapse, and he knew he would have felt this way even if there was no chance of a cave-in. "It can't be much farther," he told himself hopefully, taking some comfort in the sound of his own voice.

The floor beneath him suddenly leveled out, and Mike realized that he was no longer in a narrow passageway but in a fairly large chamber. Shining the light around, he saw that the walls of this chamber had been thoroughly worked so that it was much wider and higher than the offshoot tunnel.

"Thank you, *shih*, for coming," said a voice that was obviously strained and frightened, yet nonetheless used the formal Chinese term of respect. The disembodied voice came from somewhere in the darkness that was as black as pitch, and Mike played the beam of his lamp around, trying to find its owner.

"Where are you?"

"I am over here, *shih*."

Mike turned the beam of light toward the sound and saw a fresh pile of rubble and a large, shattered wooden beam. Beneath the collapsed timber and rubble was an old Chinese man with a long, wispy beard. He was pinned to the chamber floor, lying with one leg under the timber and the other grotesquely bent beneath his own body. The man's expression was pinched and drawn, and the color had left his face. Mike knew that the old man had to be in intense pain, and he marveled that he was not screaming in agony. Then he realized that he knew who it was.

"I know you. You are Kwai Fong, the powderman." Mike knew that for mine owners like St. John, the expertise of the

Chinese in the handling of explosives and dynamite—or "giant powder" as it was called—was invaluable, and frequently the man placed in charge of blasting was Chinese.

Despite his predicament, Kwai Fong managed a weak smile. "I am flattered that you recognize me, *shih*."

Mike looked around the chamber. "Are there any others here?"

"They are all on the other side of that wall of rock," Kwai Fong said, gesturing with his head. "Strike your pick against the stone three times to let them know you are here, and they will strike back to answer you. Then count the number of blows you will hear after that, and that will tell you the number of men who are trapped."

Mike knocked the pickax against the collapsed pile of rock and debris three times. His rap was answered, and then there was a series of measured raps, seventeen in all.

"Seventeen still alive," Mike breathed. He looked bleakly at the seemingly solid wall of rubble that separated the others from the passage out.

"I think it will not be too difficult to free them, once you have completed your task," Kwai Fong told him.

The old man's voice seemed even more strained, and Mike realized he must be suffering terribly. Knowing how highly the Chinese valued stoicism, he made no reference to Kwai Fong's remarkable aplomb. "My task?" he asked simply.

"One stick of dynamite did not explode. You must remove it," Kwai Fong replied matter-of-factly.

Mike played the light across the wall face and found the mound of rock denoting the location of the undetonated charge. He let out a long, low sigh. "Kwai Fong, I don't know . . . I've never worked with this stuff before."

"It must be done, *shih*," Kwai Fong insisted. "Look at the top of the rock."

Running the beam across the rock again, Mike saw a fissure at the top, opened by the blast, but part of the fissure had been squeezed closed again by the shifting rock.

"Notice that the pressure is increasing," Kwai Fong explained. "When it is great enough, the dynamite will explode. The stick must be picked out."

A rumbling came from deep down in the offshoot tunnel. The shoring that was still in place creaked and cracked, and the rock above the fissure groaned and shifted. From the other side of the wall of rubble came another frantic signal from the trapped miners. They were telling Mike he had to hurry.

Swallowing hard, Mike asked resolutely, "All right, Kwai Fong, what do I do?" When he didn't get an answer to his question, he swung the light around and saw that Kwai Fong was lying very still, his eyes closed. "Kwai Fong!" he shouted, hurrying over to him. Was he dead? Feeling for a pulse, Mike breathed a sigh of relief when he found it. He held Kwai Fong's head in his arms for a moment; the old man's eyes fluttered, and then he regained consciousness.

"Forgive me," he murmured, his voice very weak. "I must have passed out. I will not do so again."

"Kwai Fong, tell me, what do I do? How do I get the stick of dynamite out?"

"You must relieve the pressure from the top," Kwai Fong instructed, his pain so great that he spoke in Chinese without thinking.

Gently resting the old man's head on the ground, Mike stood up and made his way over to the rock face. "From the top? Do you mean here, at the fissure?" Mike asked, answering Kwai Fong in his own language.

Kwai Fong's eyes grew wide. "You can speak Chinese!" he exclaimed. "I have never known a *fan kuei* who could speak my language, and, even more, you speak the words in perfect Mandarin dialect and accent."

"Yes, I can speak it fluently," Mike assured him. "And if it is easier for you to tell me what to do in your own language, do so."

"But how is it that you, a *fan kuei*, can speak Chinese?"

"I'll explain it later. Right now, I have to get you out of here."

"Oh, yes, of course. Yes, thank you. I am an old man, and sometimes I forget the order of things." It was apparent that another wave of pain was washing over Kwai Fong, and he was forcing himself to remain conscious. With his voice cracking in agony, he pointed to the fissure at the top of the rock face. "Remove the pressure there," he said.

Mike slammed the pickax against the stone, and it rang loudly in the chamber. He struck again and again, and sweat ran in rivulets down his back, under his arms, and down his forehead, dripping into his eyes and burning them. He worked until his breathing came in great gasps and his arms and shoulders ached with the effort, but he was rewarded by seeing rock tumbling down, finally creating a substantial cavity below the fissure.

"Try to pull out the stick of dynamite," Kwai Fong instructed.

Mike started to pull. "There's still pressure on the stick. Should I yank it out?"

"No! Do not try anymore!" Kwai Fong warned. "If there is too much pressure, you must not force it. Use the pickax again."

Working feverishly, breathing heavily not only from exertion but from fear, Mike continued for what seemed an eternity. Suddenly the rock face above started to break loose and slide down in one huge slab.

"Quickly!" Kwai Fong shouted. "Pull the charge out now!"

Taking a deep breath, Mike closed his eyes and jerked the stick of dynamite out of the hole just as the entire wall collapsed. He jumped back and then stood still for a long moment, holding the stick of dynamite in his hand and looking at the pile of rubble on the floor. Finally it dawned on him that he had been successful.

"We did it!" he shouted gleefully, holding the stick of explosive out for the powderman to see. "Look at this, Kwai Fong, we did it! Have you ever seen anything so beautiful?" He laughed loudly, the sound rolling back in echoes from the far corners of the chamber.

With the danger of imminent explosion removed, Mike was able to concentrate on levering off the large timber that was pinning down Kwai Fong. Freeing him, he picked the frail old man up in his arms and carried him back through the mine to the opening.

Several miners were gathered around the front of the mine, looking on anxiously as Mike made his way through the entrance. Holding out the stick of dynamite for their inspection, he announced triumphantly, "The missed shot!" Then he told them, "Seventeen men are still alive on the other side of the collapse. It's loose rubble, so we should be able to have all of them out within a couple of hours."

"Do not let our brothers die in there," Kwai Fong said to his fellow countrymen, and several of the Chinese miners immediately started down into the shaft.

A big, red-haired miner grabbed a pick and hefted it over

his shoulder, saying, "I ain't gonna let it be said that Pat O'Grady stood by the coward while a bunch of Chinese coolies took all the chances." Taking Mike's lantern, he started into the mine shaft with the Chinese workers. Almost immediately a dozen other American miners followed his example, and within minutes a full-scale rescue operation was under way.

After quickly taking Kwai Fong to the company doctor, Mike returned to help with the rescue of the trapped miners. He was handed a head lamp as he went back into the shaft, and he made his way to the chamber at the end of the offshoot tunnel. The air was heavy with the smell of earlier blasting and the dank smell of wet support timbers, for water was leaking into the mine in several places.

Reaching the chamber, Mike found that with all his fellow rescuers also equipped with lamps, they were able to labor in comparative brightness. He studied the faces of his fellow workers; fear was written on every one of them—but determination was there as well. Surprisingly, although Mike was an outsider, everyone looked to him for leadership in their mission. He had been the one to retrieve the missed shot and save Kwai Fong, and the other miners recognized and respected that.

Mike closely examined the wall of rubble that separated the rescuers from the trapped miners on the other side. Listening to the desperate tapping, he asked one of his fellow rescuers, "Can we let them know we're coming for them?"

Pat O'Grady answered, "Sure. We can tap out a message with a pickax, or better yet on a spike driven into the rock."

"Okay," Mike ordered, "do it."

O'Grady drove in the spike and then tapped out a code—not Morse code, Mike knew, but a miners' code that had been evolved over the years of hard-rock mining. Then answering taps came back from the other side.

"Seventeen alive, just like you said," O'Grady reported. "Twelve Chinese, five Americans, and they're grateful we're here. Two of the Americans are hurt."

"How is their air?" Mike asked.

O'Grady tapped again and again received an answer.

"No problem with the air as of now. But if they have to stay in there more'n a day, it might get bad."

"All right," Mike said determinedly, "then it's up to us to

see that they get out today. Do they have operable lamps on the other side, and picks? Or was everything buried or damaged?"

O'Grady tapped his question and got his answer.

"Yeah, they've still got 'em."

"All right, tell them to find out where the wall is thinnest on their side and start working their way through. We'll start on this side in the same place."

A few more taps determined the spot on the wall. There was some discussion as to whether that particular spot would stand up to being worked without collapsing further; then one of the miners got the idea of bracing it with the broken timbers. O'Grady signaled the other side to use whatever shoring they could find, and the digging began.

For more than four hours, the cavern rang with the sound of steel on rock, and sweat poured from the men's bodies, adding to the dank heat of the chamber. The stifling closeness began to get to Mike Wakefield, but he kept at the job along with the others. They worked in shifts, spelling each other after a half hour of brutal labor, and the wall was knocked down bit by bit, chunks of rock falling to their feet. Finally, O'Grady shouted, "We're through, boys! Blessed God, we're through!"

The workers cheered, and when the trapped miners came through the opening, Americans embraced Chinese, and Chinese embraced Americans. O'Grady was quick to point out that Mike was the leader of the operation and its real hero. When rescuers and rescued alike emerged from the mouth of the mine into the fresh air, several of the men, to Mike's embarrassment, seized him and lifted him to their shoulders, and he was carried around the camp to the cheers of all the miners.

It took quite a few minutes before the men would put Mike down, and even after they did so, he had to push his way through the crowd to get to the office, accepting numerous pats on the back and congratulatory handshakes. Finally reaching the office, he stepped up onto the porch and paused to look back over the camp. The sun had recently set, but there was still enough light to see the men as they moved about the grounds. Here and there some lanterns were already lighted, and a dozen golden bubbles of light shone on the mountain-side.

Mike turned and knocked on the door of the mine shack. Lon Dumey opened the door, wordlessly looked at Mike, and then turned and walked back to the small table that served as his desk.

The mine manager was drinking whiskey, and the bottle he held was nearly empty. He took another swallow and then wiped the back of his hand across his mouth. "So the big hero returns," he slurred. "What do you want?"

"I want your signature on the bill of lading," Mike told him. "I presume the steel bracing has been unloaded?"

Dumey rummaged through a pile of papers on his desk and finally found the document. Scrawling his name on it, he handed it to Mike. "Yeah, it was," he finally said testily, "for all it's worth. I'm sure that when St. John hears about our little . . . incident . . . out here, I'll be without a job."

"That's not my problem," Mike muttered tonelessly.

"You could help," Dumey whined. "You could tell St. John it wasn't my fault."

Mike stared at Dumey coldly. "But it *was*."

"How do you figure that? How could I know that dumb old Chinaman would miss a shot? He caused it . . . not me."

"Dumey, you know very well you should have had more shoring in place before you began blasting. And worse, you were willing to let those men stay down there and die, just because they were Chinese."

"Sometimes hard decisions gotta be made," Dumey said defensively. "I didn't want to put the lives of a lot of miners on the line just to save a few—and I was thinkin' of the Chinese who would be on the rescue party."

"Yeah, I'm sure you were," Mike said caustically.

"Wakefield, if you tell St. John it wasn't my fault, he'll listen to you."

The driver ignored the mine manager's plea. "I'll be going now," he told him, starting for the door.

"He needs me!" Dumey yelled drunkenly after him. "You hear me? It takes a special kind of man to work these coolies he keeps sendin' up here. It takes someone who understands how to get the most out of 'em. If he wants to get any ore out of this mine, he's gonna have to keep me! You tell him that, you hear me? You tell him that!"

Stepping back outside, Mike found it was completely dark. As he made his way to his wagon along the pathway lighted by lanterns, he listened to the sounds of the miners' celebration, which was now well under way. Over in the Irish camp someone had brought out a fiddle, and its high, dancing music drifted across the mountain, borne by the light breeze. The night air was cool and refreshing after all the time spent in the close, dank quarters of the mine, and as the driver walked he breathed deeply, enjoying the air as much as a long drink of cold spring water.

Reaching the wagon, Mike saw that standing next to it, waiting for him, was a young Chinese worker. When the driver approached, the man bowed and then spoke, his words soft and almost musical—a tone used when the speaker intended to show the utmost respect.

"*Shih*, Kwai Fong has chosen this miserable one to extend greetings and to ask if the venerable Mr. Wakefield would honor us by visiting our humble quarters to dine with us this evening. He wishes to thank you for risking your worthy life to save so many worthless persons."

In manner and speech, this was called "kowtowing," an honorable behavior among Chinese who wished to show respect. Mike knew, though, that among many Americans even the term "kowtow" had taken on a connotation of extreme servility. But he accepted the young man's approach without embarrassment, for to be embarrassed by the behavior would have in itself shown contempt. Putting his palms together, he then bowed his head. "I am not worthy to receive such an invitation," he said in equally exaggerated terms, "but I accept with gratitude the honor Kwai Fong has extended to me." With the young man leading the way, Mike headed to the Chinese workers' camp.

It was not just good manners that led Mike to accept the invitation. The Chinese miners, like the Chinese workers on the railroads a generation earlier, retained their own culture no matter where they were. Although the mine company provided cooks and food, the Chinese, at their own expense, maintained their own cooks and bought their own foods. While many Americans were put off by the strange-looking concoctions the Chinese ate, Mike had learned to enjoy Chinese food many years before.

"We are deeply honored to have you join us," Kwai Fong said when Mike arrived.

Looking at the array of food laid out on the long refectory table, the driver saw that it was much more than a normal evening meal. They had prepared a banquet for him. "The honor is mine," Mike replied sincerely.

Young women, hired by the Chinese miners as cooks, serving girls, and laundresses, had prepared and were now serving the meal. Slipping back and forth around the heavily laden table on whispering feet, they carried heavy bowls and trays to the table, adding to the elaborate viands already present.

Mike was given the position of honor at the head of the table, and the dinner started when he began eating. When he picked up the pair of chopsticks beside his plate, ignoring the fork, there was a whisper of appreciation and respect from the Chinese, who were honored that a Westerner chose to eat with their utensils.

The driver was aware that the repast was unusually bountiful, in celebration of the rescue operation. But while it was not standard fare, he knew that to the Chinese, honorable work that was well done, card games and other games of chance, and good food were all that was needed for a full and rewarding life. Indeed, there was an old Chinese proverb that declared, "The lowest peasant is an emperor at his own banquet table."

During the meal, Kwai Fong told the other workers that Mike could speak their language. Many of the workers had never socialized with a white man before, and they found this American fascinating. Shaking his head, Kwai Fong said, "To find a *fan* . . ." Then he smiled in embarrassment, knowing that Mike understood the term, and began again. "To find a Westerner who speaks our language is indeed a rare thing. How is it that you can do this?"

Mike's face took on a faraway expression, and he explained, "Many years ago, when I was very young, I worked as a cabin boy on a clipper ship—and we sailed to China."

"And did you like China?"

Looking down at his plate, Mike paused for a long moment before answering. Finally he responded, "I found China to be a very beautiful country, and I was treated warmly by your people."

"And yet there is something about your trip to China that troubles you," Kwai Fong declared.

Mike smiled at the old man's perceptiveness. "It's nothing."

"I am sorry if I have made you uncomfortable," Kwai Fong said. "Please, forgive me for prying into your past. I fear I have awakened a memory that is not pleasant."

"You've said nothing that requires my forgiveness," Mike assured the old man, "and, if anything, it is I who have committed the offense by behaving in such a way. An event of much sadness happened while I was in China, and thinking about it has caused me to remember it, that's all."

"Was that why you left the sea?" Kwai Fong asked.

"I suppose it was—though in a way, I have always thought the sea left me."

"I do not understand."

Mike smiled again. "Forgive me, I am speaking in riddles. I am referring to my captain. Shortly after the *Thunderbolt*, the ship I served on, returned to California, it was seized by the sheriff, and Cap—that's what we called him—disappeared."

"What do you mean, disappeared?"

Shrugging, Mike responded, "He just vanished. We were tied up in San Francisco harbor, and I left the ship one morning to do some errands. When I returned, Cap was gone. I searched for him for many months, but I never saw him again."

"Perhaps he went to sea on another ship," Kwai Fong suggested.

"No. I've often checked with the ship's registry in San Francisco. The name of every officer and crewman is on record there, and if Cap had been on any ship sailing the Pacific, I'd have known it. I believe he left the sea, too."

"Do you feel he is still alive?"

"Yes," Mike said firmly. Deftly wielding the chopsticks, he picked up a slender piece of spicy beef and ate it before speaking again. "Over the years I've heard stories of a man who fits his description. I've probably come close to him many times. Perhaps we've even passed on the street—but the years have made us blind to each other."

"Do you believe your captain looks for gold in the mountains?" one of the miners asked.

"A prospector?" Mike replied, surprised by the thought.
"Yes."

"Why do you ask if the captain could be a prospector? Have you heard of such a man?"

Nodding his head, the miner said, "I have."

Then Kwai Fong spoke quickly to the man in a dialect that Mike could not understand. When he mentioned that he did not know what they were saying, the old man smiled and apologized. "We were speaking of a tall man with white hair and beard who wears the hat of one who has been at sea. Some say he is crazy, some say he was once a man of great power. He speaks to no one, but on occasion he comes down from the hills."

"Please, if you hear or see such a man again, will you tell me?" Mike asked urgently. "I would like to meet this prospector."

"Of course. And we will tell all the workers that you wish to meet with this man," Kwai Fong assured him. "If he is your captain, we will find him."

"Thank you."

"And now, we would be honored if you would stay the night with us," Kwai Fong offered. "It is too late for you to travel back to San Francisco tonight."

Waking just after dawn the next morning, Mike Wakefield got off to an early start, and without a heavy load he was able to make the return trip in just under three hours. After leaving the wagon and horses in the care of the stableman, he walked to the rear of the stage and freight depot, unlocked the door to the single room that he called home, and went inside. The room was not very large, but it had everything Mike needed—a bed, a desk, and a shelf of books. He had developed a love of reading during his days at sea and passed many a pleasant evening with a book.

There were no cooking facilities in his room, but he did not need any, for when he was in San Francisco, he ate all his meals in the stage depot's dining room. After changing out of his grimy clothes, he went around to the café to have his breakfast.

As he entered the dining room, a stout woman in her midforties exclaimed, "Well, hi, Mike! I'll have your breakfast for you in a jiffy." She piled a mound of eggs and potatoes onto a large plate and added a couple of biscuits. Coming around the serving counter with the plate in one hand and a cup of coffee in the other, she smiled broadly at him. "The word is that you're quite a hero," she said. "I want you to sit yourself down right here and tell me all about it."

Somewhat embarrassed by her effusiveness, Mike said, "Hannah, why would anyone say such a thing?"

"What do you mean, why! Because of what you did at the mine yesterday," Hannah told him, gentle exasperation in her voice. "Too bad you weren't around seven years ago to rescue my late husband."

"It was nothing, but . . . when did you hear about it? I know Lon Dumey wasn't in any hurry to file a report."

Hannah smiled. "I'm sure he wasn't. But one of the mine foremen sent a wire to Mr. St. John right away, and the news got around. The boss is upstairs in his office, by the way, and he wants to see you as soon as you've finished eating."

"All right, thanks, Hannah," Mike said, putting butter on a biscuit and then hungrily digging in.

Walter St. John's office was on the second floor, above the café. When Mike knocked on the office door, St. John called for him to come in, and the driver pushed open the door and stepped inside.

The businessman was standing by the windows, looking down North Point Street toward the bay, where a forest of masts, spars, and rigging from a dozen windjammers made a confused tangle against the skyline. Walter St. John had started his adult life as an able-bodied seaman, and like Mike, he had sailed to China. He lost the little finger on his left hand when the mizzen cable fouled one icy morning off Point Barrow, Alaska, and he wore that wound almost as a badge of pride. Now in his early fifties, the distinguished man with well-trimmed, silvering sandy hair and beard was one of the wealthiest men in California, but he never forgot his past. Leaving the sea, he had tried a variety of jobs; then, with barely enough for a grubstake, he tried prospecting. He struck gold, mined enough to make himself rich, and then invested wisely; he now owned several gold and silver mines, a stage and wagon line, and an elegant hotel. As he turned toward Mike, the morning sun enhanced the colors of the light-brown suit and dark-brown silk vest that he was wearing, and the gold watch chain stretching across his chest glittered brightly. He was a very wealthy man, and while he was not ostentatious with it, he enjoyed his money—as do most men who come into wealth later in life.

Smiling broadly, St. John declared, "I don't have to tell you how proud I am of you for your heroics at the mine yesterday." He walked over to a silver serving set, poured Mike a cup of coffee, and handed it to him before sitting at his desk, putting his hands behind his head as he observed his driver.

"I didn't do much," Mike responded, sipping the coffee.

"You're being far too modest. Why, you're the talk of the entire district."

"It was all an accident," Mike said blithely. "I just happened to be there at the right time."

"Maybe. All I know is it's a good thing for those miners that you were. From all I've been able to determine, no one else seemed willing to do what you did—least of all Dumey. That's why I've sent him packing."

Mike chuckled. "You fired him, huh? He seemed to think you would."

"I got off a wire this morning," St. John said, nodding. He leaned forward and put his hands on his desk. "His job is yours, anytime you want it. And at double your present salary."

Mike sighed. The job—or one like it—had been offered many times before, and doubling his salary did make it attractive. But not attractive enough. To give himself a few moments to collect his thoughts, he got up from his chair and walked over to stand at the window from which St. John had been gazing a few moments before. Looking down on the street, he watched one of St. John's stagecoaches pulling away from the depot. A man, probably a drummer, was waving out the window of the coach at a child who was running down the road in pursuit, waving back. After a few feet, the child apparently realized the futility of his chase, and he stopped. His mother came out into the street, picked him up, and carried him in her arms back to the depot. It was a tender good-bye scene, one that invariably was repeated every time a coach pulled out of the depot. Mike enjoyed such scenes; although poignant, they were always tinged with excitement.

Turning to the businessman, Mike finally said, "I appreciate your offer, Mr. St. John, honestly, I do. But I like driving a stage too much. I wouldn't be happy tied down to one spot."

St. John got up and walked over to stand beside him. "Ah, you've still got too much of the wanderlust in you, lad," he said. "I'm afraid I have a bit of it myself, so I can understand what you're telling me." St. John smiled, adding, "And I suppose it would be a shame to take such a good driver off the road. Well, then, that being the case, why don't you sit down, and I'll tell you all about your next assignment. There'll be a raise in it for you."

Later that same evening, in a little town called Cacheville, about forty miles northeast of San Francisco, an old prospector with graying hair and an unkempt beard came down out of the hills. Trail-worn and dirty, he stood in the middle of the street scratching himself, trying to decide which of the saloons might offer him the most comfort. A woman crossing the street directly in front of him made a disgusted face and pulled out a scented handkerchief, which she held to her nose. The grizzled man paid no attention to her.

He finally chose a saloon and walked over to it, pushing his way through the swinging doors. Walking up to the bar, he removed the strange-looking cap from his head, set it on the bar, and ordered a drink. A few of the customers standing close to him hurriedly moved away in obvious distaste.

The bartender delivered the drink and then looked at the cap. "Looks like a sailor's hat. Where'd you come by it, old-timer?"

"Don't call me old-timer," the prospector growled, swallowing some of the whiskey. "I'm not *that* old. I'm known as Cap."

"Cap? That short for Casper?"

One of the men at the bar declared with a laugh, "Hell, maybe it's for that funny cap he's wearin'."

Cap glared at the man and then picked up his glass and moved over to a table by the wall. It was obvious that he was a man who had spent many years alone, and he had little need for company or conversation.

Just then a Chinese man entered the bar, and the bartender shouted, "Hey, you, Chinaman. What are you doin' in this bar?"

The Chinese man put his palms together, bowed his head slightly, and made a drinking motion.

"You want drinkee-drinkee, eh?" the bartender asked in a singsong voice. He smiled broadly and winked at the others in the saloon, all of whom smirked at the way the bartender was treating the man.

"Yes," the man said, smiling and bowing his head. "Drinkee, drinkee."

"Yeah, that's what I thought. Well, you ain't gonna get nothin' in here. We don't serve your kind."

The expression on the man's face showed that he did not quite understand what the bartender was saying.

"I said, get out of here!" the bartender said, this time punctuating his order by coming from behind the bar and shoving the man toward the door. "Go on, get! There's a place down the street for your kind."

As Cap watched the Chinese man leave, it triggered a vivid memory. In his mind he could see a shapely young Chinese woman being dragged out onto a raised platform, in the middle of a court square before a palace. The woman was dressed all in white, including the heavy veil that hid her face, and her hands were tied behind her back. There was a man on either side of her, wearing the gold and red robes of officers of the palace guard. Each of the men held a broad sword in one hand, while with the other he gripped the woman by her upper arm. She kept her head bowed, not looking out at the thousands of men, women, and children who surrounded the platform, awaiting the show that was about to be presented to them. Only once did she lift her head, glancing back at the palace.

In the center of the stage was a large wooden cylinder, not unlike a tree stump: a chopping block. Standing beside the block was a man in tight-fitting black trousers who was otherwise naked from the waist up, and his huge chest, broad shoulders, and powerful arms glistened bronze in the sun. He was wearing a black hood over his head and holding a large ax with a wide blade.

The woman was led to the block and forced to kneel beside it—though in fact no force was needed, for she knelt willingly. The man in the black hood placed her delicate neck on the chopping block and then raised his ax over her head and looked up toward the palace. There, standing all alone at a window high on the third floor of the palace, was the prince. He stood motionless for a long, agonizing moment, just looking down at the scene—the two palace officers, the girl kneeling by the chopping block, the black-hooded executioner, and the thousands of people who crowded the square. The shouting and jeering grew quiet . . . so quiet that the loudest sound was the song of a mockingbird perched high on one of the parapet towers. The prince raised his right arm, showing the back of his hand to the executioner. He made a very slight movement with the hand, the executioner's ax started downward, and . . .

Though Cap had replayed the scene in his mind hundreds of times, the image never progressed beyond that point. He had succeeded in blocking out the rest of the scene, never actually seeing the blade make contact with the young woman's neck. Shaking his head fiercely to clear away the terrible memory, he picked up his glass of whiskey and downed the rest of it in one gulp. Slamming the glass down hard on the table, he picked up his cap and hurried back out into the night air.

Chapter Two

The wind whipped across the water of San Francisco Bay as a large and beautiful sailing ship made its way to port the next afternoon. Standing on the deck with all the other passengers of the *Pacific Star*, twenty-year-old Ku Xuan remained slightly off to one side, smiling graciously to all who spoke to her but—as she had for the entire voyage—keeping primarily to herself.

Alhough at first glance Ku Xuan appeared entirely Chinese, she had Occidental features as well, her eyes being slightly rounded and her skin tone somewhat lighter than an Oriental's. This was because her father had been an American, and it was also because of her American father that she was a passenger on this ship. She had come to this country not to seek a personal fortune like the others, but to find the father she had never seen.

The trip from China had been quite an experience for the exceptionally beautiful young woman. Never in her wildest imaginings had she thought that a body of water could be as vast as the Pacific Ocean. There were times during the journey when sky and water were the same shade of blue or gray, so that the horizon disappeared and it seemed as if the passengers and crew were on some celestial craft suspended in space, with no heaven and no earth. During those times, Ku Xuan often sat on deck, listening to the music of their transit: an orchestral composition created by wind and sea, the instruments being the parts of the vessel. The moaning winds plucked at the tensed shrouds and straining backstays, causing them to sing like the strings of a harp. Some stays

23

gave forth a deep bass note, others a melodious tenor. Halyards rang like violin strings, while the strongest gales caused heavy blocks to beat a steady rhythm against steel spars. When the ship rolled in heavy seas, every strake and frame of the hull creaked and groaned. Beneath all other sounds was the restless crash of the sea and the deep-throated boom of canvas, soaked by the spray.

Having spent a lifetime reconciling all the aspects of time, space, and nature, Ku Xuan adapted quickly to life at sea. Her fellow passengers, however—Chinese men and women bound for California—found the voyage difficult. She heard no complaining, for they were by nature docile and therefore quietly suffered the cramped quarters lacking in privacy, the disruption of their normal routine . . . and the seasickness. Ku Xuan, who suffered from none of their maladies, watched and listened sympathetically. She helped when she was able and looked away discreetly when that was all she could do.

Alhough she had remained somewhat apart from the other passengers, she had great admiration for their having taken the drastic step of going to California. To do something as heart wrenching as leaving the country that had been home for all their years, to redirect their destinies, was a step of major proportions. In Ku Xuan's mind, there was not one passenger on board who was not a person of great courage. And now the long voyage was nearly at an end, the buildings of San Francisco growing ever larger as the ship sailed into the port.

A steam tug came out to meet the vessel, and Ku Xuan watched with curiosity as a small cannon on the afterdeck of the tug fired a rope across the bow of the *Pacific Star*. A crewman expertly caught it and then made the rope secure. Taking the ship under tow, the little tug started off, rolling in the swells, its paddlewheels losing purchase for a moment before catching the water again. Then the tug shot forward, and the resulting jerk was transferred along the line to the *Pacific Star*, causing it to lurch. The movement caught Ku Xuan unaware, and she had to grab the railing to keep from falling.

The more than one hundred passengers had come on deck to watch their passage into America, and many of them did fall, shouting out in surprise. Then they laughed merrily. Even this unexpected tumble did not dismay them, for they had come to this foreign country to make their fortunes, and they were poised on the brink of a new life.

The passengers had more in common than the fact that they were all Chinese and ambitious: They had all paid for their passage in the same way. Like Ku Xuan, they had signed a contract of indentured servitude with a businessman in Canton who represented a Mr. Wo Hamm, of San Francisco. Wo Hamm was a tong chief, and although slavery was illegal in the United States, Wo Hamm would for all intents and purposes own these workers until such time as their wages repaid him for his investment. With the interest and agent's commission, plus the tong tribute (which many of the Chinese immigrants thought was a legal tax), it would take from two to five years for even the most frugal of the workers to purchase their freedom. Therefore, their personal ambitions would have to be set aside until their obligations to Wo Hamm were discharged. In the meantime, he would have earned many times his investment on each one of them.

Three shrill toots suddenly sounded from the tug's whistle, and then the hawser was dropped. The tug pulled away sharply, leaving the *Pacific Star* to drift gently toward the pier, where three men stood ready to catch the securing lines and make her fast.

"Stand by the bow line," an officer on deck called.

"Bow line ready, sir!" came the answering call.

"Stand by abeam."

"Abeam ready, sir!"

"Stand by stern line."

"Stern line ready, sir!"

"Away all lines!"

The sailors whirled the lines over their heads for a few turns and then threw them toward the wharf. The bow line and the abeam line were caught by men on the pier, but the stern line fell into the water. Receiving a good-natured razzing from the others, the sailor on the stern line simply pulled it back in and tossed it out a second time.

Ku Xuan's heart was pounding as she descended the gangplank, herded with all the other new arrivals from the *Pacific Star* like so many cattle. She looked around, her head swimming with the new sights and sounds, wondering what lay beyond the immediate area, which for the moment was all her eyes could see.

The waterfront of San Francisco was teeming with humanity, Orientals and Occidentals alike. The Chinese passengers, dazed and confused, stood in a group on the pier, waiting to see what would happen next.

Though it had been her intention to blend with her fellow passengers, everyone noticed her. Ku Xuan was such a beautiful woman that despite the shapeless peasant smock she was wearing, she stood out from the others like a rose among cabbages. The burly dock workers, who were used to seeing hundreds of Chinese arrive, stared unabashedly at this creature of extraordinary beauty.

Standing close to Ku Xuan was another woman, even younger than Ku Xuan and also very pretty. Like Ku Xuan, she was attracting unwanted attention, and when a big American dock worker grabbed her and squeezed her painfully, the young woman cried out. Without hesitation, Ku Xuan went over to assist her.

"Please, sir," she said to the burly American in English, "she does not wish your attention."

The dock worker scratched himself obscenely and laughed. "Well, now, she don't wish my attention, huh? Then how 'bout you, little lady? You interested in what ol' Barney can do for you?"

Ku Xuan smiled seductively, and the worker, surprised by what seemed to be an invitation, let out a grunt and started toward her. She let him reach for her, then at the last moment leaned to one side, the movement so subtle that most observers did not even notice it. The man had already reached for her, but now there was nothing there, and he lost his balance. Ku Xuan's foot slipped out and touched his almost imperceptibly, then pulled back quickly, accelerating his loss of footing. Shouting and flailing his arms uselessly, the man tumbled forward off the dock and into the water. His fellow workers and the Chinese immigrants roared with laughter, but no one other than the young woman Ku Xuan had rescued realized that the man was in the water because Ku Xuan had put him there. She smiled at Ku Xuan, her eyes flashing the fact that she knew the secret, but would not tell.

As the dock worker was fished out of the bay and ridiculed by his fellow longshoremen, an elegant coach approached. Its iron-rimmed wheels hummed, and the horses' hooves clopped hollowly on the cobblestone pavement as it rolled onto the scene. Ku Xuan caught her breath as she watched its progress, for the coach was extremely beautiful. Red with black trim and decorated on the door with a raised, gilded dragon, it was pulled by four matching black horses, and at its rear stood two footmen dressed in dark green livery. A hand, its long, red-lacquered fingers adorned with rings, appeared from inside the coach, grasped the edge of the window, and then was followed by a man's face. The face had dark, rather beady Oriental eyes, plucked eyebrows, and a long, drooping mustache and beard. The man looked out over the pier and his eyes locked on Ku Xuan's. He then called out to his driver, and the coach stopped. The two footmen hurried to the side, and one placed a footstool below the door while the other opened the door and helped the occupant out of the coach. The man was richly dressed in a robe of royal blue silk trimmed in gold.

As the dock was a place of foul odors, he clutched a perfumed handkerchief to his nose with one hand; with the other he pointed to Ku Xuan. "Bring that one to me," he commanded.

The two servants hurried across the dock to Ku Xuan, and she allowed them to escort her to the coach. Recognizing at once that this was a man of wealth and influence, Ku Xuan stood before him with her head bowed and her eyes lowered respectfully.

"How are you called?" the man asked, his voice high and thin.

"I am called Ku Xuan."

"Xuan . . . pronounced like the English word 'swan.' A swan is a most beautiful bird. The Americans will think you well named, Ku Xuan, for you are most beautiful."

"Thank you, *shih*," she whispered.

"You are not like the others," he declared. "You are much more beautiful, more delicate, more . . . refined. Why are you here at the docks?"

"I have come on the ship with the others to this new country."

"Did you buy your own ticket?"

"No, *shih*. Like the others, I am indebted to a benefactor."

"I see. And do you know who that benefactor is, my lovely one?"

"Only that his name is Wo Hamm."

The man laughed triumphantly and then said, "I am he."

"You are most generous."

"Generous, yes. But not to a fault. You do understand, beautiful one, that I will expect to be repaid."

"Yes, *shih*."

Wo Hamm held out his hand. "You will ride with me," he commanded.

"Yes, *shih*."

By now nearly a dozen open wagons had arrived at the pier, and the Chinese immigrants and their meager belongings were being loaded onto them. Ku Xuan picked up her own little bundle and stepped up into Wo Hamm's coach. She sat on the red-cushioned seat opposite him, looking through the window at the scene outside. After a few minutes, Wo Hamm shouted the order to go, and the train of wagons and the coach rolled away. The coach was exceptionally well sprung, and it rode as softly as if it were cushioned by a cloud.

As they left the docks, Wo Hamm began talking, telling her of his importance in San Francisco. "If ever you want something done, I am the one you must see. But always remember," he added, showing his teeth in a smile that was without mirth, "it is good to keep me as a friend, for I am a ferocious enemy."

Ku Xuan said nothing, wanting only to watch, listen, and learn. Through the window of the coach she could see signs written in Chinese and hear people on the streets speaking her language. Familiar aromas assailed her nostrils as they passed tenements and restaurants along the way. Yet there was a subtle distortion in everything she saw. It was like a vision of home, but viewed through flawed glass. This was not Canton; this was San Francisco. And though the people she saw were of the same race and language, they were different from the people of mainland China—changed in some subtle yet distinct way by distance, time, and their association with a new culture. She wondered if they knew how they had changed, and she feared that after a short period of time she would no longer be aware of these subtle differences because she, too, would have changed.

The coach and wagons stopped in front of a large, elaborate building, and while the other Chinese immigrants were ordered into a large meeting hall where, they were told, jobs would be assigned to them, Wo Hamm signaled that Ku Xuan was to follow him toward another entrance.

"What a beautiful place this is," she breathed as she looked at the building.

"I am pleased that you find it acceptable," Wo Hamm said in mock humility. "This is where I live. It is also where I conduct all my business."

As Ku Xuan studied Wo Hamm's house, she thought that it reminded her of the Grand Temple at the abbey of Shan Tal, though this house was much larger. The red-tiled pagoda roof was of many tiers with graceful scoops and curves at the eaves. Red and gold were the main colors, but there were also decorated panels of royal blue between the leaded glass windows.

The entrance they were using was reached by a broad, tiled walkway that led through a courtyard, in the center of which was a formal garden awash with beautiful flowers and exquisite shrubbery, some of it trimmed into the shape of tiny pagodas. Dotted here and there among the flowers and shrubs were graceful marble statues, most depicting scowling lions and ferocious dragons. Ku Xuan found the scene utterly enchanting—and not a little intimidating.

After entering the building, the tong chief led her down a long narrow hall toward the back. A cloying smell permeated the hall, and as Ku Xuan passed by an open door, she peered inside. In the dimly lit room she saw a wall lined with bunks, and lying on them, oblivious to her passage—indeed, oblivious to everything except their own private dreams—were dozens of men smoking opium.

At the end of the hall Wo Hamm opened a door and ushered Ku Xuan into a room unlike any she had ever seen. It was hung with the richest tapestries and appointed with the finest furniture. Artifacts of gold and jade were everywhere—obviously the room of a very wealthy man.

Wo Hamm suddenly turned and reached for her. Having seen the lust in his eyes, Ku Xuan had been expecting this advance, and as she shifted her body just enough to avoid his hands, she reached up to grasp his shoulder. She recalled the parting words from the abbess at the Shan Tal temple where she had been born and where she had spent her entire life, mastering the skills of a Shan Tal priestess. . . .

*   *   *

"Ku Xuan, you have learned rites and practices that have been shrouded in mystery for fifty centuries," Mata Lee had told her. "You have the power to control all the resources of your body by using parts of the mind that others never develop. You are a master of *choeng-te*, a martial art more deadly than all others. Beyond that, you have mastered the most potent weapon of all, for you know the secret paths the sex force takes through the body—and the ways to use that secret knowledge to dominate any man."

Using that power now, Ku Xuan found the path of Wo Hamm's sex force, and squeezing slightly with her thumb and forefinger, she redirected the flow of sexual excitation. Suddenly, and totally without warning, Wo Hamm felt himself overcome with such intense sensations that he could not control himself. He gasped in pleasure and surprise, though Ku Xuan gave no sign that she knew what was happening.

Unexpectedly satisfied, Wo Hamm's lust was defused.

"Are you all right?" Ku Xuan asked innocently.

"What? Uh . . . yes, yes," Wo Hamm murmured. "Ku Xuan, you are a woman of rare beauty and, uh, exotic charm. Such a woman should not have to labor at menial tasks like the others. I have something better in mind for you."

Ku Xuan said nothing, merely looking at him intently with her large, liquid brown eyes.

"I can make you a very, very wealthy woman," he went on.

"Why do you wish to do such a thing for me?" she asked.

Wo Hamm smiled. "Why indeed? I will be honest with you; it is not because I have a good heart. I am Wo Hamm," he said and touched himself on the breast, "and Wo Hamm does not have a good heart. Wo Hamm has a gift for making money . . . much money." He rubbed his thumb and forefinger together, his long, red-lacquered nails glistening. "And by setting you up as the concubine of a very wealthy man, we will *both* make much money," he explained.

While Ku Xuan did not consider such a position dishonorable—indeed, other Shan Tal initiates had gone on to serve in just such a capacity—accepting it might interfere with her real purpose in coming to America. Nothing must be permitted to distract her from the mission given to her by the abbess, Mata Lee, who had raised her in the cloister from the day she was born.

"Thank you for your kindness," Ku Xuan finally responded. "But I do not wish to be a concubine."

"Ah, so you do not wish to be a concubine. . . ." The tong chief laughed humorlessly. "You belong to me, Ku Xuan. You will do as I say, and if I want you to be a concubine, you will be a concubine."

"This is true, *shih*," Ku Xuan said, her voice deferential, "but who would want a concubine who is unwilling? What pleasure would I bring a man, if he knew that I felt no enthusiasm for the act? No, I think a wealthy man would not pay much for such a woman."

Wo Hamm cursed angrily. "So you think you have won this point, do you? Very well, I concede it to you, for you are right: No man would pay much money for a woman who is unwilling to share his bed." Sneering, he said, "You will go somewhere else then, and we will see how your . . . delicate beauty can hold up under the most demeaning and back-breaking work. You will be assigned to a laundry."

Ku Xuan said nothing, but merely bowed her head in respectful obedience.

Striding over to a large gong, the tong chief struck it hard, and a moment later one of his manservants entered the room. Wo Hamm directed the man to escort Ku Xuan from the elegant room to the large meeting hall where the other indentured servants were being given their assignments.

The moment Ku Xuan entered the hall, Lai Song, the young woman she had helped on the dock, saw her and walked over to speak to her.

"Did you get a very good job?" she asked.

"I am to work in a laundry," Ku Xuan said.

The smile left Lai Song's face. "A laundry? But that is the most difficult job."

"There is honor in doing a difficult job well."

Lai Song smiled again. "Then I, too, wish to work in a laundry."

"Why would you wish to do that?"

"Because you are. And where you go, I will go. Besides," Lai Song said, smiling, "you said there was honor in doing a difficult job well." The smile left her face. "Unless you do not wish me to be your friend?"

Ku Xuan touched the younger woman on the cheek. "I will be pleased to call you my friend."

Lai Song hurried over to the man assigning the jobs. Since few wanted to work in the laundry, she was accepted immediately when she volunteered.

As the workers were allocated to their various jobs, they were loaded onto wagons. The laundry to which Ku Xuan had been assigned was about ten blocks away from Wo Hamm's house, at the edge of Chinatown. She climbed onto the wagon with Lai Song and eighteen other women and men, all of whom chatted animatedly. As they drove through the streets, the wagon passed a building that was obviously a temple, and Ku Xuan was suddenly overcome with longing and sorrow, thinking of Mata Lee. The abbess was now dead, killed by assassins who had come to the Shan Tal temple in search of Ku Xuan. A cold chill ran up Ku Xuan's spine, and the horror she had felt then was again fresh.

Returning from a market where she had briefly gone, Ku Xuan had found the abbess lying on the floor in a pool of blood, her two murderers still poised over her.

"Mata Lee!" Ku Xuan shouted in anguish.

Looking over at her, one of the assassins ordered, "Get her!" As he thrust the wide-bladed sword at her, the other swung his in a vicious arc in an attempt to decapitate her.

Leaping high to avoid the lower sword and ducking to avoid the higher blade, she was for one moment suspended in midair between the two blades. When both men missed and readied their blades for a second try, Ku Xuan fell forward on her hands and then did a flip, coming up behind them.

The murderers spun around and thrust their swords at her again, and she leaned to one side, letting the blades slip by. Then she slammed the heel of her hand into the base of the nose of the man nearer her, breaking the small bone and shoving splinters into his brain. He fell, dead before he hit the floor. Grabbing his blade, Ku Xuan spun to her left and, thrusting the sword, drove it up to the hilt between the other man's ribs. He gasped in surprise, let his own sword clatter to the floor, and then fell, dying. She immediately abandoned the two assassins and hurried to the side of her abbess.

"Mata Lee!" she cried, falling to her knees and cradling the older woman's head on her lap. "Who are these men? Why did they attack you?"

Barely alive, the abbess gasped, "They did not come for me."

Ku Xuan could see that Mata Lee was dying, but she insisted, "I must get help for you."

"No!" the older woman whispered fiercely, reaching for her. She coughed, and then added, "It is too late for me. But your life is in danger."

"My life? Why? Who would want to hurt me?"

"You were the one those men came for. They wanted to kill you. You must leave here immediately, Ku Xuan. You must get away."

"Mata Lee, why am I in danger? What wrong have I done?"

"You were born, child," the abbess told her sadly. "That was your only crime." After coughing again, she said, "Promise me, child, promise me you'll get away."

"Not until I have taken care of you."

"Promise me!" Mata Lee said forcefully.

"All right," Ku Xuan agreed. "I'll leave. But where should I go?"

"California."

"California? Where is California?"

"I do not know," Mata Lee admitted. "But you must go to this place. You must go there and find your father."

"Who is my father?"

"Your mother called him Big Cat." She said the name in English, just as Ku Xuan's mother had told it to her. Then the abbess translated it to Chinese so that Ku Xuan would understand, even though English had been one of the languages Ku Xuan had studied. "You must go to California, search for him, and when you find him, tell him who you are. Your mother told me three questions that will help you. If he can answer all three of them correctly, you will know he is truly your father."

Weakening, Mata Lee fought to stay conscious. She swallowed hard, and then continued, "One: What lies beyond the inner door of the golden pagoda? The answer is the private prayer chambers. Two: What secret is hidden by the jasmines

of the garden? Answer: a secret passageway. Three: Who was
Tsu? Answer: your mother's handmaiden."

Tears fell from Ku Xuan's eyes onto the old woman's forehead, and the young woman bit her lip hard to keep from
sobbing.

Mata Lee found her breath again and said, "Once you
know he is . . . your father, tell him that your mother wished
to go with him, but could not, for even as they spoke in the
garden that last night, her father had armed guards waiting to
. . . kill your father if she tried. Tell him that her heart was
full of love for him. She . . . wanted him to know. Tell him
also that what was seen was not seen. . . ." The abbess's
eyes closed and her voice faded. "You must flee, Ku Xuan,
before you are found . . . but you must be sure to take with
you your mother's eating set . . . in my room." Mata Lee
gasped one last time; then she died.

Overwhelmed by sadness and fear, Ku Xuan began to sob.
The abbess was the only family she had ever known. She had
no memory of her mother, for her mother had died when she
was born. She did not even know her mother's name.

Ku Xuan forced herself to regain her composure. Taking a
long, shuddering breath, she gently laid Mata Lee's head
onto the cold stone floor. She took a final, loving look at the
woman who had done everything for her but give her life,
and then she hurried to Mata Lee's room. After a short
search, she located the cylindrical carved-ivory case that contained her mother's eating set—jade chopsticks and silver
knife with an engraved handle—and made her way back to
her own cell.

As she walked through the cloister, she felt saddened at
the thought that now she could not be inducted as a priestess
of Shan Tal. Although she had all the skills and knowledge of
the priesthood, she had not yet taken the final vow. Her
entire life had been spent in training for the day she would
take the vow, and she had never considered the possibility
that it might not happen. But with her dying words the
abbess herself had instructed Ku Xuan to leave the temple
immediately. Her priestly obligations might guide her in one
direction, but the mission given her by Mata Lee sent her in
quite another. As she could be loyal to only one truth, one
way, she chose the path Mata Lee had given her. Her heart

was heavy, but she knew this was what she must do. She vowed that she would seek her father.

Ku Xuan was sure that none of the other priestesses and novitiates had been told of her need to leave the cloister, yet somehow everyone seemed to know. For the first time in her life, she saw the residents of Shan Tal as others saw them. She saw the shield that protected them from outside influences, and she realized that as of this moment, *she* was an outside influence. She did not feel anger with the others for excluding her, for she knew this was as it should be. But she did feel a sense of sadness at something having passed.

With her mother's eating case rolled securely inside her little bundle, Ku Xuan hurried through the beautifully sculptured gardens of Shan Tal to the large wall that guarded the entrance. She stood silently as the gates were opened, and then, without once looking back, she walked through them and down the rocky path toward the little village of Chiensein. There she would learn which road one must take to walk to California.

By the end of her first day of walking, Ku Xuan had learned that California could not be reached in one day—nor indeed by walking. Making her way to Canton, she found that a ship would be leaving for California shortly, and she inquired how passage might be secured. Passage was available, she was told, if she would sign an agreement of indentured servitude until the passage was paid for. She accepted the terms, and after that long ocean voyage, she now found herself in the back of a wagon with nineteen other men and women. Holding in her lap all her worldly possessions, she was going to the laundry where she would both live and work and begin fulfilling her long period of indentureship.

Glancing at the others, Ku Xuan was sure that she did not feel the same sense of violent dislocation that they did, even though she too had known only China, with its ancient culture and orderly ways. She reflected that perhaps it was because her father was American, so that a part of her already belonged to this country. Excited about discovering new things, she also had a very strong sense of obligation in carrying out her mission. But there was a pervasive feeling of nostalgia for the homeland she had left, for the place she knew she would never see again.

"I wonder how long it will take until we can repay Wo Hamm for our passage?" Lai Song suddenly asked.

"You are a pretty girl," a middle-aged woman answered. "It should not take you very long. I do not know why you and your friend agreed to work in the laundry. If I were as lovely as you two, I certainly would not work in the laundry."

"But you are not as lovely. You are as ugly as an old crone," one of the men told her, and everyone laughed, even the woman, who mugged and teased with her ugliness.

"But I do wonder, why did you take such a job?" the woman asked again.

"It is honorable work," Lai Song said, defending her decision and obviously remembering Ku Xuan's comment.

"And what about you, Silent Beauty?"

Ku Xuan had heard the term applied to her many times before, on the ship. She knew it was how all her fellow passengers referred to her, because although she always spoke when spoken to, she was otherwise very quiet.

"Why do you take such work?" the woman went on. "You are even more beautiful than this one. And you are half Westerner; I can tell by your eyes and your skin."

"As Lai Song said," Ku Xuan answered. "This is honorable work. And I have no wish to be a concubine."

"Ah, truly, there are some questions that not even the great Buddha can answer," the woman replied with an air of long-suffering patience. "Such as why it is that I, who would love to be a concubine to a rich man, am cursed with the ugliness of a toad, while the two of you, who have no such desire, are as beautiful as flowers. I ask you others, do you not think beauty is wasted on such women as these?"

Again there was laughter, and when Ku Xuan and Lai Song joined in, the others accepted them, and they all began to talk excitedly of the new life that lay ahead of them.

Early the next morning, twenty-five miles east of the city, a Concord coach belonging to the California Stage and Freight Company made its way along the main road leading to San Francisco. The wheels rolled over the hard-packed dirt road with a quiet, crunching sound. The sun was still low over the mountains, and way down in the valley a morning mist wrapped itself around the ponderosa pines, clinging to the branches in flowing tendrils like the delicate lace of a fine bridal veil.

Riding high on the box seat, looking out over the broad backs of a six-horse team, Mike Wakefield smiled happily. Loving the scene displayed before him, he thought about Walter St. John's pronouncement that he still had the wanderlust of the sea in him. That was only half true. He no longer had any desire to go to sea, but he *did* like to travel around, and nothing he had ever done had suited him the way driving a stage did.

After leaving before sunrise, he was about one hour out of Sonoma, although if he turned in his seat, he could still see that community as a cluster of tiny white buildings on the valley floor below. He would reach San Francisco by noon, take on a fresh team, and then start back for Sonoma, reaching it just at sunset.

As Mike rounded a curve a moment later, he had to haul back on the reins and push hard on the brake lever, for blocking the road dead ahead was a wall of rock. It was a dangerous stop, since the road was very narrow at this point, and the right-hand side of the stage was so close to the edge that passengers could look through the window straight down to the valley, nearly one thousand feet below. If the horses were unable to stop in time, the team, coach, driver, and passengers could be hurled over the side.

The stage slid across the road, lurching sideways, while a couple of the horses went down on their back legs in their effort to stop. A cloud of dust rose from the road, and it drifted off over the valley as the coach finally came to a halt. During the quick stop, Mike had heard screams and shouts of surprise and fear coming from inside the coach. Now that he had things under control, he called down to his passengers to calm them.

"You folks in there all right?"

"Yes, no one's hurt," a man's reassuring voice came from inside. "What is it? What happened?"

"The road is blocked," Mike explained. "I could use some help from the men." He lashed the brake handle down, although he knew the team was not going to move until he urged them. Climbing down the wheel, he stood there with his hands on his hips looking at the pile of rock. The door opened and the three male passengers got out, joining him.

One of the men was a rancher in his midforties, another was a store clerk in his late thirties, and the third was a schoolboy of no more than fifteen. The boy's mother and grandmother were also passengers in the coach.

"Well, would you look at that," the rancher said, pointing to the barricade. "How odd that the rocks should fall across the road like that."

"I don't think they fell across the road," Mike said, taking off his hat and running his hand through his thick, dark hair. "I think they were put there."

"Put there? But for what purpose?" the store clerk asked.

"Well, now, just why do you think?" a new voice asked.

Mike looked over at the small hill to his left and saw three masked men standing there, looking down at the coach. One was holding a shotgun, the other two had pistols, and all three guns were aimed at him and the passengers.

"It's a robbery!" the store clerk gasped.

"Ain't you a real smart fella," declared the one with the shotgun, apparently the leader. He worked his way down the hill while the other two remained where they were.

"You, driver—climb back up on the box and chuck down the money pouch," the robber called as he approached.

Mike shook his head. "Mister, I don't know where you got your information, but I'm not carrying a money pouch."

"The hell you say. I can see it from here. Now, I'd advise you to climb on up in that box and throw it down."

"Do what he says," the store clerk pleaded in a frightened voice. "You have no choice."

With a sigh, Mike climbed back up onto the driver's seat, reached underneath, and picked up the pouch. He showed it to the robber. "Is this what you're talking about?"

"Yeah," the robber said. "Throw it to me real easy like. You don't want to be no hero now, do you?"

Without answering, Mike tossed the open pouch to him.

Catching it by the rim, the man stuck his hand down inside and moved it around. "Damn!" he swore angrily.

"What's wrong?" one of his cohorts called.

"There ain't nothin' in it. It's empty, just like he said."

"I told you," Mike muttered. "Looks like you just wasted your time building that wall across the road."

"Cole," the man on the hill yelled, "we ain't gonna go away from this with nothin', are we?"

"Shut up, damn you!" the robber leader shouted angrily. "You want to tell them where I live, too?"

The man looked contrite, but then the other robber suggested, "What about the passengers? Maybe they got somethin'."

"Yeah, good thinkin'," the leader said. "All right, we'll take whatever you people got. Men, shell out your wallets. Ladies, empty your purses."

"Wait just a minute, Cole," Mike said coldly.

Looking toward Mike with his eyes flashing fire, the leader warned, "Mister, it ain't healthy for you to be rememberin' that name."

"If you rob my passengers, I'll be remembering more than your name. I'll be remembering you."

"Is that a fact? Well, rememberin' is one thing . . . doin' somethin' about it is another. How about you? You got somethin' to contribute to the cause? Throw down your wallet."

A second robber came down from the hill to join the man named Cole, and after taking the money from the wallets and purses, he flung them to the ground.

Cole then examined the two women, who stood shaking in fear. The older woman was wearing a cameo brooch, and he demanded it from her. Looking at the young boy's mother, he said, "What about you, ma'am? You ain't wearin' no jewelry. Your husband too mean to buy you anythin'?"

"My husband is deceased."

"Ain't that a shame," Cole said flatly. Turning to his men, he declared, "All right, boys, we got everythin' there is to get, so let's ride out of here."

With the third robber covering Mike and the passengers, the others scrambled back up the side of the hill.

The rancher looked over at Mike and demanded, "You going to do anything?"

"What do you expect me to do?" Mike replied. "They've got us covered."

"Well if you won't do anything, I will!" the rancher shouted, and his right hand sought the pistol he carried in his waistband behind his jacket.

"Look out, Cole!" the third robber shouted. "One of 'em's goin' for a gun!" At the same time he yelled his warning, he fired.

The rancher gasped loudly as the bullet caught him in the shoulder. He fell against the coach wheel and slid to the ground, the bullet hole pumping blood.

The other two robbers turned and started firing. Thinking first of the safety of his passengers, Mike shouted, "Get down!" He grabbed the boy and his mother, shoving them down just as a blast from the shotgun tore out a big chunk of wood from the door of the coach. The older woman and the clerk also flattened themselves on the ground, and that gave Mike the opportunity to pull his own gun and return fire.

His first shot hit the man on the top of the hill, the one who had shot the rancher. Blood flew from the man's thigh, and he let out a scream of pain, dropping his hand to cover his wound.

Mike fired once more and missed, but by this time all three men had scrambled over the top of the hill, out of sight. Waiting, intently watching the crest of the hill to see if they reappeared, he soon heard the sound of hooves as the robbers rode away.

"Are you all right?" the driver asked the rancher.

"Well, it didn't hit any of the vitals," the rancher said through clenched teeth, "but you better get me to a doctor. The pain's real bad."

Turning to the store clerk, Mike said, "Help me get him inside."

"All right, but I want you to know that I hold you personally responsible for this," the man grumbled. "Those robbers got my money, and you did nothing to try and stop them. You left the defense up to one of your passengers."

"Yes, and look what it got me," the rancher said tightly. "We didn't get our money back, and I got a bullet in my shoulder."

"The driver's responsible for that, too," the clerk complained. "He's the one in charge."

"Right," Mike agreed. Pointing to the wall of stones, he added, "And now the man in charge says let's get these rocks off the road so we can get out of here."

"I'll look after this man's wound," the boy's mother offered.

"And I'll help clear the road," the boy added.

"Thanks."

"You hit that robber in the leg, mister," the boy said

excitedly. "I seen it. I seen the blood flyin'. Boy, it was really somethin'. Wait till I tell my friends I was robbed."

Narrowing his eyes, Mike Wakefield told the boy, "I wonder if you'd think being robbed was so exciting if you had to face the possibility of it every day of your life." He shook his head and said, "Well, come on. Let's get to it so I can get you people to your destination. As the man said, that's my job."

Chapter Three

Wu Ho, the owner of the laundry where Ku Xuan worked, was an industrious man. Twenty years earlier he had paid his way across the Pacific by selling his services as an indentured servant. Working for five years on the Central Pacific Railroad, saving diligently, he finally amassed enough money to purchase his freedom, and then he started his own laundry. Now he had more than forty of his countrymen working for him, and he was proud of the fact that even the most affluent citizens of San Francisco used his laundry.

Though the washing machine had been invented a few years earlier, neither Ku Xuan nor any of her fellow laundry workers had ever heard of the device. They toiled so efficiently, they did not need machines to help them. Indeed, in the several weeks that she had been working there, the laundry had become as familiar to Ku Xuan as Shan Tal had been. Even in her sleep she could see the long, unpainted room at the back of the building where all the work was done. Along the four walls of the room were stands where a dozen washtubs sat, laborers toiling at them, scrubbing the clothes on metal washboards in soapy water that smelled strongly of lye. Other workers took the wet wash to the back porch, where they wrung as much water from the clothes as they could and hung them out to dry. Still others gathered in the dried laundry, ironed it, and packed it into bundles for delivery back to the customers.

Work started in the laundry before dawn and ended after dark, with breaks for lunch and supper. The laundry room smelled of wet wood and sweating bodies as well as lye. It rang with noise from the constant chatter of the workers, from the scrubbing of the washboards, and from the banging and sloshing of buckets and tubs. It was not a pleasant place to be—yet Ku Xuan never heard one word from anyone suggesting regrets for having come to California.

Picking up a large bundle of soiled laundry, Ku Xuan began dropping it piece by piece into the vat of hot, soapy water. Hers was the most distasteful of all the jobs in the laundry, for it embodied everything that was bad about working in such a place—the unpleasant odors, the backbreaking toil of bending and lifting, the burning alkaline fumes—and yet Ku Xuan did it uncomplainingly. And although the other workers still called her Silent Beauty because she continued to speak only infrequently, they did not call her that disparagingly. She knew they had grown to respect her and admire her because she was so quick to offer help when asked—and many times even before being asked. This morning as she stood over the large, steaming tub, her arms plunged up to her elbows in the harsh suds, she thought of her time at Shan Tal. It had been a life dedicated to study and preparation and contemplation . . . a life of gentleness and ease. The contrast between her former life and her present one was amazingly great—and yet, like her fellow workers, Ku Xuan did not regret her decision.

As she paused briefly in her labors to push a wayward strand of hair out of her face, her eyes met Lai Song's, and the two young women smiled at each other. They were becoming close friends, and although Lai Song did not realize it, she was only the second friend Ku Xuan had ever known. In the cloister, the byword had been, "Friendliness to all . . . friendship to none," a policy designed to make it difficult for the novitiates to develop close friends.

"Ku Xuan. Ku Xuan!"

She was dimly aware that her name had been called several times before she let go of her thoughts of the past. Looking over at Lai Song, she saw her pointing to another bundle of dirty clothes.

"Wu Ho just left this, but I am going to take it to one of the other tubs. You have done more than your share today." Lowering her voice, Lai Song told her, "You are the most even-tempered person I have ever known. And sometimes I think perhaps you are too much so. I have seen the way the other workers take advantage of you—knowing that you will never complain. Well, I will not let that happen. It is my responsibility to look out for you . . . just as you looked out for me that first day we met."

Ku Xuan smiled gently. "I assure you, dear Lai Song, that I can take care of myself."

Lai Song shook her head resolutely. "That may be, but look at all the wash sitting here in front of your tub." Gesturing with her head, she added angrily, "I heard those other two give you some excuse about why they were falling behind and so were unable to do their assigned work. And I heard you agree to take on the extra work yourself."

Ku Xuan smiled again. "It is no trouble for me to do the work. If the others are unable to do it, whatever the reason, and I am able, then I shall do it."

Lai Song was due shortly to be reassigned to ironing, but she had a few minutes with nothing to do, so she volunteered to help at the tub. Ku Xuan accepted the offer, and as they worked side by side, Lai Song's face took on a look of astonishment. "I cannot help but notice that you work so quickly and with so little effort that my presence makes no difference, except to provide company."

Laughing sweetly, Ku Xuan said, "I am not worthy of all your compliments—nevertheless, I thank you for them."

"You have not mentioned where you came from, but I think you must have been raised in a small hamlet," Lai Song decided. "No girl from a big city would let others take advantage of her like this."

"Yes, the place I come from is small."

"What is the name of your village?"

"Chiensein," Ku Xuan replied, naming the small settlement above which Shan Tal clung, like a white flower, to the wall of the mountain that guarded the Chiensein Pass.

"I do not know the place."

Ku Xuan was aware that Lai Song wished to know more, but despite the friendship that had grown up between the two young women, there were still many things about herself that Ku Xuan had not revealed to Lai Song—things she was sure Lai Song found strange. For example, Ku Xuan always kept her wrists covered. When it was very hot and they had a few moments to stand out in the alley behind the laundry to catch the faint breeze, Lai Song would pull her sleeves up and let her arms cool, but Ku Xuan never did. Ku Xuan was aware that her friend had noticed this, and although Lai Song was far too polite to ask, she perhaps thought her friend had a disfiguring scar on one or both of her wrists. She concluded that Lai Song undoubtedly perceived this as an odd sort of vanity, for the younger woman had exclaimed that she had never known anyone as beautiful as Ku Xuan . . . or as seemingly unaware of her beauty. Why, then—she must wonder—would Ku Xuan be so protective of a scar?

Later in the day, after the washing was done and Ku Xuan and Lai Song were riding in the wagon back to their lodgings, Lai Song let her curiosity about Ku Xuan overcome her.

"Forgive me for asking, my revered friend, but I have noticed that every time you get a new bundle of laundry, you very carefully examine the laundry mark. Why is this?"

"I am searching for someone named Big Cat," Ku Xuan explained. "If he lives here in San Francisco, and if his laundry is done by Wu Ho, I will see his name in the marks."

"Big Cat? Who is he? And why do you wish to find him?"

"He is my father."

Lai Song looked at Ku Xuan in surprise. "Your father?"

Gesturing with her long, slim fingers to her eyes, Ku Xuan asked, "Have you not seen by my eyes that I am one-half Chinese and one-half Westerner?"

"Yes," Lai Song admitted. "Some say that is the secret of your beauty."

Ku Xuan smiled graciously. "This I do not know," she replied demurely, "but I do know that my father is an American. I have never met him, and all I know other than his name is that he lives in California."

"California is a big place," Lai Song declared pragmatically. "I do not think you will find your father by examining laundry marks."

"Do you believe there are many Americans with the name Big Cat?" Ku Xuan asked.

"I have never heard of such a name," Lai Song confessed. She laughed and added, "But then I have not met many Americans."

"Then perhaps there is one with such a name. And if so, perhaps I can find him by examining laundry marks."

"Even if you find him, I fear he will not accept you. It is not likely that an American would wish for a Chinese girl as a daughter—even one who is only half Chinese and as beautiful as you."

"That may be true. But this American loved my mother, and I must tell him that my mother returned his love."

"Did your mother tell you much about Big Cat?"

"I did not know my mother. She died when I was born."

"I am sorry to remind you of your sorrow," Lai Song murmured.

"It is all right," Ku Xuan assured her friend, touching her hand. "I do not feel sorrow for someone I never knew."

They were quiet for a few moments. Finally Lai Song said softly, "Now I can understand why you are so private. Not to have known your father and mother . . . My poor Ku Xuan. What a lonely childhood you must have had."

Ku Xuan looked off into space. Finally she replied, "My childhood was many things, my good friend, but it was not lonely."

Two days later, Ku Xuan and Lai Song were assigned the job that all the workers felt was the most pleasant of all. They were to leave the washroom and deliver the finished wash to all the wealthy customers.

Wu Ho allowed the workers who did this job to clean up and put on fresh clothes so that they would make a good impression for his laundry. Thus it was that, feeling fresh and clean and enjoying the pleasant warm air, Ku Xuan and Lai Song walked through the streets of Nob Hill, chattering happily and feeling excited about the future.

As it was to everyone who came to San Francisco, including the Chinese immigrants, Nob Hill was by far the most impressive part of the city. Not just because of the rolling streets, huge estates, and beautiful homes, but because there were so many of them all grouped together. The Chinese had seen homes of great splendor, for their princes, wealthy merchants, and warlords spared no expense in the building of their palaces. But Nob Hill was not just one, or two, or even a dozen such dwellings; it was several dozen beautiful mansions—surely proof that in America, anyone who worked hard and was thrifty could live like a prince.

With each delivery, Ku Xuan and Lai Song grew more astonished at the luxury in which their customers lived. As they walked along, they pointed out particular homes to each other, selecting the ones they especially admired and wondering about the people who lived inside.

They had already made six deliveries, and now they reached a flagstone walk leading to the front door of the house that was their seventh and last stop. Teasing, Lai Song declared, "This one is very beautiful. Perhaps the good gentleman who lives here will invite us in for tea."

"We should not count on such a thing," Ku Xuan replied, looking around the grounds. The house was one of the grandest and most beautiful they had seen today, and yet there was something about it that was unpleasant. "There is a disquieting feeling about this place. I sense we are not welcome here."

"But we have his clothes," Lai Song announced, holding up the large bundle. "Surely even a rich man would welcome the return of his clean clothes."

"I think we should be careful here," Ku Xuan warned.

They started up the walk, but they were stopped by low, menacing growling. Standing before them were two large, vicious dogs, their fangs bared and their ears flattened against their heads.

"Ku Xuan, we are doomed!" Lai Song gasped in terror, starting to tremble all over. "They will surely rip us apart!"

Reaching her hand out to steady her friend, Ku Xuan commanded, "Do not move." It was an order she did not need to give, for Lai Song was immobilized with fear.

"We will be killed!" Lai Song whispered frantically.

"No," Ku Xuan replied calmly. "It will be all right."

Ku Xuan organized her mind, concentrating the mental power she would need. Harnessing the energy, she then projected it through her eyes at the two dogs, holding them with her gaze. They stood their ground, growling quietly, as if unsure of themselves. Then the growls ceased. As they looked at her in bewilderment, the dogs quickly succumbed to the strange power of her stare. They whimpered once and then lay on their stomachs with their heads on their paws.

"What have you done to my dogs?" a man shouted angrily, pushing through his front door so hard that it slammed back against the front of the house. "What are you up to?" The man's shout frightened Lai Song, and she dropped her basket

of clothes. A shirt fell onto the ground, and she quickly
picked it up and brushed it off as best she could.

"Sic 'em!" the man shouted at his dogs, pointing at the two
Chinese girls. "Get 'em!"

The dogs remained motionless.

"Then get out of here, you worthless mutts," he screamed.
"Go on, get!"

The dogs still did not move.

"Get, I said! Get!" Fairly boiling with rage, the man kicked
the two animals in the side—first one dog, then the other.
They still refused to move.

The man looked at Ku Xuan, who was still holding the dogs
with the power of her gaze, and demanded, "What did you
do to them? What did you give them?"

Ignoring the man, Ku Xuan nodded her head once at the
dogs. They got up and ran around the corner of the house
with their tails tucked between their legs.

He then turned his anger on Lai Song, who was still trying
to brush the dirt off the shirt, and he began shouting again.
"Is that my laundry?"

Ku Xuan answered for her. "My friend does not speak
English. Yes, it is your laundry, sir."

The man sniffed in derision. "I suppose it's too much to
expect that all you people would learn our language. Oh,
well, at least one of you can speak properly—so let me teach
you something, girlie, and you can pass it on to your friend.
You should have come around by the side door. I don't allow
tradesmen—especially Chinese—to come to the front door.
And I won't take laundry that has been soiled."

"We would be glad to stay and wash the shirt again," Ku
Xuan offered.

"Stay and wash it!" the man shouted incredulously. "What
do you think I'm running here, my own laundry? That's why
I send it out, thank you. Besides, you've probably ruined the
shirt for good!"

"Ed, Ed, don't get so upset," a new, deep male voice
suddenly spoke up. "If it bothers you that much, I'll be glad
to take the shirt—buy it from you, in fact."

Ku Xuan looked over her shoulder toward the street. Coming up the walk was an elegantly dressed, handsome middle-
aged man. He doffed his hat politely and smiled at her. Ku
Xuan studied his face. She saw kindness and humor in his

eyes, and a goodness about him that she liked. She knew at once that he was a man of honor and integrity.

"Buy it? What do you mean?" Ed asked.

"I mean just that: I'll buy the shirt," the man repeated. He took a bill from his pocket. "Will you sell it for five dollars?"

"Five dollars? But it only cost one dollar when it was new."

"Then you should hasten to avail yourself of this opportunity for profit," the man told him, laughing. His laughter had a pleasant, warm quality to it, and it apparently did a great deal toward calming the laundry customer's anger. That and the "opportunity for profit."

Ed took the money and stuck it in his pocket. "I'll take your money," he said grandly, "though you're quite the fool to make the offer."

"I hardly feel the fool. In fact, I feel rather the victor. For although I was merely out for a pleasant stroll, it seems by some good fortune I have come by at just the right moment to prevent these lovely young women from being subjected to your ire."

"Are you talking about these here women? They're Chinese."

"And they are lovely," the stranger said again.

"This one's also a menace—or maybe a witch," the man declared, pointing at Ku Xuan. "She did something to my dogs. I don't know what it was, but she must've given them something to make them act real strange."

"If it were up to me, Ed, I'd give your dogs poison. They're the terror of the neighborhood, and they ought to be put away."

"Ah!" Dismissing them all with a wave of his hand, Ed pulled the soiled shirt from the basket and gave it to the stranger. Then, taking the rest of the laundry, he went back to his house, going inside with a slam of the door.

After the man had retreated, Ku Xuan faced the kind stranger. "Thank you for your help, sir," she told him, and then she and Lai Song turned to leave.

"Ladies," the man said, stopping them, "I am Walter St. John. May I ask, what are your names?"

"I am called Ku Xuan, and this is my friend, Lai Song."

"Ku Xuan and Lai Song. Those are beautiful names for beautiful women," he exclaimed. "And you speak English so well, may I presume that you were born in this country?"

"You are most gracious," Ku Xuan told him, lowering her

eyes demurely. "However, I have been in your country but a few weeks. I was taught your language at school."

St. John's eyebrows rose. "Then I am doubly impressed." He paused, studying the two women, and then asked, "I take it you work for a laundry?"

"Yes, we are indentured to Wo Hamm, and he has assigned us to work in the laundry of Wu Ho."

"And you deliver the finished work?"

Shaking her head with a smile, Ku Xuan informed him, "Oh, no. This we do but once in a while. Normally we do the washing and ironing."

St. John looked shocked. "But you are far too refined and genteel to perform such drudgery day after day! You will get old before your time."

Smiling at his concern, Ku Xuan assured him, "It was the work we requested." She lowered her eyes, knowing the Western sensibility about such things, and added, "We preferred it to concubinage."

The man looked thoughtfully at her for a long moment. "I fear that a scoundrel like Wo Hamm will not allow you such a choice for long . . . and you are bound to end up as a prostitute at one of his bordellos. That would in effect sentence you to an early grave, for in order to escape the unrelentingly terrible circumstances, you would no doubt turn to opium." Pausing as if assessing the matter, he then asked, "You know, I would be delighted to have two such beautiful ladies in my employ, and I'm sure I can find something for you to do. Would you two like to work for me?"

"I am sorry, Mr. St. John. We cannot work for you. We cannot repay Wo Hamm, and therefore we cannot quit."

"I see. Well, don't you worry, my dear. Wo Hamm owes me a favor. In fact, he owes me a great many favors. I shall visit with him and arrange to have you work for me. How would you like that?"

"It is not for me to say," Ku Xuan said. "I shall go wherever Wo Hamm tells me to go until I am out of his debt."

"By nightfall you and your friend *will* be out of his debt and working for me. That is, if you wish to."

"It is kind of you to offer."

"I shall take that as a yes. Very well, I know where Wu Ho's laundry is, and I shall come for you later. Until then." Nodding graciously, he turned, walked up the path, and left.

As the two young women walked the streets of Nob Hill, heading back to the laundry, Lai Song was very excited. "Did you see the elegant clothes Mr. St. John was wearing? And he must live here in one of these fine houses, for he knew the man whose laundry we soiled. That means he must be a very wealthy man."

"Yes," Ku Xuan agreed, without elaboration.

"Do you not see, Ku Xuan? Working in the house of a wealthy American will bring honor to us both."

"That is true," Ku Xuan replied, although her words carried much less enthusiasm than Lai Song's.

"You see this, yet you do not seem pleased."

"I told you of my search for my father," she explained. "Working in the laundry, I could examine the laundry marks. I will not be able to do this working for Mr. St. John."

"Mr. St. John is a good man," Lai Song pronounced. "Maybe going to work for him will be a good thing for you. Maybe he can help you find your father."

"Perhaps. We shall see."

When a phaeton with a liveried driver appeared at the laundry that evening just at sundown, all the Chinese workers buzzed excitedly. Lai Song had told them all of her and Ku Xuan's encounter with Walter St. John—and, in fact, that meeting had caused her to forget completely the nasty episode with the dogs. Ku Xuan had been relieved that the one event had overshadowed the other, because she did not wish to have to explain to Lai Song what it was that had taken place with the vicious animals.

As the two woman prepared to depart, they said their farewells to their coworkers.

"So the silent beauty will be a courtesan after all?" the old crone said slyly.

Ku Xuan said nothing.

"I thought you would not work at the laundry for long," the woman went on.

"It was not we who asked to leave," Lai Song explained. "Mr. St. John asked for us. I do not know if we are to be his courtesans."

"What other kind of work would a man like him want from two young women?"

"Perhaps it is housework."

"And perhaps pigs will speak," the crone replied, and the others laughed.

With the laughter of the others still ringing in their ears, Ku Xuan and Lai Song went to their dormitory room and bundled up their meager belongings. Then they left Wu Ho's laundry building—with its heavy smells of sweat, lye, and damp wood—for the last time. The carriage was waiting for them outside, and the driver nodded to them formally, touching the brim of his hat. Climbing into the phaeton, they settled into their seats for the long ride through San Francisco to the house of Walter St. John.

The softly cushioned carriage rolled through the brick and cobblestone streets on rubber-tired wheels. For the first few minutes the coach was still in Chinatown, and everything was familiar to Ku Xuan, from the ideograms painted on the signs and windows of the shops and cafés to the traditional clothes of the people in the streets. She heard the sounds of her own language and, from an upper window, the plucking of a stringed Chinese instrument, accompanied by the nasal sounds of a song whose origins were lost in history. Smelling fried pork and dried fish, she idly wondered if she and Lai Song would continue to eat their own food or that of the Americans.

Then they passed from Chinatown into the American part of San Francisco, and the sights and sounds, although just as loud, changed in tone and tint. Now the signs were in English, and though Ku Xuan could read English as easily as she could read Chinese, seeing every word written in English was a new experience for her. In just a matter of moments, she and Lai Song had changed worlds as dramatically as they had when they crossed the ocean on the *Pacific Star*. And then another drastic change took place, for the phaeton left the commercial district and entered Nob Hill.

It had grown darker, and Ku Xuan realized that this was the first time she had ever seen Nob Hill by night. She was amazed at how much artificial illumination there was in this part of town. In Chinatown, the streets at night were long and forbidding black corridors, relieved only by scattered islands of light—golden bubbles around lanterns carried into the street, or the sparse light coming from an occasional open doorway. On Nob Hill, there was a streetlamp every fifty feet, which as far as Ku Xuan was concerned was wasteful, for there were very few pedestrians to be seen anywhere.

Unlike the jarring world they had just left, it was tranquil on Nob Hill, and only the call of the insects and the singing of a night bird disturbed the stillness. The harsh smells of food cooking and commercial enterprise were also absent. In their place was the aroma of flowers, such as jasmine, sweet shrub, and night-blooming verbena.

Lai Song had uttered a few, hushed words when they began their journey, but both women were so overwhelmed by everything that was happening to them that they had ridden the rest of the way in complete silence. Now, as the coach turned up the long, curving driveway that led to Walter St. John's house, Ku Xuan was certain that Lai Song's heart was pounding as hard as hers was.

The first thing she saw was an elaborate fountain, at least fifteen feet tall. It had three scalloped tiers, with statues of naiads, cherubs, and birds gracing each tier. There were also dozens of brightly burning gas lamps about the grounds, although if the lamps were for security they were wasted, because there was a maze of shrubbery on the vast lawn providing enough concealment to hide an army of burglars. The house itself was huge and white, with walks and turrets, spires and cupolas, and practically every window glistened with golden light.

A smiling Walter St. John came down the broad steps and met the carriage as it pulled up to the front of his house. Ku Xuan studied the man who had just purchased her from Wo Hamm. She could tell by looking at him that he was a man of great virility and a great lover of life—and she knew also that he found her very desirable sexually, yet was trying to suppress that desire. What she did not know was why he was trying to suppress it, although she was certain it was not because of prejudice, not because she was Chinese. She decided it was from some sense of propriety. The biggest question in her mind now was if he gave in to his desire for her, would she allow him his way with her? He was much older than she was, but she knew that age was unimportant. She had learned that basic tenet at Shan Tal. . . .

*   *   *

"The pleasures of a man for a woman and a woman for a man are not reserved just for the handsome and the beautiful, nor for just the young and not the old," Mata Lee had explained. "There flows between all men and all women a river. As men and women begin to know each other sexually, they are on opposite sides of the river. But as they grow in knowledge, they come into the river until finally both are in midstream. It is when both are in midstream and the river of pleasure surrounds them that sexual pleasure is at its greatest.

"There are many things that can put men and women in the middle of this stream. One is knowledge of all the sexual arts, such as are taught at Shan Tal. Another is well-spent years of unselfish feeling in a man or a woman of advanced age. The final and most exquisite way for a man and woman to share in the river of pleasure is to know love. But this last is not to be for the priestesses of Shan Tal."

Ku Xuan knew that she could give Walter St. John pleasure, but she felt quite certain that he would not provide her with the opportunity. She waited to see why.

"Come, ladies," St. John said, gesturing toward his house. "Let's go inside, shall we?"

"Mr. St. John, your home is truly beautiful," Ku Xuan told him appreciatively.

He smiled proudly. "Thank you. I confess that its opulence is a little embarrassing to me sometimes—but I must also admit that I enjoy living here."

They walked up the broad steps and through the double doors into a huge foyer. Directly in front of them, in the center of the foyer, was a grand stairway ascending to the second floor. Elsewhere the visitors saw polished marble floors, rich wall hangings, beautiful paintings, and a collection of fine statuary. As they stood admiring everything, servants seemed to materialize and then disappear again, almost like ghosts.

"By the way, there is an excellent view of the city from the second floor, if you wish to see it," St. John invited.

He led the way upstairs and then down a long hallway and out onto a huge balcony that ran along the back of the house. The back lawn, like the front, was exquisitely landscaped, with boxed hedges forming geometric patterns and statues and fountains surrounded by beautiful flower beds. Ku Xuan had never seen so many artificial lights winking and sparkling in one place, and she felt that they put the sky and its stars to shame. But the most breathtaking sight was the rest of San Francisco, for from this vantage point it seemed as if the entire town was spread out at their feet, put there only for their pleasure.

"It is very beautiful," Ku Xuan breathed.

A woman suddenly joined them on the balcony, and St. John turned to her. "Ah, Mrs. Adams. Good." Turning to Ku Xuan, he introduced them. "This is my housekeeper, Martha Adams, and Mrs. Adams, this is Ku Xuan." Gently touching Lai Song's elbow, he said to the middle-aged woman, "And this young lady is Lai Song. Would you please show her to one of the empty servants' rooms?"

"Certainly, sir," she answered. Gesturing to the two young women, she said, "This way, please."

Ku Xuan and Lai Song started to follow the woman, but St. John put his hand on Ku Xuan's arm. "No," he told the housekeeper. "Only the one. This young lady will have the Rose Room."

"The Rose Room?" Mrs. Adams asked with raised eyebrows. "Surely you don't intend to put her in the Rose Room!"

"Surely you don't intend to question me," St. John replied coolly.

Mrs. Adams looked down. "No, sir, of course not."

"Then kindly do as I ask."

"Yes, of course, sir." Speaking to Lai Song in pidgin Chinese, Mrs. Adams started to lead her toward the servants' quarters, and with a glance back at Ku Xuan, the young woman followed.

When they had left, St. John turned to Ku Xuan. "Your room is right down here. Come, I will show you."

Ku Xuan followed St. John back into the house. They walked along the spacious hallway, which was wide enough to accommodate the entire women's dormitory at the laundry where, until barely an hour earlier, she had been living and working. Passing a number of rooms, at last they halted before carved double doors.

St. John pushed the doors open, allowing Ku Xuan to step into the bedroom, and she caught her breath. Like the rest of the house, it was elegant beyond comparison, and as she stepped into the room, her eyes were wide with disbelief. The floor was covered in a plush dark-blue carpet, the walls were white with a series of carved panels trimmed in blue and gold, and the ceiling was vaulted and decorated with paintings of flowers. A large rosewood dresser with a mirror sat on one side of the room, and St. John crossed to the other side to open the door to a spacious closet-dressing area. A delicately painted table with two matching chairs formed a cozy eating area in front of a large bay window, which offered essentially the same view as was enjoyed from the balcony. Dominating the room was an enormous canopied bed, and two servant girls stood beside it.

Gesturing to the two, St. John told Ku Xuan, "These girls will take care of anything you might need."

She did not understand her position. She had thought she was to be a servant, and yet he had just assigned two servant girls to her. She wondered, but she did not question.

"You may leave now," St. John said to the two servants, and they both left quietly. Then he walked over to the window and looked out for several moments. Finally he turned to look at Ku Xuan and cleared his throat. She saw the look of desire in his eyes again, and then she saw that he again quickly suppressed it.

"I suppose you are wondering about all this."

"Yes."

"My wife died ten years ago," he said. He paused and took a deep breath. "Like you, she was a beautiful woman. I promised her a house like this—and clothes, beautiful things—but she died before I could give any of it to her. Now that I have all the material things a man could want, I find that this house needs the presence of a beautiful woman."

"I see," Ku Xuan said quietly.

"No, I don't think you do. I'm not proposing anything to you, Ku Xuan. I do not want you to become my wife; I do not want you to become my mistress. I want only for a beautiful, intelligent, gracious woman to be the hostess in my house—and I'll demand no more of you. Will you accept this position?"

"You have purchased me from Wo Hamm," Ku Xuan stated. "I have no choice."

"Oh, yes, you do have a choice," he told her emphatically. "I purchased your contract, but I didn't purchase you. If you wish, you may walk out my front door this very minute. I will make no claim on you."

For a moment, Ku Xuan thought of the mission of finding her father. Without being tied down to the laundry or any other job, her search might be easier. But then she realized that her being brought here was her destiny—and one cannot, after all, alter the river of destiny. Smiling serenely at Walter St. John, she said simply, "It is my wish to stay."

Chapter Four

Walter St. John spent a few more minutes with Ku Xuan, pointing out the various appointments of her new quarters before going back downstairs. After he had gone, the Chinese woman continued to investigate everything. Entering the huge closet, she closely examined the rich, elaborate clothes, the most beautiful she had ever seen. She had been very surprised when St. John told her that a number of the dresses were not his wife's, but had been hastily bought especially for Ku Xuan after he had negotiated with Wo Hamm for her contract.

The closet with its large dressing area led to what St. John had called her private bathroom. Larger than the room that had been hers at the temple of Shan Tal, this room was filled with white and gold porcelain fixtures. She had marveled when St. John reached for the golden spigots over the bathtub and twisted one of them, telling her, "If you turn these knobs, you'll get all the water you need; this one is hot, that one is cold."

She smiled to herself as she recalled St. John telling her, "I warn you, my dear, you could become quite intoxicated by all the trappings you may find here."

"I'll try to keep a level head," Ku Xuan had replied.

St. John had laughed aloud, saying, "By heaven, I believe you will."

When he had left, he had said that they would dine in a little over an hour, which would give her plenty of time to get ready. He told her to feel free to pick out whatever dress appealed to her, and that he looked forward to seeing her choice.

Just as he was about to leave the room, she had asked, "Shall I prepare the meal?"

"No, no, my little one," St. John had said, holding his hand out toward her and laughing. "You must get used to the fact that all that will be done for you now."

As Ku Xuan stepped out of the gleaming bathtub, she picked up the thick towel left for her by one of the servants. The young woman—she had told Ku Xuan that she was her personal maid, and that her name was Sarah—was to help Ku Xuan with her dressing, but Ku Xuan had dismissed her, feeling uncomfortable as yet in the presence of a stranger.

After a vigorous toweling, her body was left glowing and clean. She slipped into a yellow silk dressing gown, and the feel of the silk on her body was the most sensuous she had ever known. The robe clung to her body, and as she examined herself in a full-length mirror in the dressing area—the first such looking glass she had ever encountered—she saw herself from head to toe for the first time in her life. She observed that the dressing gown did little to conceal her body, and her nipples protruded boldly through the silk. She made a mental note never to wear the dressing gown when modesty was required.

Stepping over to the hanging garments, Ku Xuan examined the dresses. The Western style of dress was so different from the Oriental. Indeed, it looked very complicated—and not a little uncomfortable. Running her hands over the dresses, she finally decided to choose from three of them. After taking them from the closet, she laid them out on her bed and stepped back to look at them. One was white and demure; another was deep green and elegant; and the third, red and daring. She studied them closely, her finger pressed to her cheek and her brown eyes taking in every detail. Finally she decided upon the green dress.

Ku Xuan looked down at the undergarment that her maid had left for her. Sarah had explained that it was called a corset, and it was designed to emphasize the hourglass shape of the female form. Picking it up, Ku Xuan decided it more resembled an instrument of torture and chose to do without it. Besides, she reminded herself, her form was very slender and was not in need of shaping. Slipping out of the dressing gown, she put on a fine cotton lawn chemise with matching pantalets, and then stepped into the gown, pulling it up and thrusting her arms through the short, puffed sleeves that sat just below her shoulders. Then she realized that it was fastened by dozens of tiny buttons running up the back, and she knew why a maid was necessary. Sighing, she pulled the bellcord as she had been instructed and waited for Sarah to appear.

Twenty minutes later, feeling somewhat out of her element, Ku Xuan stepped into the dining room. Seated at one end of an enormous table was Walter St. John, dressed in formal attire, and he stood as one of the servants held a chair out for her along the side of the table. She bowed slightly at him and took her seat.

"Cook told me that Lai Song insisted on preparing a special dinner for us," St. John informed her. "I hope you are pleased."

"I am sure the effort will be as gratifying as the deed," Ku Xuan replied.

St. John looked at her appraisingly. "I applaud your choice of a gown."

"Thank you," she answered, smiling shyly, "although I fear this mode of dress will take a bit of getting used to."

St. John patted her hand. "I assure you, you look as if you had worn Western clothes all your life."

She sat looking down at her plate so that her long, delicate lashes shielded her eyes for a moment. Finally she looked back up at St. John and her eyes asked the question before her mouth formed the words. "Mr. St. John, I'm puzzled," she told him.

As if he knew what she was thinking, he patted her hand again. "Please don't be," he replied. "I explained to you . . . you will not be required to do anything but serve as hostess of this house."

"But will not such an arrangement cause you embarrassment?"

"Embarrassment? In what way?"

"You are an unmarried American man. And I am . . ."

"A beautiful and unmarried young woman?"

"I am Chinese."

"Then you are a beautiful woman who happens to be Chinese. I still don't understand your concern."

"Will not your neighbors think such an arrangement is unseemly?"

St. John laughed. "Ku Xuan, when you look at my neighbors, what do you see?"

"I see beautiful homes and wealthy men," she answered.

"Yes, yes, beautiful homes and wealthy men—but *new* wealth. Practically everyone out here is just like me . . . men who made their fortunes through labor and sweat. There is no old money out here, so there are no old, firmly established social rules. Half the men out here have spent their lives prowling brothels . . . and half the women came from those brothels. Most have a live-and-let-live attitude, and those that don't—those who are trying to anoint themselves the watchkeepers of society—must do the anointing very quietly lest the skeletons in their own closets be exposed. I assure you, my dear, you needn't worry about my neighbors."

"Then I have one more area of concern," she admitted.

"And what would that be, my dear?"

"Your servants. Are they not offended by me? Are they not envious of my position in this house? And you say that Lai Song is cooking our meal. What does your cook say about that?"

"My servants are very well paid and well treated," St. John said. "Those who harbor jealousies and resentments have been weeded out long before now, for I want only cordiality and happiness surrounding me in my own home. You will find none among my staff who will complain—or skulk about in silence. They won't envy you, Ku Xuan. You'll even discover that they'll be your friends. And as for Cook, well, she and Lai Song were laughing and having a good time when I overheard them earlier. Lai Song is a pleasant young woman who offends no one. Worry not, your stay in this house will be a tranquil one."

A moment later a parade of servants began bringing in trays of food, and Lai Song, also wearing a new Western dress, smiled broadly as she supervised.

"I hope my humble efforts have pleased you, my mistress," Lai Song said in her own language.

"Why do you call me your mistress?" Ku Xuan asked. She was glad for the opportunity to speak Chinese and thus be able to speak freely.

"I am told that you are so, and I see that it is so," Lai Song replied as she began to serve Ku Xuan. "And I am truly glad, for never would such a wonderful thing have happened to me without you."

Ku Xuan smiled and then lifted her napkin from the table to place it on her lap. She heard Lai Song draw a sharp breath, and looking at her, she realized that Lai Song was staring at her exposed wrist and what she had always before taken pains to hide—the tattoo of a tiny blue chrysanthemum.

"Oh," Lai Song whispered, and quickly set the dish she was holding on the table, dropping to her knees. Bowing low, she touched her forehead to the floor. "Now I know why you could work such magic with the dogs. You are a priestess of Shan Tal."

"What is it?" St. John demanded to know. "Why is the girl bowing to you so?"

Thinking quickly, Ku Xuan replied, "She is impressed with my status," wording it in such a way that St. John would think she meant her place within the house.

"Oh, to think you once washed clothes like a peasant," Lai Song murmured.

"As I told you, there is only honor in honest work." Ku Xuan was embarrassed. "Please, Lai Song, do not kowtow before me. It will make our host uneasy."

"But you are a priestess," Lai Song insisted.

"No, I am not. I took no vows."

"But the chrysanthemum."

"It was placed there at my birth, for I was born in the temple of Shan Tal."

"Then you are a priestess. It matters not that you took no vow. I will be your servant forever."

Giving her friend her hand and almost forcibly raising her up, Ku Xuan told her, "If you would serve me, you will not speak of this to anyone. And you will make no action that would betray me."

"I will do as you ask," Lai Song humbly assured her. "But if someone else sees the chrysanthemum . . ."

"The Americans will not know the meaning of the chrysanthemum if you do not tell them."

"I will honor your wishes and not tell them. But I shall serve you secretly," Lai Song declared. She stood up straight, finished supervising the serving, and then withdrew from the room.

Turning to St. John, Ku Xuan explained, "I have told her that she embarrasses me by showing such respect when I, too, am but a servant. She means well, and she is a good person who is my friend."

"I thought as much. That's why I had her come as well. I thought you would be less lonely if your friend was with you."

They finished eating, and the servants pulled out their chairs for them as they stood up.

"Come, my dear," Walter St. John said, "I'll show you the rest of the house."

"I would very much enjoy that," Ku Xuan said, smiling.

As they crossed to the door, she noticed a shield on the wall, and she walked over to it to examine it more closely. What held her attention was the design in the middle: a lion rampant, holding a sword in one hand and an olive branch in the other.

"That is my family crest," the businessman explained. "Though recent generations of my family have been common folk, we have some remote noble connections going way back. In the old days, many people couldn't read signs, but they would always know the St. John family when they saw that big cat snarling at them."

Ku Xuan suddenly gasped and paled.

"What is it, Ku Xuan? Is something wrong?"

"Big cat," Ku Xuan whispered.

"What? It's just a picture, that's all."

"Yes, I understand that," Ku Xuan said, composing herself. "It is my father. My father's name is Big Cat." Ku Xuan then explained her mission to St. John. However, she omitted the details of her days in Shan Tal, passing off the cloister as merely a type of orphanage, and she also said nothing about discovering the assassins standing over Mata Lee's body—or the fact that she had to kill them.

"And so you've come to America to find your father?" he asked, when she had finished her story.

"Yes, if I can."

St. John sighed. "I don't know, Ku Xuan, this is an awfully

big country, and there have been a lot of Americans who went to China. I even went there myself."

"When?" Ku Xuan asked, intensity evident in her voice.

St. John looked at Ku Xuan for a long moment with a very strange expression on his face. Finally he stroked his chin thoughtfully and told her, "My dear child, nothing would make me happier than to believe I was your father—and while I was there, which was just about the right time, I must confess to having met a beautiful young woman, the daughter of a very wealthy merchant. Though I wouldn't want to go into any details, I will tell you that while I'm not aware of any children, it *is* possible." He looked at his family crest. "However, it seems to me that we'd need a lot more than a cat to go on before we could make up our minds."

"I have some questions," she stated.

"Questions? What sort of questions?"

"Questions that only my father can answer."

"All right, girl, fire away," St. John said, crossing his arms over his chest and smiling. "And I hope I can answer every one of them."

"What lies beyond the inner door of the golden pagoda?" Ku Xuan asked.

"I . . . I don't know the answer to that."

"What secret is hidden by the jasmines of the garden?"

St. John just shrugged his shoulders.

"Who was Tsu?"

He shook his head sadly. "I'm sorry, my dear. None of those questions means anything to me."

Ku Xuan looked down at her hands for a moment. When she looked back up, her eyes were shining brightly from a sheen of tears. Smiling wanly, she told him, "It would have been nice to call you Father."

St. John walked over to her and put his arms around her, then pulled her to him.

"I can think of nothing sweeter," he said tenderly. "In the meantime, until you find your real father, I'd be very honored to be your substitute father."

"Even when I do find him," Ku Xuan answered, trying very hard not to cry, "I shall continue to regard you as my father."

"I would like that," he replied, his voice cracking. "Very much."

*   *   *

About two hours before Ku Xuan and St. John sat down to
dinner, Mike Wakefield was sitting on the driver's box of his
stagecoach heading north, roughly midway between the tiny
town of Half Moon Bay and San Francisco. Only one passenger was on board, but there was a canvas and leather bag in
the boot that was stuffed with five thousand dollars in green-
backs being transferred from the bank in Half Moon Bay to
the Bank of America in San Francisco. More wary than ever
of robbery attempts since he and his passengers had been
robbed at gunpoint a few weeks earlier, Mike now made
every trip with his gun loaded and his eyes searching the
terrain.

St. John had offered to send a man riding shotgun along
with him, but Mike figured that it might be safer to decline
the additional protection and proceed as if everything were
normal. Therefore, although he was carrying a great deal of
money, he was unguarded except for his own weapon.

The road between Half Moon Bay and San Francisco was
wide, flat, and straight for much of the way. However, there
were stretches that passed through mountains, and one particular section that went through a narrow canyon with high
walls, known to the drivers as Ambush Pass. Once inside this
narrow defile, a horse and rider could turn around and back
out, but a wagon or a stagecoach had no choice but to pass all
the way through.

Although the whole stretch was called Ambush Pass, in
truth there was only one spot where an effective ambush
could be staged, and that was three-quarters of the way
through, where the western wall of the canyon lowered until
it was a jumble of boulders near the left side of the road,
forming a natural vantage point and place of cover. At any
other section of the pass, potential attackers would have to be
on the road in plain sight, or far away, at the very top of the
canyon walls and beyond effective firing range.

Starting through Ambush Pass, Mike drew his gun and
held it by his side. The minutes went by, and he had traveled
three-quarters of the way through without incident. He looked
to his right. The sun was low, coming from just above the
canyon wall to his left, so that it cast elongated shadows along
the east wall of the pass. There Mike could see the shadow of

the coach and the shadow of the stand of boulders . . . and if anyone were concealed behind or on top of the rocks moved, their shadows likewise would appear, giving Mike advance warning of their presence. Ready for action, he cocked his pistol.

Peering over the top of the stand of rocks, Cole Granger watched the coach as it started through the pass. He turned to the two men who were with him and chuckled, saying, "This here's gonna be like takin' candy from a baby."

"I don't know, Granger, there ain't no shotgun ridin' with him. Maybe he ain't carryin' nothin'."

"I got it on good word that he's carryin' five thousand dollars," Granger told his accomplice, pulling his revolver and cocking it. "He figures to fool us, is all. Now you two get ready."

Granger waited a few more moments until he was absolutely certain the stagecoach was committed to the narrow pass. There was no way of escaping him now, and he smiled broadly.

"All right, boys, let's get him," he hissed.

Although to anyone watching him Mike Wakefield would have appeared concerned only with the task of negotiating the team through the narrow ravine, in fact he was paying acute attention to the shadow of the boulders on the canyon wall. Suddenly the shadow changed shape, as three distinct forms detached themselves and went into motion along the main shadow. He knew that ambushers were swinging into action, and he raised his pistol, gauging where the men would appear.

He fired just as the first head showed itself. The would-be bushwhacker fell face forward, his unfired gun clacking down on the rocks beside him. All hell broke loose as both remaining ambushers opened fire. Little flashes of orange light exploded like fireballs on the rocks as their bullets raised sparks and dust.

Peering at the two remaining confederates, Mike was sure that one of them was the man who had robbed him earlier in the month. He had since learned that his full name was Cole

Granger, and he was wanted all up and down the state for similar robberies.

The two men had apparently been frightened and surprised by Mike's sudden and unexpected firing, and in their confusion their aim was ragged. Flying lead whistled through the air, whined off stone, and rattled through tree leaves like hail—but every shot missed its target.

"What the hell?" Mike heard the man with Granger scream. "What is this? How'd he know we were here?"

"Shut up!" Granger shouted. "Just shoot the son of a bitch!"

Mike had dropped down into the bottom of the box and was offering a small target. As the coach continued on through the pass beyond the stand of boulders, Mike had a clear shot at one of the two men. He aimed carefully and shot again, and the outlaw standing beside Granger clutched his chest and fell. Realizing then that he had not only lost his advantage in numbers but was also exposed, Granger turned and scrambled up over the top of the boulders, no longer interested in robbery, concerned now only with getting away.

The driver sent two more shots after the retreating bushwacker. His bullets kicked up stone dust and chips just behind Granger as the outlaw disappeared behind the rocks. He had gotten away, but the two bushwhackers who were with him were stopped, and the money satchel was still safe in the bottom of the boot.

Sitting erect on his seat, Mike whipped the horses. The animals, frightened by the shooting, needed no encouragement. They pulled the coach through the rest of the pass at breakneck speed, finally calming down on the other side. Reining them to a halt, he let them have a rest while he climbed down to stretch his own legs. The door to the passenger box opened, and a heavyset gray-bearded man stepped out of the coach, took off his hat, and wiped his forehead with a red bandanna.

"Whooeee!" the passenger exclaimed. "Mike, you certainly upset their applecart. I liked the way you got two of them and set the other one a-running."

"The one that got away robbed my passengers a few weeks ago," Mike said. He reloaded his pistol as he spoke, although he did not really believe there would be another try. "I was determined he wasn't going to do it again."

"So that was him," the passenger said. "Yes, I heard about

that." He laughed and slapped his knee. "But I'll bet it'll be a while before he tries you again. I've never seen such good shooting."

"I was lucky," Mike declared.

"I don't believe in luck," the passenger responded. "If I did, I'd be a gambling man. I figure a man makes his own luck. I don't know how you got on to 'em so fast, but you sure got my hand and my thanks for a job well done." The passenger reached out to shake the driver's hand, and Mike took it, grinning at the compliment.

"I just wish some of the passengers I carried the last time I was attacked felt the same way," Mike said ruefully. Pointing to the coach, he suggested, "Best you climb in now, so we can get going again. We have a ways to go before we reach San Francisco."

It was dark by the time the coach arrived in San Francisco, and Mike drove the team through the streets to the stage depot. A number of people were milling around, waiting expectantly for the stagecoach's arrival.

"We were robbed!" the portly passenger declared as he stepped down from the coach.

"What? Robbed?" one of the bystanders asked, looking up at Mike with concern.

The passenger held up his hand and laughed. "Maybe I should say some varmints *tried* to rob us." Pointing to Mike, who was climbing down from the driver's seat, he added, "But Mike killed two of them and ran off the third one."

A buzz of excitement swept through the crowd, mingled with awe over the exploits of the coach driver. The young hostler, in particular, gazed admiringly at the driver.

"Then the robbers didn't get anything?" another bystander asked.

Mike handed the man the leather and canvas bag. "No, sir, Mr. Barnes, everything is here. You can take it over to the bank now."

Barnes, who was the bank's regular messenger, smiled and took the bag. Then he nodded toward the front of the stage office, and two armed security men came over and flanked him. "Well, Mr. Wakefield, on behalf of the bank, allow me to extend my gratitude."

"Just sign this receipt," Mike told him, shoving a paper across to him. "That's all the gratitude I want."

The man quickly scribbled his name on the release form and then left, accompanied by the two guards. After seeing to it that the hostler took charge of the coach and horses, Mike started up the street. He paused in midstep when the passenger called out to him.

"Mike, come on over to the Nugget and let me buy you a drink."

Turning, the driver said over his shoulder, "Thanks. Maybe I'll stop by later. First, though, I've got to report to Mr. St. John. He'll want to know what happened."

"What happened? I'd be glad to tell him what happened!" the passenger exclaimed with a laugh. "The bushwhackers were outnumbered, that's what. There were only three of them to the one of you."

As Mike walked through the cool streets toward Nob Hill, he thought how it always gave him a thrill to visit Walter St. John at his house. Of all the stately mansions in that prized neighborhood, St. John's was the most elegant, sitting like a crown jewel atop an exquisitely landscaped hill and overlooking the entire city.

When he reached his destination, he paused and stared at the house for a few moments, wondering what it must be like to live in such a place. He shook his head, as if to clear it of the thought, and then strode up the drive to the front door. His knock was answered by a servant, who ushered him inside.

"Ah, good, you're back," St. John said when Mike was shown into the parlor. "All went well?"

"Everything turned out all right." He paused to clear his throat. "We were ambushed just as we came through the narrows, but I managed to fight the bushwhackers off."

"Was anyone hurt?"

"Neither the passenger nor I was hit, but I, uh, may have killed two of them."

"You managed to fight them off you say; then you tell me you may have killed two of them? Son, you are much too modest. Well, thank God you and the passenger were unhurt. That's far more important to me than the money getting through safely—though I must confess that I am pleased you accomplished that task as well. Come, sit down and have a drink with me."

"Don't mind if I do," Mike answered.

St. John picked up a small bell and rang it. A few moments later the most exquisitely beautiful woman Mike had ever seen in his life appeared in the doorway of the parlor.

"Oh, Ku Xuan, won't you join us for a drink?"

"Of course, sir," Ku Xuan answered, her voice as melodious as a wind chime.

The girl came farther into the light, and Mike stared at the girl for a long, frozen moment. He was struck by her beauty, to be sure—but there was something more about her, a haunting presence that stirred a memory buried deep in his heart.

"Ku Xuan," St. John said, "I'd like to introduce Mike Wakefield, my top driver. Mike, I've asked Ku Xuan to join the household and act as my official hostess."

"I'm sorry—what?" Mike replied, not having heard.

"I said, Ku Xuan is my new hostess."

"Oh, yes. I'm sorry. Pleased to meet you, ma'am."

"And I am pleased to make your acquaintance, Mike Wakefield," the beautiful Chinese woman replied.

"Mike's been to China, too," St. John went on.

"Oh? Did you like China, Mr. Wakefield?" Ku Xuan asked, smiling pleasantly.

"Yes. No. It was a long time ago."

She smiled. "You say yes and no. Which was it?"

"I don't know," Mike admitted.

There was something about this girl that he found very unsettling, and he could not put his finger on what it was. He thought about his voyage to China with his old captain, and he felt a sense of uneasiness. Without understanding why, he knew that he had to put some distance between himself and this beautiful Chinese girl.

"Surely you would know whether the experience was pleasant or unpleasant?" Ku Xuan gently insisted.

"I don't remember," Mike answered, his voice raised and sharp, almost to the point of rudeness. The pleasant expression on Ku Xuan's face suddenly changed, and she became guarded.

"Mike, Ku Xuan was just trying to make friendly conversation," St. John said testily.

The driver looked at his employer, aware that he was surprised by Mike's attitude. He had always admired Mike's affinity for the Chinese, and now here he was acting like a perfect boor with Ku Xuan.

"I'm sorry," he apologized. "It's just that it was a long time ago, that's all. Something unpleasant happened then . . . and I don't like to be reminded of it."

"And I am sorry if I am the cause of an unpleasant memory," Ku Xuan replied, looking upset. "If you will excuse me . . ." She bowed slightly, then left the room.

Mike watched her go and then asked, "Who is she? I mean, why is she here?"

"She's looking for her father."

"I beg your pardon?"

"She came to America to search for her father," St. John explained. "She knows only that he is an American, and she has come to find him."

"Why?"

St. John shrugged his shoulders. "Why? That I can't tell you." He took a swallow of his drink. "She briefly thought it might be me. She saw my family crest and the lion intrigued her. It seems her father's name is Big Cat."

"Big Cat? That doesn't sound like an American name."

"I know, but it's all she has to go on. That and a few questions Big Cat is supposed to know the answers to."

"And she's living here, in your house?"

"Yes. I purchased her contract from Wo Hamm."

"I see. Well, I understand that you're, uh . . . lonely."

St. John laughed mirthlessly. "You, too, eh? Well, I suppose I can understand that everyone would immediately jump to the wrong conclusion. But I assure you, I just wish to help her. And she is providing me with delightful company."

Mike Wakefield was quiet for a long moment. Finally he said, "Mr. St. John, it's none of my business, but do you think you should have an unmarried young woman living here in the same house with you? And a Chinese girl at that? You're bound to be hurt by malicious gossip."

"I have a dozen women and nearly as many men living here . . . all servants," St. John answered.

"Yes, but—"

"But what?"

"None of the others are so . . . so beautiful."

St. John smiled. "Well, so you noticed she was beautiful, did you?"

"How could anyone help but notice?"

"That's true. And in answer to your question, Mike, you're right when you say it is none of your business—but you're wrong if you think I'll be hurt by gossip. In the first place, I seriously doubt whether anyone will have the audacity to bring it up. And if they do, I care not one whit what they might say." He smiled slyly and added, "As a matter of fact, I think I'll rather enjoy watching how some of our pillars of society deal with their disapproval and discomfort. They're far too hypocritical to object openly—and I know full well that none of them will dare to ostracize me, because I'm too damn wealthy."

Mike grinned. "In other words, to hell with them?"

"To hell with them," St. John agreed, nodding vigorously.

On the San Francisco docks the following afternoon another shipload of Chinese immigrants had just landed. As the newly arrived workers milled about in confusion, waiting for someone to come and take charge, one man stood apart from the rest. In fact, his only similarity to the others was that he was Chinese. This man did not have the same anxious and uncertain look that everyone else had—quite to the contrary, his face reflected tremendous self-confidence, almost to the point of arrogance; his attire was clearly elegant and expensive; and he had about him the air of a man with a definite mission.

His name was Li Chen, and he had not come to San Francisco as one of Wo Hamm's indentured servants. Here at the behest of Ma Phat, the supreme warlord of the Canton district, his mission was to find and kill the only surviving relative of Lo Ching, the Manchu prince Ma Phat had overthrown and murdered to assume power. The warlord felt lucky to have Li Chen working for him—not only because of his command of English, but because he was absolutely ruthless.

"You," one of the burly American dock workers suddenly called to him. "Get over there with the others. Wo Hamm will be coming down here soon to take charge of all you Chinamen."

Li Chen looked at the dock worker as if he were something unclean, and then looked away, remaining exactly where he was.

"Didn't you hear me, Chinaman? I told you to get over there with the others."

Li Chen still did not respond.

"Hey, Carl, maybe he don't understand our lingo," one of the other dock workers said to the first.

"Yeah? Well, he'll understand this," the man named Carl replied. He walked over to Li Chen and stood right in front of him, towering over the much smaller man. "If you don't get over there now, I'm gonna pick you up and *throw* you over there."

Li Chen stared at him impassively.

"All right, Chinaman, you asked for it," Carl said, and he swung at Li Chen. But Li Chen pulled his head back, avoiding the blow, and his movement was so quick and so subtle that it looked almost as if the big dock worker had just missed.

"Haw! You can't do much if you can't hit him," one of his companions called, laughing.

Carl swung again, and again Li Chen moved out of the way.

"Why you chink bastard! I'll break you in two!" Carl sputtered. Again he lashed out, and again he missed.

"You want me to show you how it's done, Carl?" one of the other workers chided, and then he, too, came over and took a swing at Li Chen. Now both men were trying to punch him, and Li Chen, whose hands were still folded across his chest, moved this way and that, easily avoiding the attempted blows of the frustrated dock workers.

By now the incident had attracted the attention of several other bystanders, and a crowd began to gather—both Chinese and American—to watch the two men trying to hit Li Chen.

"Come on, guys," someone else declared to his fellow workers. "This is embarrassing, having a Chinaman do that to a couple of our friends. Let's take care of him."

With that, two other dock workers joined the first two, so that now four men surrounded Li Chen, but he evaded the attempts of all four as easily as he had just the two. The Chinese began to cheer for their champion, while the other dock workers jeered at the four men, who were being made to look so foolish. Finally Li Chen thrust his hands out to either side of him, catching two of his adversaries. Surprised by his sudden movement, both men went down, unconscious. With a spinning motion, another thrust of his hands, and a lashing foot, Li Chen knocked out the other two. Bringing up his arms into a fighting pose in front of him, he stood for a moment longer, looking around through narrowed eyes.

With his arms so positioned, the tattooed dragon of a Shal Minh priest was clearly visible on his wrist. Although it meant nothing to the Americans who were looking on, every Chinese man and woman recognized it at once, and as awe and fear spread through their ranks, they all bowed respectfully. Perceiving that there was no danger of being attacked again, Li Chen lowered his arms and relaxed his pose, making absolutely no effort to acknowledge the homage being paid him by the others. It was clearly his due.

The Chinese who had come to America as indentured servants were well aware of the forces that governed their lives. They had been victimized by poverty, by the warlord or province chief, by the landlords whose land they worked, by the wealthy merchants who took what little money they did make, and by the tong leaders who robbed and terrorized them. And the personification of all that was evil to them, those who in Western cultures would be regarded as "angels of Satan," were the priests of Shal Minh.

Although Shal Minh was, like Shan Tal, a religious abbey and place of learning, dedication, and self-discipline, it espoused a philosophy wholly different from that of Shan Tal. The Shan Tal order held that the secret skills and knowledge learned at the abbey should be used only for good. The priests and priestesses who were the products of the temple were taught that they were the protectors of the weak and the servants of the people. They learned that the harmony of nature was the guiding principle of the universe, and the life of a flower that bloomed and died in one day was as important to that harmony as the life of a tree that endured for hundreds of years. The beauty of a butterfly's wing was to be as much respected as the strength of an eagle's talon.

But the priests of Shal Minh took the opposite view, preaching honor to the strong and contempt for the weak. They did not serve the people; they were served by the people. Founded more than eight hundred years earlier by a Shan Tal priest who had tried and failed to take control of that religious order, Shal Minh was dedicated to the principle of evil, and its priests took pride in their power, demanding and receiving heavy tribute from the people. They served no one but themselves and accepted tasks—such as the one Li Chen had agreed to—only if the tribute was high enough. Priests of the Shal Minh, such as Li Chen, owed allegiance to no one. The positions of warlords, princes, and wealthy merchants were of no consequence to Li Chen—except insofar as he could benefit from them.

And now he stood patiently on this American pier, waiting for the tong chief, Wo Hamm, to come for his latest shipment of human cargo. Ma Phat had known of the tong chief and informed Li Chen of him. The Shal Minh priest immediately realized that he could make very good use of Wo Hamm. As he watched for the tong chief's arrival, he recalled the circumstances that had led him to this American pier in pursuit of the Manchu princess.

After the uprising he had staged, Ma Phat had seen to it that Lo Ching, the Manchu prince, and all of his relatives were beheaded. All had gone according to his plan for a time, but soon the warlord was himself plagued by revolutionaries. It was then that his adviser, Li Chen, decided to use to his advantage knowledge that only he had.

He had informed Ma Phat that, unknown to anyone, the prince still had one living descendant. "She is not only the last surviving relative of Lo Ching," he had explained, "she is trained as a Shan Tal priestess and is very skilled, for she killed the men I sent for her."

"And why did you send them?"

"Because I knew you would wish her dead."

Nodding, the warlord agreed. "You were correct. Tell me, the men you sent . . . were they priests of Shal Minh?"

"No, but they were from my personal bodyguard, and they were men of great strength and skill."

"And yet they were bested by a young woman."

"Yes. That is why I have decided to fulfill the mission myself."

"Where is the girl now?" Ma Phat had asked.

"She has gone to America to find her father."

"Why did her father flee to America? Why did he not stay and fight for what was his?"

"Her father is American," Li Chen explained. "He was a ship's captain."

"That means the girl is one-half American?"

"Yes."

"I do not like Americans. It will be a pleasure to have you find her and kill her. A Manchu of mixed blood must not be allowed to live, in case she ever decides to rally support and try to assume the throne. Yes, she must be found and dealt with. The people demand it."

"I do not care what the people demand," Li Chen had said coldly. "I will perform this task because you will pay well for it—and because I will enjoy destroying one of the Shan Tal."

When Wo Hamm's coach arrived at the dock to oversee the new shipment of indentured servants, Li Chen walked over to meet the tong chief. He stood silently for a long moment, studying the man who was so elegantly dressed in silken robes of blue and gold.

Wo Hamm was obviously disconcerted by the man's unwavering stare, and he started to order two of his bodyguards to send Li Chen away. Then someone whispered something to him, a bit of information he had picked up from the others, and Wo Hamm's eyebrows rose. Looking at Li Chen, he forced a smile.

"I am told you are a priest of Shal Minh."

"That is correct. I am called Li Chen."

"I am puzzled, Li Chen. Why would a priest of Shal Minh come to America? There is nothing for you here in this country."

"But there *is* something," Li Chen said. "There is a girl—a very beautiful girl. I am told she came to America recently. I must find her."

"Perhaps I can help," Wo Hamm said. "Many beautiful young women have come to America, and most come through me."

"The girl's name is Ku Xuan."

Wo Hamm recognized the name. And Li Chen was right when he said she was beautiful. As Wo Hamm recalled her, she was a woman of exceptional beauty.

"Why do you seek her?"

"She is my cousin," Li Chen lied. "I must return her to China. . . . It is a matter of family business."

Wo Hamm thoughtfully stroked his chin, his long, red-lacquered fingernails reaching up beyond his long mustache as he did so. "I shall endeavor to discover what I can about the young woman," he promised. He smiled ingratiatingly and added, "And if I locate her, I will inform you at once."

"That will be most appreciated," Li Chen said, bowing slightly. "And now I must make my way and find suitable lodgings. Until we meet again . . ."

Later that evening, one of Wo Hamm's lieutenants came to see him. Wo Hamm was lying on silk pillows, completely nude, while two young women pulled apart the blossoms of freshly cut roses, dipped the petals in warmed oil, and then carefully placed them on his body. He was smoking a pipe of aromatic tobacco blended with a tiny bit of opium, not enough to cause him to slip into narcotic dreams, but enough to heighten the sensuousness of the rose petals against his naked skin.

"A thousand pardons, honorable master," his lieutenant said, sinking to his knees and bowing his forehead to the floor.

"Yes, yes, what is it?" Wo Hamm said angrily, his mood destroyed. He sat up quickly; some of the petals fluttered to the floor, but others stuck to him, so that his body was a patchwork of skin and rose petals.

"I have heard a most interesting story from some of those who just arrived from China."

"It had better be as interesting to me as it is to you to warrant this interruption," Wo Hamm warned. Motioning with his hand toward one of the young women, he then pointed to a robe of purple silk. He stood, and most of the remaining petals fell from his body as he held out his arms to allow the women to put his robe on him.

"That will be all," he said to the two women, and they

backed out of the room, their heads bowed low. Then he turned back to his lieutenant. "Now, what is this . . . *interesting* story I should hear?" he asked, weighing the word heavily.

"Do you recall Lo Ching, the prince of Canton?"

"Of course. It was because of Lo Ching that I had to leave China." He sneered, adding caustically, "I cannot say that I grieved when he was killed."

"His throne was taken over by Ma Phat," Wo Hamm's lieutenant said.

"Yes, yes, as disagreeable a fellow as Lo Ching. I know all that. Tell me something I do not know."

The lieutenant smiled. "Perhaps, *shih*, you do not know that a granddaughter of Lo Ching survives, and it is she, not Ma Phat, who is the legitimate ruler of Canton."

"A granddaughter? Ah, Ma Phat must not like that."

"No, he does not. He has offered a very large reward of gold to anyone who would find her, kill her, and provide him with proof of her death."

"How large is this large reward?"

"In American money, the gold would be worth one hundred and fifty thousand dollars."

"That is indeed a lot of money," Wo Hamm declared, impressed with the figure.

"Yes, *shih*," the lieutenant agreed. Then he smiled broadly. "And here is the interesting thing, master. The girl the Shal Minh priest seeks is not his cousin. It is she who is the granddaughter of Lo Ching."

Wo Hamm was nonplussed. "The girl Ku Xuan?"

"Is a princess."

Wo Hamm smirked. "And worth one hundred and fifty thousand dollars in gold." Suddenly Wo Hamm told himself, *And I know where she is!* He remembered the girl vividly now. He had assigned her to work in Wu Ho's laundry, but she was no longer there because he had sold her to Walter St. John. That was information he would keep to himself. If there really were that big a reward out for the girl, he intended to claim it all for himself. There was no sense in including anyone else—certainly not Li Chen, not even this fool lieutenant who had brought him the news.

"Go," Wo Hamm ordered. "Send four of my best bodyguards to me."

"Yes, *shih*," the lieutenant said, bowing respectfully.

Wo Hamm watched the lieutenant leave and then rubbed his hands together in eager anticipation. In half an hour, he would have his hands on Ku Xuan—or perhaps he should say Princess Ku Xuan. And then the reward would be his . . . all his.

Chapter Five

There were three kinds of drinking establishments in San Francisco. First, by the waterfront, were the bars frequented by the dock workers and sailors. Since the sailors came from all over the world, these bars had no racial or national restrictions. One heard conversations in French, German, Spanish, Russian, and Chinese; black sailors from Jamaica hoisted drinks with blond Scandinavians; and Chinese and American dock workers shared the same tables.

Second, in the lobbies of the finest downtown hotels, there were elegant drinking and gambling salons, where women in butterfly-bright dresses and flashing earrings drank fine imported wines and champagnes while they watched well-dressed men gamble hundreds and sometimes thousands of dollars at the gaming tables.

Finally, there were the ordinary saloons, frequented by prospectors and hardrock miners, draymen and cowboys. These were similar to the saloons found all over the West, and a man arriving from Wyoming or Kansas would feel right at home in them.

One such saloon was the Bloody Bucket, where Cole Granger was a steady customer. He had been there all afternoon, sitting morosely at a table near the back wall.

Rose, one of the bar girls who worked the Bloody Bucket—sometimes hustling drinks, sometimes agreeing to go upstairs with a customer if the price was right—came over to stand beside him. "Hello, Cole. Buy me a drink?" She knew Cole Granger and had been upstairs with him a few times, although he always seemed to have more mouth than money.

Granger raised his glass and looked at her over the rim. "Don't have any money," he mumbled.

Rose put her hands on her hips and leaned back contemptuously. "Oh, you don't have any money, you say? Well, now, what happened to that big deal you said was comin' through? You do remember the big deal, don't you? The other night you told me you'd be comin' back with your pockets bulging. You'd buy me the moon, you said. Ha, what a liar you are. Buy me the moon? You can't even buy me a drink."

"The deal fell through," Granger growled.

"Deal? What deal? There wasn't any deal; you were just trying to make yourself look good."

"No, I had plans," Granger said defensively. "Really."

Rose turned away from the table and called back over her shoulder. "Sure you did, honey. You had big plans. You be sure and come see me again—" she paused, looking around the rest of the saloon to make certain everyone was listening—"but not until you have some money." It got the laugh she was looking for.

Granger took another gulp of his drink. Rose had made him feel small, but what else could he expect? He had told her he would have money next time she saw him, and he really did intend to have it. He would have had it now—all the money he could ever hope for—if Wakefield had not spoiled his plans. It was Wakefield who had kept him from getting the money . . . and it was Wakefield who had killed his two confederates. Now Wakefield was a hero in everyone's eyes, and his name was on everyone's lips. In every saloon in the city where draymen and cowmen hung out, they were talking about Mike Wakefield, and how he had shot it out with three would-be stage robbers; about how he had killed two of them, and sent the third one skedaddling off with his tail tucked between his legs.

At least no one knew who the third robber was, Granger told himself, taking another swig of his whiskey and feeling the fire burn all the way to his gut. Although he had barely enough money left to keep himself in food, he tossed down the drink and slammed the glass down on the table.

Mike Wakefield. How Granger hated that man. How he would like to see him dead.

Thinking back, he was not exactly sure when he had stopped

just wishing Wakefield was dead and started planning for it, but he suddenly knew that was what he had to do: He had to kill Mike Wakefield. That would not only take care of the great hero, it would also make the next coach easy pickings for another robbery.

When Granger had begun casing the stagecoach operation for the robbery, he had learned that Wakefield had a habit of visiting Walter St. John after the last run of the day. He had also learned where St. John lived—in a big house over on Nob Hill. His curiosity getting the better of him, Granger had walked by the house earlier in the day and studied the lay of the land.

As his plan had taken shape, Granger had decided that what he needed was a place to hide, so he could shoot Wakefield from ambush. He then realized that Walter St. John's estate offered the ideal setup, with dozens of places where he could lie in wait. All he needed to do was hide in the bushes outside the house until Wakefield had finished his report to St. John, and then he could shoot him when he came outside. After that, it would be a simple matter to melt into the darkness, using the maze of shrubbery to cover his escape. He would then turn up in one of the saloons, drinking and minding his own business, and no one would be the wiser.

Turning in his seat, he peered through the dusty window at the front of the saloon. Seeing that it was now quite dark, Granger tossed down the last of his drink and then stood up, adjusting his holster, and went outside.

The Bloody Bucket was on Washington, and it was just a short walk from Washington to Nob Hill. As he walked along the sidewalk in the cool dampness, he listened to the cacophony made by two or three pianos and half a dozen singers competing with each other. Although San Francisco was the most substantial and sophisticated city west of St. Louis, it had grown so fast—thanks to the silver and gold taken from nearby mines—that some of its districts still had the atmosphere of a rough and raucous boomtown.

When Granger reached the edge of Nob Hill, he looked around cautiously. Keeping to the shadows as much as he could—no easy task with all the streetlamps—he reached Walter St. John's house and stood under a tree, studying the grounds. A half hour passed before he saw what he was waiting for: Mike Wakefield arriving to give his report to St. John. Granger figured he had at least ten minutes to get across the road and into position behind one of the sculptured hedgerows, where he could wait and surprise the driver when he emerged from the house.

Granger pulled his pistol and checked the load in the chamber. It was ready. Slipping the pistol back into its holster, he drew a deep breath, looked around to make certain that he was not being observed, and then darted across the street and behind a row of shrubbery. Crouching low, he ran along the hedgerow until he was about fifty feet from the front door. There he drew his pistol and waited. From that position, he could not miss.

Four Chinese men, tong warriors sent by Wo Hamm, were waiting behind the hedgerow for their opportunity to snatch Ku Xuan. When they heard someone approach, they slipped farther back into the shadows, intending to wait until he was gone.

But it did not appear as if the American were going to leave, for he pulled his pistol and waited, staring at the front door. The four tong warriors were puzzled. Was this man also here to kill the girl? If so, what would Wo Hamm do to them?

The men looked at each other, asking the question silently with their eyes. Finally, without a word passing between them, they reached a consensus: They would not kill the American, but he would have to be taken care of. Sneaking up behind him, they knocked him out and carted him off to Wo Hamm's house. The tong chief could decide what to do with him.

"Tell me," Wo Hamm demanded of Cole Granger when the American was revived in front of him. "Why were you planning to kill Ku Xuan?"

Granger could not remember anything beyond waiting outside St. John's house for Mike Wakefield. He had no idea what had happened next, or how he had gotten here . . . or, for that matter, where "here" was. The only thing he knew for certain was that he had a terrible pain in the back of his head.

He looked around in confusion. He seemed to be in a room full of Chinese. "Where the hell am I? How did I get here?" Granger asked angrily. He tried to raise his hand to rub the bump on his head, but he discovered that his arms were tied to a chair, as were his feet, and he could not move at all. "What the hell? . . . Why am I tied up?" Granger demanded. "Who are you?"

"I am called Wo Hamm," the tong chief replied smoothly as he raised a long, ebony cigarette holder to his lips. He took a deep puff and then let it out in an audible sigh.

Granger stared unabashedly at the man. He had never seen anyone—man or woman—with fingernails as long as Wo Hamm's, nor had he ever seen a man with painted nails. And it was not only Wo Hamm's nails that were painted. Between his perfectly plucked eyebrows and his eyes there was a dark blue dab of color; his eyes were outlined in black with a splash of silver at each end, and he had deep red rouge spots on his cheeks. He looked not a little like an elegantly painted whore, and part of Granger wanted to laugh. But he had enough presence of mind to know that to laugh might very well be to sign his own death warrant.

"Why am I here?" Granger asked again.

"*I* shall ask the questions," Wo Hamm told him. "Why were you waiting to kill Ku Xuan?"

"Who is Ku Xuan?"

Wo Hamm nodded, and one of the Chinese bodyguards standing nearby slapped Granger across the mouth. Granger tasted blood. He strained at the ropes, but he could do nothing.

"Perhaps we shall try again," Wo Hamm murmured. "Why were you waiting to kill Ku Xuan?"

"Who the hell is Ku Xuan? I don't know any Ku Xuan. I was waitin' to kill Mike Wakefield," Granger said angrily. "He's the stage driver."

"And why would you want to kill this man?"

"That's none of your business," Granger growled.

Wo Hamm nodded, and one of the men alongside Granger hit him again.

"Anything I want to know is my business," Wo Hamm declared in an oily voice. "Now, tell me, please, why do you want to kill the stage driver?"

"The other day I tried to hold up his stage," Granger

confessed with a sigh. "I didn't get nothin', but he killed two of my men. I was plannin' on gettin' even with the son of a bitch. I don't even know who this Ku Xuan fella you keep talkin' about is."

One of the men standing close to Wo Hamm leaned over and whispered something to him. Wo Hamm listened attentively and nodded his head.

"I am told that what you say is true. There was an attempt to rob the stage and it was unsuccessful. You were that miserable person?"

"Yeah, that's what I said," Granger admitted, his voice a mixture of regret and embarrassment.

"What is your name?"

"Granger, Cole Granger." He did not know what Wo Hamm wanted with him, but he decided to answer all the questions to keep from being hit again . . . or worse. Glancing at each of the men, Granger realized they were all wearing daggers, and if they wanted to cut him, there was nothing he could do about it. He felt a little like a lamb, all trussed up for slaughter.

Wo Hamm studied Granger in silence for a long moment, as if contemplating something. Then he spoke again, in the same oily voice.

"Mr. Granger, I have a proposition for you—a business proposition. I think you should listen to it."

"Right now it don't look like I got much choice."

Wo Hamm smiled. "To be sure, Mr. Granger, you have no other choice. Here is my proposition: There is a young Chinese woman who is staying in the house of Mr. St. John. Her name is Ku Xuan. I would like her killed." He paused, waiting for this to sink in. "I would like her killed, and I would like proof of her death."

"That's it? That's all you want, for me to kill some woman?"

"I trust you have no problem with killing a woman?"

"Hell, no, that won't bother me. Especially a chink woman. Oh, uh, no offense, Mr. Hamm."

"And the fact that she is only one-half . . . chink"—Wo Hamm set the word apart distastefully—"and one-half American . . . does that bother you?"

Granger smiled and then said, "Can't kill the Chinese half without killin' the American half, too. Anyway, it don't matter. You want her killed, I'll kill her. That is, if the money is right."

"Ah, yes, you will have to be paid for your job."

"In American."

"Of course, in American." Wo Hamm reached down into a deep pocket of his green silk robe and pulled out a bundle of cash.

"Here are two hundred and fifty dollars, Mr. Granger. You can have this money now and another two hundred and fifty when you bring proof of the young woman's death."

"Untie me, and you got yourself a deal," Granger announced.

At a nod from Wo Hamm, the ropes were undone, and Granger stood in front of the tong chief, rubbing the circulation back into his arms.

Looking sharply at Wo Hamm, Granger declared, "I'll kill the girl for you—but I'm also gonna kill Wakefield. For me."

"What you do with Wakefield is of no concern to me," the tong chief assured him. "My only concern is to see the young woman killed. Kill her swiftly, if you can—although I must warn you that I also intend to send some others to do the job, just in case you fail."

"What makes you think I'd fail?" Granger asked with a sneer. "Sure can't be much to killin' a woman."

"Not most women, perhaps, but Ku Xuan is a priestess—a priestess of Shan Tal."

"Oh, she's a religious woman, is she? Well, that don't bother me. I once killed me a Mex priest, so I reckon I can kill a religious woman from China."

Wo Hamm smiled. "I take it, Mr. Granger, that you do not fully understand what it means to be a priestess from Shan Tal?"

Granger counted the money, shoved it in his pocket, and said distractedly, "It don't mean nothin' to me—but I don't care, either." His mind wandering, he was thinking about Rose, the bar girl at the Bloody Bucket. When he got back there in a short while and spent a little money on her, she would not think him such a fool anymore.

"Very well," Wo Hamm said, shrugging, "I will make no attempt to explain it to you. I shall merely wish you good luck, Mr. Granger."

"You just have that other two hundred fifty dollars waitin' for me when I come back."

*   *   *

It was early the next morning, and as Ku Xuan stood at the bay window in her room, looking out over the city and watching the morning fog roll away, she wondered if her father was out there in one of the houses or hotels or saloons. She also wondered if she would ever find him, for her search was suspended now that she was honor bound to stay with Walter St. John for as long as he wanted her.

A part of her did not mind staying here. It was certainly a wonderful house, and her position as hostess was one of great honor as well as privilege. But she had taken a vow to find her father, and even if she never found him, she felt as great an obligation to continue the search as she felt to stay. The same honor pulling her in two different ways was like Kwin and Kwan, the two-headed dragon, consuming itself within her heart. She did not know what to do.

The night before, Ku Xuan had seen a map of California. Until that moment she had had no idea how large California was or how great a task lay before her. How could she, one insignificant person, ever hope to search a land this large? And yet she had learned at Shan Tal that the size of the task is dependent only upon the size of the heart of the problem solver, and while California was a large state, Ku Xuan believed her heart was larger. With every ounce of her being, she resolved anew to fulfull her vow. It did not matter how large this land of California was . . . she would find her father.

At the sound of a soft knock on her door, she turned and called, "Yes, come in."

The door opened, and Walter St. John stood at the threshold. "I have to take a drive to take care of some business," he said. "I thought you might like to go with me."

"I would be delighted," Ku Xuan said, smiling pleasantly at the invitation. Taking a light woolen shawl from her dresser, she wrapped it around her shoulders and followed St. John into the hallway and down the regal staircase.

A few moments later they seated themselves in the rear seat of his elegant, open-topped landaulet. St. John insisted that she sit next to him—and that the top be kept down—because he wanted the world to see what a beautiful woman was staying in his house.

As they headed off, Ku Xuan noticed that the driver of the carriage was a big, quiet man who seemed to be watching either side of the road as often as he looked ahead. Unlike the other drivers who had driven her around town on the few occasions she had ventured out, this man was not elegantly uniformed—and he was wearing a large gun. She felt a bit uneasy about it, and she asked her benefactor why their driver was more like a guard.

Shaking his head, St. John replied, "I'm sorry his being armed makes you uncomfortable, but there have been several robberies and robbery attempts of late, and one can never be too careful."

"I understand," Ku Xuan assured him, and then she relaxed and settled back to enjoy the outing.

She found the ride delightful. They made several stops in town and then went out into the country along a deserted stretch of road bordered on their right by low cliffs. The scenery was beautiful here, and Ku Xuan was enchanted by everything. She was reveling in her sense of inner peace when seemingly from nowhere, four Chinese men leaped down onto the road in front of the carriage. Their sudden appearance startled the horses, and the animals reared, making it difficult for the driver to control the team.

"What is it, Billy?"

"Four Chinamen, Mr. St. John," the driver answered, after he had the team under control. "I don't know what they want, but I don't aim to find out. That shouldn't be too hard to do, since they don't seem to be armed."

"Stop!" one of the Chinese men yelled.

"The hell I will," Billy answered. He reached for his pistol, but he never cleared leather. Before he could pull his gun, one of the four bandits flipped a multibladed knife shaped like a star toward him. The knife buried itself in Billy's chest, and with a life-surrendering gurgle, Billy went down.

"Stay behind me!" St. John warned Ku Xuan. "I'll try to fight them off."

Though Walter St. John was much older than the Chinese attackers and though he was outnumbered by them, Ku Xuan saw that he was a man of courage. He climbed down from the coach and stood on the road, ready to meet them.

Suddenly and unexpectedly, Ku Xuan put her hands on the side of the carriage and vaulted out of the seat. She went high into the air, turning a flip over the top of St. John's head and landing on the ground in front of him, between him and the four bandits.

"Ku Xuan, what . . ." St. John shouted, but before he could even finish his question, Ku Xuan lashed out with her foot toward one of the assailants, knocking him out with a kick to the face. As St. John watched with a look of utter disbelief, two of the other men charged her. She calmly stood her ground, moving only at the last instant and doing so as gracefully as a matador avoiding the charge of a bull. The two thugs were left grabbing thin air. Turning toward her to charge again, their movement caused them to be slightly off-balance—exactly as Ku Xuan had planned. Whirling, she knocked one of them out with a kick to the head, while the other warrior caught the knife-hard edge of her hand in his throat. He went down on his knees, clutching his throat as he coughed and gasped for breath.

Now only one of the four assailants remained, and he pulled a long dagger. He started toward Ku Xuan, and she raised her hands into fighting position. When she did so, her attacker saw the tiny blue chrysanthemum tattooed on her wrist and apparently recognized it as the symbol of Shan Tal, for he dropped his knife and fell to his knees, bowing and touching his forehead to the ground.

Speaking in Chinese, the attacker kowtowed before her. She spoke to him sharply in return, commanding him to help his three companions to their feet. He did as he was told, and the four of them limped over to their horses and rode off.

"Ku Xuan, what . . . what was all that?" St. John asked in bewilderment. "Things happened so fast that I'm not sure I even followed it all. Except I do know that one minute I was about to be killed, and the next I was watching a beautiful, unarmed woman fighting off four armed and powerfully built men. And though I don't understand a word of Chinese, I could hear the groveling, pleading tone in that man's voice, and he obeyed all your orders."

"I told them who you are," Ku Xuan said solemnly. "I told them you are a man of great power and to do harm to you would be a very bad mistake."

"And you mean to say that they stopped because you told them I am a man of great power? I'd say that you're the one with the power. How did you do those things?"

"The orphanage trained me in acrobatics," she told him airily. Though she disliked telling her employer an untruth, she had no intention of revealing to him her entire background. Changing the subject, she knelt beside the driver's body, saying, "I am sorry about Billy." Standing, she looked into St. John's eyes. She could tell that he did not believe for one moment that the men had abandoned their attack for the reason she had given, but he was allowing her the subterfuge.

The two of them lifted Billy's body into the landaulet, wrapping it with the carriage blanket. St. John helped Ku Xuan up onto the driver's seat and then climbed up beside her. Clucking to the horses, he turned the vehicle around and headed back to San Francisco.

They were both silent for a long while, each lost in thought. Then St. John turned to Ku Xuan and said, "Ku Xuan, I have been trying to think of some way to reward you for what you did for me back there."

"No reward is necessary," she replied. In truth, she had already figured out that the four assailants were after her, not him. Far from saving his life, she had placed it in danger. But she thought it best not to tell him.

"You let me decide that," St. John said. "Now, you've said that you've come to America to search for your father."

"Yes."

"Then this is what I will do for you. I will make a stagecoach available, and I'll give you my best driver—Mike Wakefield. Take as long as you want, and search as far as you wish. You can even take Lai Song with you as a traveling companion and personal servant. If your father is here in this country, I want you to find him."

"You would do that for me?"

"Yes, gladly," St. John declared fervently. "And even that would not be enough to repay you for my life."

Reaching over, Ku Xuan put her hand on St. John's. Her eyes gleamed with tears, and she smiled at him. "Thank you for allowing me to fulfill my vow," she whispered.

.at evening, Mike Wakefield stood in Walter St. John's parlor, staring at his employer's back while the older man poured each of them a drink. Invited by St. John for dinner,

Mike was not dressed in his normal denim and buckskin, but rather—in honor of the occasion—in a dark-blue suit and vest, a white shirt, and a tie. To a casual observer his appearance was fairly refined, although if one were to look closer, one would see that his shoulders were a little too broad for his suit jacket, his hands a bit too callused to look natural holding a crystal goblet, and his neck a bit too unused to a high starched collar.

By contrast, St. John looked very polished and very much at home in his black suit and ruffled shirt. Although he had spent years laboring at sea, on the railroad, and in the mountains, several years of affluence had worked subtle changes in his demeanor, so that he was no longer awkward in fine dress.

St. John turned and came toward his driver holding a tumbler of whiskey, saying, "Mike, I want to get this matter resolved before Ku Xuan comes down and joins us."

Shaking his head, Mike complained, "Mr. St. John, you've got other drivers you could send with this woman. I think it's very nice of you to want to help her in her search and that you want to supply her with a driver—but why does it have to be me?"

"That's true," St. John agreed, handing the drink to Mike, "I do have other drivers. But I want to use you."

"Frankly, I don't understand why. If you'll pardon my saying so, sir, that seems a waste. You've got cargo to move and people to transport. With all due respect, you shouldn't be using your most experienced driver to help some Chinese girl look for her father. The chances are she'll never find him anyway."

Taking a sip of his own drink, St. John studied his employee over the rim of his glass. "I must say, Mike, I'm surprised by your reaction to all this. I've always been impressed with your demeanor around Chinese, yet when you met Ku Xuan, you were practically rude to her. And now you tell me you don't want to make this trip."

"I'm sorry if I appeared rude," Mike said somewhat contritely, "but you're right. I *don't* want to make this trip. It seems to me a waste of time, energy, and money, and I could serve you much better doing what I usually do."

"You'll serve me best by making the trip." St. John's voice was tight. "Look here, Mike, Ku Xuan saved my life and I want to do this for her. If I didn't use my top driver, I wouldn't feel I was doing right by her. I know that if you take charge of the search—even though you might not want to—you'll do the best job you can. Do you understand? This is something I *must* do."

"Mr. St. John—" Mike started to protest, but he stopped when St. John held up his hand.

The older man looked toward the door to make certain Ku Xuan was not there before he went on. "Mike, I want you to get to know this girl. There's something about her, something I can't explain. . . . I don't mind telling you that when I first met her, I was strongly attracted to her. I still find her the most beautiful woman I've ever seen, and I still have very deep feelings for her—but the . . . sexual attraction is no longer there. I know she isn't my daughter, but the feeling I have for her now is almost the same. I'm pleading with you, Mike. Do this for me."

Mike gulped his drink down and set the empty glass on a table. "All right," he said. "If that's what you want, that's what I'll do."

"Thank you, Mr. Wakefield," declared a woman's voice, and Mike looked toward the door, surprised that Ku Xuan was standing there and that she had heard the conversation. Looking at her, Mike gasped for breath, for never in his life had he seen a more beautiful vision than that which greeted him at this moment. She was wearing a Western gown of golden silk, cut low at the bosom, pinched in at the waist, and flaring out into many tiers. Her hair was fashioned into one long braid that fell softly across her left shoulder, and her skin glowed and her eyes sparkled in the soft lamplight. She smiled at him, and her teeth were perfect and brilliantly white. When she turned her head toward Walter St. John, a flash of light twinkled from the dangling earrings he had given her.

"Tell me, lad," St. John said, smiling broadly as he looked at the vision of loveliness standing before them, "have you ever seen a more beautiful lady?"

"Never," Mike agreed.

"Come," St. John invited, ushering them out of the parlor. "We'll eat dinner and discuss the journey. You two can get an early start in the morning."

During dinner, Ku Xuan told Mike about her quest, explaining that her mother had died giving birth to her, leaving her to be raised in what she described to him too as an orphanage. She informed him that all she knew about her father was what the abbess had told her as she lay dying. Describing her mother's eating set, she told him that it was the only memento she had of her past.

Mike listened politely to her story, although he was strangely quiet. Finally, St. John commented on the fact.

"Mike, I'll admit that Ku Xuan is a beautiful young woman and therefore might render you quite speechless, but you've scarcely said a word, and you've stared at her the entire meal. What is it?"

"I don't know," Mike confessed. He looked at Ku Xuan. "I'm sorry if I've been staring, but there is something about you . . . something haunting. You remind me so much of the girl that my captain fell in love with in China. Of course, it's impossible for you to be that girl—or that girl's child."

"How do you know it's impossible?" St. John asked sharply, his interest piqued.

"Because that girl is dead, and she died long before any child could have been born," Mike told him.

"Oh. I'm sorry," St. John apologized.

"Yes, well, it happened many years ago," Mike said. "When I was a cabin boy on the *Thunderbolt*."

"Would you tell us about it?" Ku Xuan asked.

"All right, if you want to hear."

Mike's words wove the story so thoroughly that Ku Xuan and St. John could practically see the tall ships rocking at anchor and the large warehouses that the Chinese called factories on the shore, just as the twelve-year-old boy had seen them as he entered the harbor at Canton. He then described an elegant dinner he had attended with his captain.

"I had gone for a walk in our host's garden. There I met a very beautiful young woman, probably six or seven years older than I. She had seen my captain on a few occasions and asked me to arrange an introduction, cautioning it must be kept secret. I did what she asked, and with my help and that of her personal servant, the captain and the girl met many times over the next few weeks—though each time the meetings had to be very carefully arranged, for the girl's father couldn't find out."

"Why not?" St. John inquired.

"Because her father was a Manchu prince."

Both Ku Xuan and St. John looked at Mike askance.

"What happened?" Ku Xuan asked, caught up in the story.

"She was a very determined young woman," Mike answered. "And as she knew he would, the captain succumbed to her beauty and charm and fell in love with her—and she with him, he was sure. After a period of time, she went to him with the news that she was carrying his baby."

Ku Xuan gasped and then asked, "And her father still did not know about them?"

"No."

"That must have made matters even more difficult for them," St. John said.

"It certainly did. But since Cap couldn't go to her father and explain that he loved her and wanted to marry her, he made plans to sneak her away from China. He was going to bring her back to America and marry her here."

"And did he?" Ku Xuan asked.

Mike sighed deeply. "No."

"Why not?"

"When Cap went to get her, her maidservant appeared with a letter explaining that his lover would not leave China. Cap was certain that that was not her wish but her father's, so he demanded to see her."

"And did he see her?" Ku Xuan asked.

"Yes. She told him that she didn't really love him, that he had been a diversion for her and nothing more."

"How cruel," Ku Xuan exclaimed.

"No," Mike replied, shaking his head, "I don't think she meant to be cruel at all. I think she knew what was going to happen, and she was just trying to spare Cap."

"And what *did* happen?" St. John asked.

Mike was quiet for a long moment. Finally, he went on. "After thinking about it all night, Cap decided to go back for her the next morning, to give her one more chance to come to America with him. He took me along so that if he had to smuggle her away, I could help. When we got there, we saw an enormous crowd gathered in the courtyard square. We had no idea what it was about, so we moved closer to see— and there on a raised platform in the middle of the crowd, her arms tied behind her back, was the captain's sweetheart. Her face was covered, but there was no mistaking her. For the high crime of falling in love with an American, she was forced to kneel in front of the people of Canton, put her head on the chopping block and . . ."

"Mike, stop!" St. John shouted, interrupting the story. "I don't want to hear any more."

Looking down, Mike put his hand to his neck. "Although I was only twelve years old when I saw it happen, I've never forgotten it. The barbarity of a man who would condone the execution of his own daughter. . . ."

"Where is Cap now?" St. John asked softly.

"I don't know," Mike answered, shaking his head. "He scarcely drew a sober breath on the voyage home, and the cargo spoiled. When we docked in San Francisco, the sheriff seized the ship for nonpayment of tariffs and fees, and the captain disappeared. I haven't seen or heard from him since then, though I ran into a man recently who'd heard about a man who's now prospecting in the hills who may have been a sea captain." Shrugging, Mike told them, "Maybe it's Cap."

"That is a very sad story," Ku Xuan murmured, tears glistening in her eyes.

"I'm sorry to have upset you. It wasn't my intention to make you cry."

"Do not apologize," she assured him. "I am sorry for your captain for losing his love and his child." She smiled tenderly at him, adding, "But your story has made me more determined than ever to find my own father."

St. John put his hand on Mike's arm. "You'll go with her, won't you, son? You'll give it your best effort?"

Mike looked at Ku Xuan and then smiled warmly at her. "Yes," he agreed. "I'll give it my best effort."

Chapter Six

Cole Granger woke from his alcohol-fueled sleep and sat up, looking around. It took him a few moments to realize where he was: in Rose's room over the Bloody Bucket. It then took him a few minutes longer to realize that except for getting up to eat and relieve himself every so often, he had not left her bed since the night before last, soon after leaving Wo Hamm's house. Reaching for his dungarees, he thrust his hand into the pocket and pulled out a few coins and even fewer bills, and then he looked over at the nude, still-sleeping form lying next to him and smiled. He had spent just about every cent of the two hundred and fifty dollars he had received from Wo Hamm on Rose—but it had been worth it. Although Rose was still young, dissipation had worked its effect on her, and in the harsh light of day, he could see every imperfection in her body and features. But she sure knew how to satisfy his lust . . . as long as he could pay for the satisfaction. Just thinking about the night before inflamed him, and he promised himself that he would return for some additional pleasure just as soon as he collected the rest of the money for killing that chink girl.

He got out of the bed and pulled on his dungarees. It was still very early, the sky outside Rose's window just becoming light. As he slipped into his shirt and then his socks and boots, he planned his next move. He would go back to Walter St. John's house and wait there for the opportunity to grab the girl—what was her name?—Ku Xuan. He would take her someplace private where he could kill her and then bring her body as proof of her death back to Wo Hamm's.

Fully dressed now, Granger hurried down the back stairs
and through the deserted streets toward St. John's house. He
had gone there last time to kill Wakefield. Now he would go
back and kill the Chinese girl—and there was no time like
the present to take care of it.

A short while later, Granger was standing at the edge of
the St. John estate. The other night, in the dark, getting
close to the house had been easy. But it was almost completely light now, and if he wanted to make his way up close
to the house without being seen, he would need the cover of
shrubbery the whole distance.

"Here, you!" someone called, and the startled Granger
looked around to see who it was. A big policeman wearing a
high-domed helmet and carrying a menacing-looking nightstick was walking toward him, glaring at him.

"What do you want?" Granger asked.

"The question, laddie, is what do *you* want? There ain't a
house out this way that ain't lived in by a man o' means.
Now, I'm a fair judge of character, and I'd be willin' to bet
that you ain't a man o' means."

"It's a public street."

"Aye, that it is, as long as you keep walkin'. But I'll not
have you loiterin' by Mr. St. John's place."

Although except for the nightstick the policeman was not
armed, Granger could not use his pistol—not here in the
middle of the city. "All right, all right," he muttered, walking
away. "I ain't gonna cause no trouble." As he scurried off
across the road, he looked back over his shoulder and saw a
stagecoach driven by none other than Mike Wakefield turning into St. John's driveway. Fortunately Wakefield did
not see him. Checking to see that the policeman had
gone, he raced back across the street and stood in the
shadows where he could see what was going on without being
seen.

When he saw a couple of young Chinese women standing
with what looked like provisions and suitcases, he knew that
one of them must be Ku Xuan. *So they're going to take a
little trip, are they?* Granger asked himself. He smiled. Maybe
he was going to be able to take care of two little jobs at the
same time—kill the girl for money . . . and kill Wakefield
because he wanted to.

*   *   *

Mike halted the stage in the circular drive in front of St. John's house and then climbed down to open the boot while Ku Xuan and Lai Song watched the household servants put the luggage and supplies aboard.

Walter St. John came out and supervised the operation, explaining to Mike, "I want you to be as self-sufficient as possible. There's food, a tent, extra lanterns . . . anything you might need."

"You seem to have thought of everything," Mike offered.

"I hope so, because I want Ku Xuan to find her father— although the hard part is up to you, Mike."

"If he can be found, we'll find him," Mike promised.

Ku Xuan came around to where they stood, saying that all was ready, and as Mike helped her to board, he was again struck dumb by her beauty. As he held her hand while she climbed into the coach, it felt hot and cool at the same time. Clearing his throat, he looked away, cursing himself silently. Why was he letting this woman affect him so?

"Miss Ku Xuan—"

"Please, Ku Xuan will be simpler," she interrupted.

"All right. Anyway, I thought we might start by driving out to the Silverado mines. There are many Chinese there, and a number of them have been in America for over twenty years. It could be that some of them may know of this man Big Cat."

"What a wonderful idea!" she exclaimed, smiling happily. "Mr. St. John was right when he said you would be a help in finding my father. You are a man of much wisdom."

"We'll see how much wisdom I have," Mike mumbled to himself as he closed the door behind her. Climbing onto the driver's box, he released the brake and then snapped the reins, starting up the well-trained team.

When the coach arrived at the mine several hours later, the coolies greeted them excitedly, showing a special regard toward Mike Wakefield for having risked his life to save many of them. Ku Xuan was pleased to see the warmth with which her people regarded Mike. It spoke well of him, and it reinforced the opinion she had already formed of him.

"You have come just in time for lunch," one of the workers said to Mike. "I hope you will do us the honor of being our guest."

"Are you kidding?" Mike asked, grinning. "I would never miss the opportunity to eat with you. You have the best food in California."

His compliment was passed around to the others, and his praise of their food made him even more welcome.

During the meal, Mike watched Ku Xuan. He felt that, for some reason, here among the Chinese she seemed even more beautiful than she had before. Her long blue-black hair falling loosely across her shoulders framed a delicate face in which were set deep brown eyes, high cheekbones, and lips that were full and sensual. And her smile—and a charming twinkling of the eye—made it appear as if she was drawing intense pleasure from the meal. Not having revealed to Ku Xuan that he knew her language, Mike was flattered that she was speaking in English in deference to him. Her English was perfect, with just the suggestion of an accent, a subtle softening of the vowels that tended to caress the language.

Mike noticed that when one of the Chinese saw the tattoo on her uncovered wrist, he pointed it out to a friend. Then others saw it, and he heard the word about the tiny blue flower being spread through the camp. Suddenly the coolies began showing an exceptional respect toward her. He understood why they would receive a woman of such beauty so warmly, but he did not know why they were suddenly showing such deference to her. When he asked one of the coolies about it, the miner pointed to Ku Xuan's wrist.

"Have you not seen the symbol?"

"You mean the tattoo? The little blue flower? Yes, I saw it. What about it?"

"That means she is a priestess. She is a priestess of Shan Tal."

"You mean, like a nun?" Mike asked, suddenly feeling oddly pained. He looked over at her. "She can never get married or anything like that?"

The Chinese man laughed. "No, my friend. A priestess of Shan Tal is nothing like a nun of your Jesus church. It is something very, very different."

"How different?"

"She has powers," the coolie said.

Powers, eh? Mike thought, laughing to himself. *Maybe they believe she can foretell the future or something like that.*

After Mike had asked several questions about Big Cat and

received no information, one of the miners suggested that he
speak with Kwai Fong, the old powderman he had rescued.
Kwai Fong had been in America longer than any of the other
Chinese, and he might know the answers to Mike's questions.

"I believe he is down in the number four shaft right now.
Do you know where that is?"

"Yes I do, and thanks for the suggestion. I'll go look for
him." Getting up from the long table, Mike walked over to
where Ku Xuan sat with Lai Song and told her what the
worker had suggested.

"Can we go find him now?" she asked hopefully.

"Certainly. But are you sure you want to go down into the
mine?"

"I am sure."

"Okay . . . but don't say you weren't warned. It's pretty
spooky down in the shaft."

She looked into his eyes and smiled. "I am not afraid."

Feeling his whole body tingle from the power of her gaze,
Mike swallowed hard and led her toward the mine entrance.

From his vantage point inside a small supply shack a dozen
yards from where Wakefield and the two women had eaten,
Cole Granger peered through the partially open door and
watched with interest. He had followed the coach all the way
from San Francisco. At first he had intended to attack the
coach on the road, but then he had thought better of it.
Having already attacked the coach twice, with Wakefield
coming out on top each time, this time he intended to wait
until he was sure there was absolutely no chance of failure.
Only then would he make his move. Now, although he was
too far from them to hear what was being said, he kept his
eyes open and waited for that perfect moment.

The moment seemed to present itself when Wakefield and
the Chinese girl left the table and went down into the mine.
Granger chuckled and told himself, *Well now, Mr. Stagecoach Driver, you just made it awful easy for me to do what I
gotta do.* He would wait a few minutes until they were far
enough down in the mine, and then he would sneak up
behind them and kill them. Suddenly his glee lessened. How
would he prove Ku Xuan's death to Wo Hamm without a

body? Then he realized that the newspapers would surely report their deaths, giving him all the proof he needed.

As he looked around the shack, searching for a weapon he could use that would be quieter than his gun—perhaps an ax or something, he thought—he noticed for the first time what was being stored there. "Explosives!" he whispered harshly. Chuckling again, Granger slipped several sticks of dynamite into his shirtfront and then carefully opened the door. Walking without undue haste across the dusty yard, trying to appear as if he belonged there, he slipped into the mine and saw Wakefield's light, far down in the shaft. He followed along until he saw the light turn. From the brief time he had worked in a mine himself, he realized that Wakefield and Ku Xuan had gone into an offshoot shaft. All he had to do was close the mouth of that shaft, and his job would be accomplished.

Looking back to make certain there were no other miners' lamps visible, Granger struck a match. It flared up in the dark of the mine, and he held the flame to the fuse. A second later the fuse started hissing and popping. Granger hurled the dynamite bundle as far down the offshoot shaft as he could and then turned and ran back. He was nearly back at the mouth of the main shaft when the explosion went off, deep and distant, a hollow, resonant sound that carried through the whole mine. Granger felt a huge puff of wind from down inside the mine, a sure indication that there had been a cave-in.

He hurried to the mouth of the mine, making it appear to everyone else now arriving that he had reached the scene mere moments before they had.

"Cave-in! Cave-in!" someone shouted, and seconds later there was a series of short, repeated blasts on the mine whistle, the universal signal for emergency. That was followed by so much turmoil and confusion that Granger was able to slip away unnoticed. Miners, both American and Chinese, rushed past him inside the mine, where they peered anxiously. Many had seen Mike and the girl go in, and they began to speculate as to what had happened—and whether Mike and his friend were still alive.

Down inside the mine, the supporting timbers snapped in a series of pops like a string of firecrackers. Rock and mud fell from above, and Ku Xuan was suddenly grabbed by Mike and backed up against the wall, apparently the safest place to be during a collapse. Finally, after what seemed like an eternity of sound and fury, the mine was silent. It was also dark, because the lamp Mike had been carrying had been snuffed out.

"Ku Xuan, are you all right?" he asked.

"Yes," she answered in a small voice. "What happened?"

"I don't know. I thought I heard a dynamite blast go off just before the cave-in, but that couldn't be possible, because it came from nearer the mouth of the mine, not from down inside where blasting would be taking place."

"Can you make the lamp work again?" she asked.

"I can try." There were a couple of zipping sounds as Mike rubbed the friction wheel to get it to spark. That was followed by a pop and then light. "There," he breathed.

He flashed the light around, and they assessed the damage. Ahead of them, deeper into the mine, there had been a total collapse, and the shaft was completely blocked with tons of rock and dirt. Behind them, a collapsed support timber prevented them from exiting the mine, but from beyond the timber, Mike could feel the free flow of air, telling him that the mine shaft was open all the way to the mouth.

"Do you think they will come for us?" Ku Xuan asked, surprised at how tremulous her voice sounded.

"I don't know," Mike admitted. "I would hope so, but this shaft is pretty unstable. The rest of it could go at any time. They might not want to risk rescuing us."

"Will we be able to escape by ourselves?"

"I don't know that either. Let's wait a few minutes to see if everything stabilizes; then we can try. At least the air is good."

Mike slid down the wall onto the floor, and Ku Xuan sat down with him. She shivered once.

"Are you cold?" he asked solicitously.

"Yes."

He put his arm around her and pulled her close to him.

"Your arm feels good around me," Ku Xuan said, not even knowing herself if she meant it was warm, or if she just enjoyed the feeling of his arm. Before she even realized what he was doing, he had turned toward her, bringing his lips to hers in a kiss. It was natural and fulfilling, and she let the kiss become more ardent. When finally their lips parted, Ku Xuan's head was almost spinning with the pleasure of it.

"I . . . I'm sorry," Mike stammered. "I didn't mean to force myself on you."

"You did not force yourself," Ku Xuan whispered. "Could you not tell that I wanted to do that?"

Mike smiled self-consciously. "Well, I sort of hoped you did," he confessed.

They sat quietly for a few more moments, and then Mike stood up and brushed off the seat of his pants. Helping her to her feet, he said, "We've got to get out of here." He walked over to look at the timbers that blocked the way.

"Do you know how to do that?" Ku Xuan asked, watching as Mike shone his lamp on the timbers and pushed against them, testing them with his hand.

"If I just had an ax," he declared, "I could chop through these three pieces. Then we could slip through."

"What three pieces?"

"These," he told her, pointing to two two-by-four timbers and a four-by-four. "I could probably break the two-by-fours, but the jarring of my weight against them might bring the rest of this down. Then we would really be in trouble. No, I need something to cut through them, something sharp that won't jolt everything."

Ku Xuan looked at the two-by-four and asked, "Where would you cut it?"

Putting his hand against the timbers, he told her, "This one, here; and this one, here. You see, that wouldn't cause a shift in pressure. And the four-by-four I'd cut right here. *If* I had an ax."

Ku Xuan looked at the boards; then she raised her hand. With a loud shout, she brought the edge of her hand down sharply, slicing through the board as cleanly as if it had been sawed. She smashed through the other timber as easily as the first.

"What the devil?" Mike's face registered complete shock. "How did you do that?"

"It is a simple thing," she stated. She then looked at the four-by-four.

"You don't plan to attack that one too, do you?" Mike asked in astonishment.

Ku Xuan took her shoes off. "Come here," she said, directing Mike where she wanted him.

"What is it? What do you want me to do?"

"You will have to support my weight," she told him. When he stepped over to her, she took his hands in hers and placed them under her arms, instructing, "Keep your hands here and hold me firmly. Are you ready?"

"Ready for what? I don't even know what's going on."

Ku Xuan suddenly leaped up so that her body was parallel with the floor, being supported entirely by Mike. Drawing both legs in and assuming a tucked position with her left foot on top of her right, she shot her feet out toward the four-by-four, and they went through the board as cleanly as her hand had gone through the two-by-fours.

"My God!" Mike exclaimed, looking at her in awe as he put her down.

"It is a simple trick," Ku Xuan murmured, dismissing her ability.

Putting his hand to his forehead, Mike said, "I don't know what it is, but it sure isn't simple." He paused and then asked, "It's the priestess thing, isn't it? The coolies told me you were a priestess . . . someone with special powers . . . but I didn't know what they were talking about."

"Please, Mike, do not misunderstand," Ku Xuan asked softly, feeling the distance that he had suddenly placed between them. "It is but a simple thing," she repeated.

He just stared at her for a moment. Then, pulling her hand, he ordered, "Come on. We need to get out of here before any more of those rocks fall." There was a hard edge to his voice as he added, "Though I don't know why I should worry, since a priestess like you could probably break up rocks as easily as boards." Pointing, he told her, "Squeeze through there."

Ku Xuan started to tell Mike that he should go first, fearful that in exiting he might bring down another timber, carrying with it more rock and other debris. She would be able to deal with it, but if she exited first and was then blocked off from him on the other side, she might not be able to help. However, she decided to hold her tongue, because she knew that to suggest it would be another blow to Mike's self-esteem.

"Thank you," she said quietly, and she got on her hands and knees and scrambled through the small opening.

Ku Xuan waited anxiously on the other side until Mike also slipped through. Relieved, she said nothing as she trudged behind him while they headed toward the mine entrance— although she thought to herself that for the first time in her life, she regretted having the special powers her training had given her.

When Ku Xuan and Mike Wakefield finally emerged from the mine entrance, Lai Song rushed over, tearfully embracing her. "I was so worried for you," the younger woman declared in Chinese, hugging Ku Xuan tightly. "Are you all right?"

"Yes, I am fine. Although some things occurred in the mine that have left me most disturbed—and confused, as well."

Tilting her head, Lai Song looked into her friend's eyes. "What kind of things?" she asked.

Ku Xuan shook her head. "I will tell you later, when we are alone."

Looking over her shoulder, she smiled at Mike, who was conversing with a young Chinese worker. Then she looked past him to an old man coming toward them. "Oh!" she exclaimed in English. "This must be Kwai Fong, the man we were trying to locate."

"You're absolutely right," Mike told her. "I've just learned from Kwai's assistant here that the other miners escaped long before we did, by exiting through another shaft. And Kwai Fong was among them. I guess he'd heard that we wanted to speak with him, so he's come to meet with us."

As the old powderman approached, he smiled warmly at his American friend, and bowed in respect to Ku Xuan.

Because of his demeanor, Ku Xuan told herself that Kwai Fong had apparently also heard about her tattoo. Worried that he might put unwanted emphasis on her Shan Tai training, she immediately told the old man in Chinese, "Please, honorable sir, make little of my priesthood. I fear it offends the American, although I do not know why. I used my skills only to help us escape."

"It is the way of the men in this country," the powderman explained. "To be rescued by your powers is to diminish his own."

"But I did not mean to do that." Ku Xuan's voice was filled with regret.

"You are a woman of great beauty and many skills, and I know you did not mean to make him feel small. If your heart is good, you will soon find a way to make him feel that he is the protector."

Standing to one side, watching them closely, Mike understood every word they were saying, and he realized that Kwai Fong must have forgotten that he could speak the language. He remained absolutely silent, until Kwai Fong began speaking in English.

"My friend, I am told that there was someone at the entrance of the mine . . . someone who may have touched off the giant powder. It was an American. Have you made an enemy?"

Shrugging his shoulders, Mike responded, "I don't know. It's possible, I suppose."

"I think you must be extra careful as you continue your travels," Kwai Fong cautioned.

"Thank you for the warning, Kwai Fong. I will do as you suggest," he agreed.

Turning back to Ku Xuan, the old man continued speaking in English. "I am told by some of my countrymen that you are looking for your father."

"Yes. His name is Big Cat."

"Big Cat is not an American name," Kwai Fong stated.

"That's what I told her," Mike put in. "But that's all she has to go on."

Kwai Fong smiled and held up his finger. "Perhaps I know the answer," he suggested.

"And what is that?" Mike wondered.

"As you may know, we Chinese do not have an alphabet as the Westerners do. We use ideograms. Perhaps Ku Xuan's father had the name of a big cat, and the ideogram represented it in that way."

"What do you mean?" Mike asked.

"Take the name of this beautiful creature." Kwai Fong smiled at Ku Xuan. "It is Ku Xuan. How would you portray her name if you had no alphabet?"

"I don't know," Mike started to say, and then smiled. "Oh, of course! I would draw a picture of a swan."

"Yes. Now, suppose there was an American named Lyons?"

"Lyons! Like a lion . . . a big cat!" Mike shouted excitedly. "Kwai Fong, do you know an American named Lyons who fits the bill?"

"I have heard of such a person, yes."

"Tell me about him," Ku Xuan pleaded.

Taking Ku Xuan's hand in his, he related his story. "His name is Daniel Lyons. He was a sea captain who fell in love with the daughter of a very important man. They had to run away and get married in secret, because the young woman's father would never approve of his daughter marrying a *fan kuei*. They lived together happily for a while, waiting for the birth of their child, when the young woman's father found them. The woman was spirited away, and the sea captain was knocked out and put on his ship. The first officer was given orders to leave port at once or have his ship burned."

"And did he?" Ku Xuan asked.

"Oh, yes. He had no choice. Later, the sea captain returned to look for his wife and child, but he never found them."

"Where is this man now?" Ku Xuan wondered.

"I do not know the answer to that question," Kwai Fong confessed.

"Never mind, it is enough that you have told us his name. That's all I need," Mike declared. "I'll find him."

Ku Xuan then translated for Lai Song what they had learned, and the young woman's face lit up. "That is most good," she said, trying out her English.

Laughing happily, Ku Xuan took the old man's hands in her own. "Thank you, honorable Kwai Fong. You have made this humble person most happy."

"I pray that you find what you are seeking." He looked over at Mike. "And what about you, my young friend. Are you still looking for your captain?"

"Yes, I am. Why? Have you heard something about him?"

"Some of my people said they saw a man with graying hair and a beard in Cacheville, not far from here. He looked worn by the years, but none could say just how old he was. He was wearing a sea captain's hat, and he had the look on his face of a man who had been in China."

That, Mike knew, was not an empty expression. It was not something anyone could explain, but among the old China hands there was a saying that a sailor wore China in his eyes for the rest of his life. Although he himself was no longer a sailor and had not been for twenty years, he could still recognize a China hand when he saw one. If the coolies said the graybeard had the look of one who had been to China, Mike was inclined to believe them.

"Where is he now?" Mike asked.

Kwai Fong shook his head. "I am afraid I cannot tell you. He has returned to the hills. They say he searches for gold."

"Well, I don't have time to look for him now, since I've promised to help Ku Xuan find her father and I will keep that promise. But afterward, I would like to find my captain, so if you hear of him again, let me know."

"I will do so," Kwai Fong agreed.

After saying their farewells, the three travelers hurried back to the stagecoach, and despite the near tragedy, they felt wonderfully elated. Now they had a solid lead to investigate. If Daniel Lyons turned out to be Ku Xuan's father—which seemed quite likely—what had at first seemed like an impossible task might in fact be accomplished quickly.

Chapter Seven

A dozen ships were tied up at San Francisco's bustling Howard Street pier when the stagecoach reached the wharf late that same afternoon. Mike Wakefield drove the coach under an elevated coal chute marked with a sign that said New Wellington Coal, then passed by the Girardeau Store and the Hotel Mohawk. He braked to a halt in front of a building on the seaward side of the street, the fading lettering on the brick reading Crowley's Marine Insurance and Registry. Mike knew that every ship, seaman, and officer working the Pacific coast would be registered in Crowley's, for in San Francisco, this was where loads were arranged and crews were signed on. Leaving Ku Xuan and Lai Song sitting inside the coach, he went into the office to search out the information he needed.

As he was about to enter, he glanced back at the coach and saw Ku Xuan and Lai Song gazing at the great ships that were loading and unloading their cargo, perhaps remembering their own long voyage across the sea. Today, at least, there were no human cargoes of Chinese—just tea, hemp, nitrate fertilizer, and other such loads.

Inside the building, a good fifty seamen bustled about, some showing their papers and signing on for voyages, others relaxing in the large reading room where many of them got their mail. For many of these sailors, this was the only onshore address they could claim.

Walking up to the long counter, Mike smiled at the harried clerk standing behind it. "I'd like to see the Captain's Registry, please."

"Yes, yes, it's over there," the clerk said impatiently, pointing across the room. "Don't take it from the table."

After thanking the man, Mike walked over to the table and opened the large, leather-bound volume. The names of the captains were alphabetized, and though he was looking for Daniel Lyons, he could not help checking to see if James Beckett's name was still in the registry.

BECKETT, JAMES E. Awarded Captain's certificate, April 1859. Last effective command: Clipper ship *Thunderbolt*, out of San Francisco. Present whereabouts unknown.

Mike had read the same entry a dozen times over the past twenty years, always hoping that some more recent information would be entered. With a sigh, he leafed on through the pages until he located Captain Daniel Lyons's name. The captain was listed as retired; his current residence was given as Monterey, California.

After writing the address on a piece of paper and sticking it in his pocket, he thanked the clerk and hurried back outside to the coach.

"Did you find anything?" Ku Xuan asked excitedly.

Smiling, Mike told her, "I found out his address. He lives in Monterey, which is several days' journey south. I suppose you'll want to check it out."

"Yes, please," Ku Xuan answered with a laugh. "That is, if you don't mind making the trip."

"I don't mind. That's what Mr. St. John is paying me to do." He paused and checked the time on the clocktower across the street. "It's already getting on toward six. Do you want to go back to Mr. St. John's house for the night and start out again first thing in the morning, or should we head off now and get in a couple of hours before making camp?"

"If it makes no difference to you, I would like to start now."

He smiled at her excitement and enthusiasm. "Sure. I understand. Well, I'll just arrange for a change of horses and send Mr. St. John a message telling him our plans. Then we'll be on our way."

*　　*　　*

The road south ran alongside the ocean, sometimes high on the hills and cliffs that overlooked the sea and other times right down on the beach. Mike Wakefield drove at a steady pace, and by the time it got dark enough, two hours later, to light the sidelamps, they had covered eight miles. They stopped and made camp just in from the road, dining on beef jerky and beans. Though the fare was very unappetizing to both Ku Xuan and Lai Song, they made no comment. The two young women giggled at Mike's surprise at how well they adapted to camping out. Then they reminded him that in their country, they had slept on simple pallets not unlike the bedrolls of blankets they spread out on the hard ground.

The following day they traveled another thirty miles, and at sunset, they stopped at an isolated Catholic mission. With their long, columned arcades and red-tiled roofs, the mission buildings bore no resemblance to the abbey of Shan Tal, but the monks who lived within them exhibited the same sense of dedication and self-discipline Ku Xuan had known her entire life, so she felt an immediate affinity for them. While Mike made arrangements for them to spend the night and have the horses cared for, Ku Xuan stepped down from the coach and walked over to watch an elderly, brown-robed monk trim shrubbery in the garden.

After standing quietly beside him for a few moments, Ku Xuan noticed an extra pair of shears, and she pointed to them, asking with a gesture of her head if she could help. The monk nodded his assent. She began clipping and trimming, matching her cuts perfectly with his, and they worked in quiet harmony for nearly half an hour. Then Mike came out of the mission and began walking toward her, leading another monk, a younger man.

The monk with Mike walked over to whisper quietly to the gardener, who nodded. Turning to Mike, the young brother told him, "Father Bustamante has given his permission for you to spend the evening with us."

"Thank you, Father," Mike said, facing the gardener.

Putting down his shears, Father Bustamante bowed to Ku Xuan. "Thank you, young lady, for sharing a few moments of serenity with me. Indeed, I can tell that you are a young woman of great peace, and I could almost believe you belonged to one of God's orders."

"I am honored by your observation," Ku Xuan replied. She put her palms together and bowed in return to the monk.

Father Bustamante looked at the monk who had brought Mike out to see him. "Tell me, Brother Elias, how is Brother Joseph?"

A shadow of sadness passed over Brother Elias's eyes.

"Father, I think he is dying."

"Should I administer last rites?"

"If you would, Father, I suggest you hold yourself in readiness, for I think that moment will soon be upon us."

"What's the matter with this man, this Brother Joseph?" Mike asked.

"He suffers from the strangest of maladies," Brother Elias replied. "Sometimes he shakes with the cold, though the sun may be at its hottest, while at other times, he complains of the heat, though it may be quite cool."

"I believe the illness was brought on by noxious vapors," Father Bustamante offered.

"Whatever the cause, he grows weaker with the passing of each hour."

"How have you treated him?" Ku Xuan asked.

"We have established a continuous prayer vigil for him," Father Bustamante told her. "One or another of the brothers is in the chapel, praying for him at all hours of the day and night."

"May I see him?"

"If you wish."

Leading the two visitors out of the garden and into the mission, Father Bustamante took Ku Xuan and Mike to Brother Joseph's bedroom, where the stricken monk lay unmoving in his bed. His forehead was wet with perspiration, and his eyes were glazed and unseeing.

Feeling his skin and looking into his eyes, Ku Xuan asked, "Father, have you a doctor here?"

"No," Father Bustamante said, shaking his head. Smiling sadly, he told her, "We are a poor order, dependent upon God and whatever healing skills we may have acquired over the years."

"Have you any quinine?"

"Quinine? No, I don't think so."

Mike gazed at Ku Xuan with a look of respect. "Of course.

He has the ague, doesn't he? I remember some of the sailors had it—but they didn't die from it."

"It's called malaria now," Ku Xuan informed him, "and the sailors you knew undoubtedly had only the recurring fevers, for it is most dangerous when first encountered. Father, please have someone get some bark from the trees that are just outside the abbey. Then make a strong tea from the bark. Also, is there any whiskey here?"

"We have wine."

"Wine won't do; I must have whiskey. Mike?"

Mike smiled. "I believe Mr. St. John did pack a bottle."

"Good. We'll make a tea of bark, mix it with whiskey, and give it to Brother Elias."

"And will that cure him?" Father Bustamante asked, a mixture of hope and surprise in his voice.

"Not by itself," Ku Xuan responded. "But if we administer it along with your prayers, he may be spared."

Father Bustamante smiled, and put his hand on Ku Xuan's shoulder. "Little one, you shall have your bark tea and our prayers, as you have requested."

When the tea was prepared, Ku Xuan mixed it with some of the whiskey. Then, using a spoon, she gave a generous dose to Brother Joseph. When she had finished, she quietly left the monk's cell, turning his care over to Father Bustamante and God.

Lai Song cooked supper for the travelers that night, managing to augment the dried beef with rice and spicy vegetables so that it was turned into quite a good meal. After they had eaten, during vespers, Lai Song and Ku Xuan retreated to the room they had been given, needing the time for quiet meditation. Mike walked around on the grounds outside, where, attracted by the booming of the surf, he stood on a flat rock and looked out over the ocean.

The moon was hanging like a great golden lantern, spilling its light onto the surface of the sea from the horizon to the shore. The long smear of silver shimmered brightly against the blackness of the water, like the wake behind a ship. Mike remembered something Cap had told him once . . . about a theory he had. A ship's wake, Cap believed, was a direct and visible link with the past. Somewhere, on the other end of that wake, everything that had ever happened was still happening, and if one had a flying machine swift enough, perhaps a thousand times faster than the swiftest ship, one could follow the wake backward and reach the other end of it before the shifting sea carried it away.

Mike wished that were true. He could follow Cap and see what had happened to him . . . and he could find out who Ku Xuan's father was—and where he was. Then Ku Xuan would be . . . He let the thought drop. She would be what? Impressed? She could hardly be impressed with him, considering all the strange powers she had. And now he knew that her powers also included the art of healing, for just before vespers, Brother Elias had told Mike that he thought he saw a slight improvement in Brother Joseph's condition.

Why did Ku Xuan's powers disturb him so? He did not believe in mysticism, or shamans, or fortune-telling, or anything of the sort. Besides, she had told him the things she did were simple tricks, and she had explained that the bark mixture was merely a substitute for quinine. So why did he keep dwelling on it?

Maybe it was because she was the most beautiful and desirable woman he had ever known. Except for the kiss they had shared in the mine, nothing overtly sexual had occurred between them—but he sensed a tremendous sexual vitality in her. And yet, even that had a touch of the unreal about it, as if the thing that made her so maddeningly desirable was itself a part of her strange powers.

Hearing the brothers wandering around behind him, Mike knew that vespers were over, and he continued his walk through the grounds. He strolled down the long colonnade toward the room Ku Xuan and Lai Song were sharing, saw that the shutter to their window was open slightly, and walked toward it.

Inside the small room, unaware that anyone could see in from the outside, Lai Song was pouring water into a tub while Ku Xuan, highlighted by the golden light from a lantern, sat completely nude on the edge of her bed, waiting for her bath.

Seeing the girl in her unabashed nudity, Mike was struck by an amazing realization. Although her nakedness stimulated an almost irrepressible desire in him, there was about her a sweet innocence that made him feel strangely protective. Suddenly disconcerted, he hurried by the open window to his own room, went inside, and lay on his bed.

Half an hour later there was a knock on his door, and when he answered he saw Father Bustamante, Brother Elias, and—amazingly—the ailing Brother Joseph. The monk was somewhat shaky on his feet and leaned on Father Bustamante for support . . . but still he was on his feet.

"It is a miracle!" Brother Elias said, smiling broadly. "Brother Joseph would like you to escort him to the young lady so that he may thank her personally."

"All right," Mike agreed.

The three of them walked down the colonnade and, reaching Ku Xuan's room, Mike knocked on the door. When Ku Xuan opened it and saw Brother Joseph standing there, she smiled broadly.

"I am so happy you are feeling better," she said.

"Thanks to you," Brother Joseph replied.

Ku Xuan reached out and took the monk's hand. "Not just me," she insisted. "You had some very good people saying some very powerful prayers for you."

Father Bustamante reached out and touched Ku Xuan gently on the cheek. "Nevertheless, I will say a special prayer for you before I retire—and we shall all pray that you will soon be reunited with your father. I was so moved by your story at suppertime. I would like to believe, too, that it was more than just good fortune that brought you to us this evening. And now I should let you get your sleep so that you may continue your journey well rested in the morning. Good night, my child."

At the same time that the three travelers had made camp their first night on the road, Li Chen had stood in the shadows as the cold fog rolled in off San Francisco Bay, keeping watch at Wo Hamm's house, believing that the tong chief would eventually lead him to Ku Xuan. He had noticed an American visiting twice; then the day before, the man had paid another call. Growing very curious, he learned his name. Now, that same Cole Granger furtively left Wo Hamm's again.

Though Li Chen had been in California only for a short while, he already understood that relationships between Ameri-

cans and Chinese were based solely on business. The West-
erners were looking either to buy or to sell something. Several
Americans came to Wo Hamm for the opium dens, but Cole
Granger was not one of them. Why, then, did he come? Li
Chen decided to find out.

Assuming the demeanor of a meek merchant, he shuffled
across the street to the two men Wo Hamm had standing
guard. He approached the men and, in a stance of groveling
respect, whined, "A thousand pardons, honorable sirs, but
from your appearance, I believe you to be tong warriors."

"What of it, old man?" one of them growled.

"I beg your forgiveness for my unworthy intrusion, but I
am a merchant, trying only to make an honest living, paying
my tribute to the tong as it should be. However, tonight I
was robbed by that big American who just left your venerable
chief's house."

The two young men looked after Granger.

"Why tell us?"

"Because, honorable ones, even as we speak, he has a
small leather bag that is filled with gold. Almost a thousand
dollars."

Li Chen could tell that the two men were interested in
what he had to say, because their eyes sparkled with
excitement.

"You say he has a thousand dollars in gold?"

"Yes," Li Chen lied. "I thought perhaps you could over-
take him and get my money from him. I would gladly double
my tong payment."

The tong warriors laughed, and one of them declared, "It is
not your money anymore, old man. It belongs to the American."

"And soon it will belong to us," the other added.

"But surely you won't take it all?"

"Go away now, and you won't be hurt," one of the men
warned. Leaving him, they hurried down the street, keeping
to the shadows, until they were a good block ahead of Granger.
Slipping into an alleyway, they waited.

Li Chen crossed the street and walked behind Granger,
laughing to himself at his plan. Granger had not taken any
money from him—in fact, he had never seen him before—
but if everything went as he expected . . .

As Granger passed the alley, the two tong warriors jumped out in front of him.

"What the hell?" Granger shouted, going for his gun.

One of the two was holding *num chucs*, a weapon consisting of two fighting sticks connected by a chain. With a quick fluid move, he used the *num chucs* to jerk the gun out of Granger's hand.

"Give us the gold," the other man demanded.

"Gold? What gold? I don't know what you're talkin' about."

Suddenly Li Chen leaped in front of the two tong warriors, and with a quick thrust of one hand, he smashed the Adam's apple of one of them. The man fell gagging, choking to death from a crushed esophagus. The other whirled the *num chucs* over his head, looking for the opportunity to make a killing blow, but Li Chen spun on his heel and kicked him in the base of the nose, sending bone splinters into his brain. Turning then to the shocked Granger, the Shal Minh priest put his hands together in a position of respect and bowed.

"I am shamed that two of my countrymen would attack you. Please, you must forgive me."

"Forgive *you?* You saved my life," Granger exclaimed as he retrieved his gun. He looked at the two men who had attacked him. "I wonder where they got the idea I was carrying gold?"

"Perhaps they just arrived in this country," Li Chen suggested. "To many Chinese, America is a country with streets paved in gold, so naturally they believe all Americans are rich."

"Yeah? Well, they sure got me wrong. Hell, I don't even have the price of a drink."

Li Chen smiled. "Perhaps you will allow me to buy you a drink to apologize for the behavior of my countrymen."

"You don't need to buy me a drink, mister."

"Is it because I am Chinese that you will not drink with me?"

"No, no," Granger assured him quickly. He smiled. "I ain't proud. I'll drink with the devil if he buys."

"There is a place near here," Li Chen offered. "It is a place for Chinese, but Americans are welcome. We can go there."

"Yeah, okay. Why not?"

The two men walked through the clammy night for a few blocks until they reached a saloon that was quieter than the places frequented by Americans. Entering, they made their way to a table and sat down. Li Chen bought Granger first one drink, then a second one, and then another. With the fourth drink, Granger's tongue loosened, and he started talking.

"This here Wo Hamm," he began, "he's what they call a tong chief, you know what I mean? He's got lots of money and he controls all the Chinamen around here like he was a king or somethin'. Anyhow, me an' him, we made a deal. There's this China girl over here that he wants killed. Well, I found her at the Silverado mine, an' she went down inside to talk to some old Chinaman about somethin', an' while she was down there, I set off a charge and caved the mine in. Then I come back to San Francisco an' asked Wo Hamm for the money he promised me."

Li Chen's heart was beating fast. He was sure that the girl Granger was hired to kill was Ku Xuan. Keeping his voice level, he inquired, "Why does he want this woman—what is her name—killed?"

Granger shrugged. "Beats me. I guess the China girl—her name's Swan somethin'—oh, yeah, Ku Xuan—I guess she did somethin' that really riled him. I don't really care. All I want is my money."

"And he did not pay you?" Li Chen asked, calmly pouring Granger another drink while all the time his mind was racing.

"He didn't pay me," Granger replied, tossing back the drink, " 'cause I didn't kill her."

"You did not? I thought you said you collapsed the mine."

"Yeah, that's what I done, all right. Only, somehow the girl got out. By the time I got back here, Wo Hamm had already found out about it."

"Do you think he is lying to you so he does not have to pay the money?"

Granger glumly shook his head. "No. I checked down at the newspaper office, and they're already runnin' a story about the cave-in. Nobody was killed; nobody was even hurt. Somehow she got away. But I'm gonna find her. I'm gonna find her and that fella she's runnin' with, an' I'm gonna kill both of 'em. The thing to do is go back to the mine. All them Chinamen there, they know somethin', you can bet on that. They know where she went. Say, is there any more whiskey in that bottle?"

"Of course, my friend." Li Chen smiled and poured another glass, only as he was pouring the liquor this time, he was also pouring a powder from a packet concealed in the palm of his hand. With a swirl of the glass, the powder dissolved, and he handed the drink to Granger.

"Yes, sir," Granger declared, gulping down the drink, "it'll be a cold day in hell when a China girl gets the best of me."

Li Chen watched Granger carefully. He could easily have killed him, but he did not want to do anything to get Wo Hamm suspicious. The potion was only enough to knock him out, although it would also make him so sick that for a few days, Granger would not feel like doing anything at all. That would give Li Chen an excellent head start.

Granger's head suddenly fell onto the table, and the Shal Minh priest smiled to himself. Standing up, Li Chen looked down at the unconscious American and then left the barroom, heading quickly back to his lodgings. Early in the morning he would go to the Silverado mine and learn where the Manchu princess was.

It was midmorning when Li Chen, riding a fast horse, made his way up the steep mountain road and arrived at the mine. Locating the office, he headed toward it just as a couple of American miners came out of the small building. Seeing a Chinese on horseback seemed to surprise them, and they just stood there, waiting for him to ride up.

As the priest dismounted, one of the Americans called, "Hey, you, Chinaman. Where'd you get that horse?"

"I have a bill of purchase for the animal," Li Chen said, using the groveling voice that he had learned most Americans expected of the Chinese and that would arouse the least suspicion.

"Yeah? Well you better have, 'cause if the sheriff comes out here lookin' for a horse what was stole, I'm gonna tell 'im I seen a Chinaman ridin' one."

Both Americans laughed and headed toward the mine entrance. As soon as they departed, Li Chen stepped up onto the porch and knocked on the door.

"Come in, come in," a voice called.

Entering the office looking completely subservient, he waited until he was addressed by the Westerner sitting behind the desk. The Shal Minh priest had learned through his sources that this man, Otto Turner, had worked at the Silverado mine for quite some time, but he had only recently been appointed to the supervisor's position, after the former manager had been fired. One of the reasons Walter St. John had promoted him was that he got along well with the Chinese.

"Yes?" the man inquired. "What can I do for you?"

"A thousand pardons for disturbing you, honorable sir," Li Chen said, kowtowing, "but I have heard that you will hire worthless Chinese."

The man smiled, and the lines around his eyes crinkled. "Well, you've been misinformed. You see, I won't hire *anyone* if he's worthless—but I will hire anyone who's a good worker. And my experience with Chinese has been that they're good workers. If you work as well as your countrymen, you've got a job with me."

"Thank you, *shih*," Li Chen murmured, again bowing in respect.

Getting up from his desk, Turner walked Li Chen to the front door and pointed to the entrance to the mine, where dozens of workers, Chinese and American, were congregated, waiting to go below.

"Go over there and find out which gang boss needs a new man. Tell 'em I sent you."

Profusely thanking Turner, Li Chen scurried over to the mine. After speaking with a couple of the workers, he reported to one of the Chinese gang bosses. The gang boss gave him a pick, and when the whistle blew, Li Chen followed the others down into one of the shafts.

For a full day, Li Chen labored alongside the other Chinese workers, quietly listening to them talk and hoping one of them would say something that would give him a lead. But he learned nothing. It was not until the morning of the second day that he heard something useful. One of the younger workers was going on at great length extolling a young Chinese woman—who was obviously Ku Xuan.

Between blows with his pickax, the young man declared to a fellow worker, "I have heard of a place where young girls are schooled in such arts and skills, but until that beautiful young woman came here, I never dreamed I would ever meet such a creature."

"She is truly a woman of great beauty."

"And great skill. Did you see the timbers? She cut through them with her hand as if her hand were an ax."

"Of course, she is a woman who has powers."

Feeling the time was right to ask a pointed question, Li Chen inquired, "Was she a Shan Tal priestess?"

His question brought all the conversation to a standstill. The young worker started to answer, but the old powderman held out his hand to still him.

"Why would you ask such a thing?" Kwai Fong wanted to know.

"I am interested in finding a priestess of Shan Tal who I have heard is in California," Li Chen replied in a humble manner. "It is said that when one has troubles and goes to a Shan Tal priestess, she cannot refuse a request for help."

"What is the nature of your trouble?"

"Ah, my friend, this I shall tell only to the priestess. Do you know where she is?"

"I know of no such person."

"Are you sure? The beautiful girl the workers were speaking of sounds like the priestess I seek. Her name is Ku Xuan."

"We know nothing of a girl named Ku Xuan," Kwai Fong declared.

Li Chen looked carefully at the faces of the other workers. "I am anxious to find her. If anyone knows anything about her, I can be most generous."

"No one here knows anything about her," Kwai Fong insisted, closing the subject.

When the workers returned to the mines after their lunch break, Li Chen tried to learn more about Ku Xuan, but no one would speak to him, and it soon became evident that Kwai Fong had ordered their silence. He decided there was only one way he was going to learn about Ku Xuan—and that would be by taking care of Kwai Fong.

The Shal Minh priest got his chance when the powderman and a young assistant went deep into a mine tunnel to lay dynamite charges. Because the explosives were being placed, everyone except the two men handling them was ordered to the surface—allowing Li Chen to hurry unnoticed through the deserted tunnel to the blasting chamber.

Reaching the chamber, Li Chen stood for a moment, observing Kwai Fong and his assistant, who were busy laying the charges on the far rock face with their backs to him.

"Good afternoon," Li Chen said quietly.

Kwai Fong turned around. "You!" he gasped. "What are you doing down here? Did you not hear the order to vacate?"

"It is very dangerous to be down here," the young assistant added.

Li Chen grinned evilly. "Oh, yes, my friends. It is very dangerous indeed"—he walked toward the two powdermen—"especially if you do not answer my questions."

"Who are you?" Kwai Fong demanded. "Why are you looking for Ku Xuan?"

"I told you."

"You lied."

Li Chen smiled agreeably. "Very well, I lied. But there is nothing you can do about it . . . except to tell me what I want to know."

"I will tell you nothing," Kwai Fong insisted.

Li Chen held out his arm and pulled up his sleeve, exposing the tattooed dragon on his wrist.

"Shal Minh!" the old man whispered hoarsely.

"What is Shal Minh?" the young assistant asked, obviously perplexed by Kwai Fong's reaction.

"What Shan Tal is for good, Shal Minh is for evil," Kwai Fong explained, his voice fearful. "Shan Tal priests are of the light. . . . Shal Minh priests are from darkness."

Li Chen chuckled wickedly. "Very good, Kwai Fong. Now, since you know my power—which means you know, too, that I am not bound by any code of honor—you are also aware I will get what I want from you no matter what it takes."

"I will tell you nothing," the old man said defiantly.

"Kwai Fong, tell him," the young man pleaded. "He will kill you if you don't. *I* will tell him to save your life!"

"You will tell him nothing!" Kwai Fong ordered.

Li Chen's hand lashed out so suddenly that it was just a blur. It smashed against Kwai Fong's neck, snapping it, and the old man was dead before he hit the ground.

"Aiyee!" the young apprentice screamed, holding up his

crossed arms in front of his face and sinking to his knees. "Please do not kill me! Do not kill me!"

"Tell me about the girl," Li Chen demanded.

"I will tell you all that I know," the apprentice assured him, his voice trembling. "She searches for her father, an American known as Big Cat. Kwai Fong believed that the father must be a man named Daniel Lyons, a sea captain who had fathered a child who would now be the same age as Ku Xuan."

"Where is this man Daniel Lyons?"

"That I do not know."

"Very well." Li Chen suddenly pointed to Kwai Fong. "See to the old man. I think he is still alive."

"Alive?" The apprentice scurried on his knees over to Kwai Fong and, his back to Li Chen, felt the old man's neck.

Coming up behind the young man, the evil priest knew that Kwai Fong was indeed dead, but by the time the assistant realized it, it would be too late. With a movement so swift that the worker did not even sense it, Li Chen's hand sliced through the air, breaking the man's neck with a single chop to the base of the skull and killing him instantly.

Li Chen worked quickly. Finding the set charges, he lit the fuses and then ran through the shaft and out of the mine. When the others found the two miners, they would think they had been killed in an accident. Making his way to where his horse was stabled, the priest slipped out of the mining camp and rode hard for San Francisco, where he would make inquiries on the docks.

Just south of San Francisco early the next day, a loud report rolled down the hillside, picked up resonance, and then echoed back from the neighboring hills. With the smoke from his pistol blowing away in the postdawn breeze, Cole Granger stood smiling broadly. Though he had been feeling ill for a couple of days, barely able to move, he was better now, and his aim was as good as ever. He had just shattered a tossed whiskey bottle with his marksmanship, and as he looked over at his audience of two, he declared, "There now. I'd like to see one of them bastard Chinamen do that."

"I thought you said we'd be workin' for a Chinaman."

"It's a Chinaman that's gonna pay us for killin' the girl, true enough. But he's a tong leader, and he's got some of his own kind out there lookin' for her as well."

"He must really want the girl dead. What'd she do?"

Granger tossed another bottle into the air and pulled the trigger. Like the first, it shattered into pieces, although the echoing shot drowned out the sound of the exploding bottle.

"Now how the hell do I know what she done?" the outlaw responded as he pushed the empty shells out of the pistol's cylinder and began reloading it with fresh charges. "Anyhow, I don't care what it was. All I care is that I get to her before them heathens do, so's I get the money . . . an' I get to kill that stage driver that's with her."

One of his two cohorts chuckled. "Seems to me like you've run into him before—and you was lucky. If I was you, I'd leave him alone and—" Suddenly the barrel of a pistol was pressing against the end of his nose.

"Brewster, I wonder how you'd look without a nose?" Granger asked coldly.

"Hold it, hold it!" Brewster cried. "I didn't mean nothin'. Tell him, Finley. Tell him I didn't mean nothin'!"

Finley put his hand on the outlaw's arm. "C'mon, Cole. You know his mouth is too big for his own good sometimes."

Granger pressed the pistol so hard against Brewster's nose that it started to bleed. Finally, he pulled the weapon away, and Brewster held the cuff of his sleeve up to the trickle of blood.

"I didn't mean nothin'," Brewster whined again.

The outlaw holstered his gun and warned, "Then watch your mouth from now on."

They were all silent for a few moments, and then Finley asked, "Cole, you got any idea where that China girl has gone to?"

"No," Granger admitted, "but I think that chink who got me drunk is after her too."

"Him and that old tong fellow must really want her bad," Finley murmured.

Granger grinned. "Yeah, that's just the way I see it. Fact is, I think our tong friend wants her *so* bad that if we catch her and hold on to her for a while, he'll pay two, maybe three times what he told me he would." He looked off into the distance. "The way I figure it, it'll be easy to pick up Wakefield's trail—hell, everybody seems to know him, since he's been drivin' that stage so long. We'll just get on back to town and ask down at the stage depot which way he went. If they won't tell us, we'll just ask around. With somethin' as noticeable as St. John's bright red coaches, somebody's bound to have seen the one Wakefield's drivin'—then we'll light out after him." Looking at his two cohorts, he declared, "Whaddya say we get started?"

Standing at the rear of the coach, Mike Wakefield looked toward the eastern horizon. A bright band of rose preceded the rising sun, and the blanket of darkness was already thrown off the hilltops. Over the small grassy meadow hovered a shroud of mist, seemingly pinned to the earth.

The monks of the mission were long awake, moving quickly and silently through the early morning shadows, attending to the details that occupied their lives. Father Bustamante materialized from one of the shadows and asked, "You will be leaving soon?"

"Yes. How is Brother Joseph this morning?"

"Much better. The shaking and the fever have stopped. He is still weak, but I think he is regaining his strength. Your young woman has a rare gift for the healing art."

"Father, you have no idea how many gifts she has," Mike told the monk.

Bustamante looked around, as if making certain that Ku Xuan was not there to hear him. "My son, please be especially careful with her. I sense a great danger."

"What kind of danger?"

"That I cannot tell you. But I know there is danger about her."

"Well, if there is, she can take care of herself. Like I said, you don't know this woman, Father. She . . . she has special strengths and powers that an average person like me could never understand."

"I know she is a holy woman."

"You mean a priestess? Yes, a priestess of Shan Tal, whatever that means. But I wouldn't exactly call her holy . . . at least, not the kind of holy you mean."

Father Bustamante looked intently at the driver. "I know she is not of our faith, but she is of *a* faith . . . and who is to say that God cannot be approached by ways other than our own? Even if the message of Jesus has not been heard, the enlightenment of Buddha can lead one to God, and then God has still won. And as we all witnessed with our own eyes last night, she is a holy woman . . . a good woman. Still, I sense great danger. You must be on the lookout. You must protect her."

"I'll do what I can, Father," Mike promised.

The door to the mission opened, and Ku Xuan and Lai Song started walking toward the coach.

Smiling at them, Mike called, "Good morning, ladies. I hope you slept well."

"Very well, thank you, Mike," Ku Xuan assured him, smiling warmly.

"Very well," Lai Song echoed.

Ku Xuan looked at her friend proudly and then said to the two men, "It is just a short while since we came to this country, and she has already learned much of the language."

Holding out his arms expansively, Father Bustamante said to the two young women, "I hope that you will both return here soon. Lai Song, you can show us what remarkable progress you have made in your mastery of English; and Ku Xuan, I pray that you will have wonderful news about your father."

Ku Xuan bowed slightly, saying, "Your kindness to us is most welcome."

Mike took their luggage and stowed it in the boot of the stagecoach, and then he helped them board. As he walked to the front of the coach to climb into the driver's box, he turned to the friar. "Again, thank you for allowing us to stay here, Father."

"No thanks are necessary, my son. All travelers are welcome in our house—especially those with goodness in their hearts, like you and your companions." Making the sign of the cross, Father Bustamante intoned, "*Vaya con Dios*, my friends." Then he smiled and told Mike softly, "Oh, and in case you did not already know it, I sense one other thing about the beautiful young woman."

"What's that, Father?"

"She is in love with you."

There was only one hotel in Cacheville, and although Cap

had passed by it many times, he had never been inside it before. But the afternoon when he had come down out of the hills, he decided he would take a room—it would be the first time he had slept under a roof in well over a year.

There were two seabags thrown across his mule's back. One of the bags contained Cap's clothes. The other was also an ordinary canvas bag, and its innocuous appearance was its security. It was heavy, but if one were to peer inside it without lifting it, one would see just a coffeepot, a skillet, a bag of coffee, a bag of dry beans, some salt and pepper—nothing more. But in fact most of the bag was filled with gold nuggets, the result of three months of digging. He was not sure how much money it represented, but he was reasonably certain that it was enough to buy another ship . . . if he had wanted to.

Taking the bags from the back of his mule, Cap started toward the front door of the hotel, but as soon as he stepped up onto the porch, he was accosted by a Chinese coolie.

"Please, are you called Cap?"

The prospector ran his hand through his beard, squinting at the man. During the last twenty years he had not made more than a dozen acquaintances, none of whom he had kept up with. How would this young man know him?

"Yes," he admitted. "Is there something I can do for you?"

"There is a young man, a *fan kuei*, who asks about you," the coolie said.

"What does he want with me?"

"This I do not know. I was asked to look for a man with a cap such as yours who works in the mountains."

Turning toward the hotel door, the prospector said over his shoulder, "Well, if you don't know what he wants, I'm not interested."

"His name is Mike," the coolie called after him.

Cap stopped and then turned back toward the Chinese messenger.

"Mike?"

"Yes."

"Where can I find him? Is he here, in this place?"

"I am told he lives in San Francisco. He is a driver for Walter St. John, the owner of the Silverado mine."

"For St. John, eh? Yeah, I've heard of him."

The Chinese smiled; then he put his hands together beneath his chin and bowed. "I have informed you," he stated.

"Yes, thank you."

The prospector watched the retreating messenger for a long moment, and then he pulled open the door and stepped into the hotel lobby. Crossing the polished floor, he plopped down his seabags in front of the desk and rang the bell for service. The clerk came from a back room, and as he approached the desk, he gave Cap a disdainful look. Ignoring it, Cap requested and paid for a room and a bath, and then signed the register. With a weary sigh, he picked up his two seabags and slowly climbed the stairs to the second floor.

It was two days later when Cap entered the Seaman's Bank in San Francisco, his appearance entirely changed from what it had been when he had first come down out of the hills. He was clean, his hair and beard were both neatly trimmed, and he was wearing a pressed blue captain's uniform. The uniform was the only decent suit of clothes he owned, and he wanted to look as good as he could when he did his banking.

"Well, Captain," the teller said with a broad smile, looking up from the tablet where he had been making his calculations. "You have eight hundred ninety-six ounces of gold, which at the current rate of exchange comes to the sum of fifty thousand, one hundred seventy-six dollars. Now, how will you want that?"

"I'll open an account. By the way, would you happen to know where my old friend Walter St. John lives?"

"But of course, sir," the teller answered. "You mean you haven't been to his house?"

"It's been a long time since I saw him," Cap replied. In fact, that was not entirely a lie, for he had been acquainted with Walter St. John when St. John had been an able-bodied seaman, though St. John had never sailed aboard his ship.

Handing a passbook over to his new depositor, the teller smiled and told him, "The bank has a carriage, sir. I will instruct the driver to take you to Mr. St. John."

"Thank you. That's most kind." Winking at the young man, the prospector added, "Looks like I chose my banking institution wisely."

Picking up his seabags, he followed the teller through the

bank and outside to the waiting carriage, an elegant closed landau. He climbed in and settled back onto the rich black leather seat. Barely ten minutes later, the carriage rolled up a long curved driveway past statuary, fountains, and gardens. Giving a low whistle, Cap said under his breath, "I'll sure say this for you, Mr. St. John: For an ordinary seaman, you've done all right for yourself."

Cap dismissed the driver and then pulled on the bell rope at the front door. A few moments later a servant appeared, and the prospector stated his business.

"Please follow me, sir," the servant said, showing the visitor into the parlor. "If you'll wait here, I'll get Mr. St. John."

Nervously walking around the formal room, Cap examined several of the beautiful objects lying on various small tables. Many of them seemed to be mementos from St. John's travels. Hearing someone approach, he put down the model ship he had been looking at and walked toward the door.

"Good afternoon, sir," an elegant middle-aged man said. "I'm Walter St. John. How may I help you?"

Holding out his hand, the prospector said, "Mr. St. John, the name is Beckett, James Beckett. I'm known as Cap."

The polite smile on St. John's face was immediately replaced by a wide grin. "Cap! I'm delighted finally to meet you! Please sit down. Would you like a drink?"

"That I would, sir. A brandy, if that's all right."

"Coming right up." St. John poured two snifters of brandy, and as he handed one to his guest, he declared, "So, you are Mike's mysterious Cap. I take it Cap is short for captain?"

"It was once—but I have to confess that I'm being dishonest by wearing this uniform now, as I am no longer a ship's captain, or even a sailor. However, it's the only proper suit I own for doing business in."

"Mike has searched for you for many years," St. John told him. "He'll be very pleased to see you again."

"Where is the lad?" Cap asked. He chuckled and added, "Of course, he wouldn't exactly be a lad now, would he?"

"Not exactly," St. John agreed, smiling. "He's a fine figure of a man, Captain, and my best stage driver."

"Well, I'm not surprised by that," Cap offered, and then took a sip of the brandy. "Though only a boy, he was the most valuable member of my crew—and I'm not exaggerating about that. Tell me, is he working nearby?"

"He's off driving a coach on a private mission right now," St. John explained. "You see, the young woman I have hired as my hostess is searching for her father."

"He deserted her, did he?"

"She doesn't know all the facts, only that her Chinese mother died when she was born, and her American father may not even know of her existence."

"Well, I presume she knows the man's name."

"Not exactly," St. John confessed, shaking his head.

The prospector looked startled. "Well, then, assuming she finds a man who generally fits the bill, how would she know he's her father?"

"She has some questions to ask," St. John explained. "Truth is, it wouldn't have been all that impossible that I would be her father, so she asked the questions of me. I'm sorry to say that I failed the test. But right now they're en route to Monterey, to talk to a Captain Daniel Lyons."

"Lyons, eh? Yes, I know him. He's a good man."

"I'm pleased to hear that," St. John admitted. "Tell me, do you think Lyons might be her father?"

"I can't say . . . though I do recall some tale about how he married a rich merchant's daughter. Seems to me like there was a child from that. If she's his daughter, he'll own up to it right enough."

"I don't think it's a question of owning up to it," St. John assured him. "Ku Xuan is the most beautiful and charming young woman I have ever met. Believe me, it would be an honor to be her father."

Something dark and deep crossed Cap's eyes, and he looked off, as if staring at something far back in time. "Aye," he said solemnly, "there are those of us who would give anything to have known such an honor."

"Captain—" St. John started. Then Cap held up his hand, and St. John smiled. "Sorry. The title seems to fit you."

"Don't mind admitting that it sounded pretty good, too," the prospector declared.

"What I was going to say is that your knowledge of China and the old China hands of the time might be of some help to the girl. And I know Mike would love to see you again. If you had the time to help in the search, I would be glad to make it worth your while."

"I don't need your money," Cap assured him. "I'm not as

wealthy as you, Mr. St. John, but I've had a run of luck in the hills. Now, with that out of the way, I'll say that I would like to help Mike if I can. I may just go down to Monterey to see if I can find them."

St. John walked over to his desk, took a sheet of paper from the drawer, and began writing on it. "Here," he finally said. "If you won't take my money, at least take this. Go to the livery stable at my stage depot. This slip will authorize you to choose the finest horse we've got, and to choose other good mounts at any of the swing stations between here and Monterey."

"Thank you," Cap replied, touched by the generous offer. He finished his brandy and put the empty snifter down on the table. "Well, no time like the present, as they say." He held out his hand. "It was a pleasure meeting you, Mr. St. John. I'm sure we'll meet again sometime."

Clapping the prospector on the shoulder, St. John told him, "I'll hold you to that. Good luck."

Chapter Eight

It was nearly six o'clock in the evening, and the three travelers had been on the road since dawn, when the coach suddenly lurched violently to one side. After pulling the team to a halt, Mike set the brake and leaped down from the box to discover that a front wheel had worked its way off because the hub that held the wheel on was missing.

"Are you two all right in there?" he called through the window.

"Yes," Ku Xuan answered. "We were tossed about but not injured. What happened?"

"The damn— Pardon me. The wheel fell off. And unfortunately it's badly bent."

"Should we come out?"

Sighing, Mike replied, "You may as well. We're going to be here a while." Cursing his stupidity for not having checked the hubs, he helped the two women out of the lopsided coach, and then he sat down on a boulder beside the road, trying to decide what to do.

They were about midway between swing stations, meaning help was ten or twelve miles away in either direction. He would have to unhitch one of the horses and ride to the station—bareback, Mike realized with a grimace—and that would take a good four hours round trip. It would be long past dark before he was halfway back.

He stood up and walked over to the two women. "I guess there's nothing else to do but make camp now, and at first light I'll ride to the swing station and get another wheel and hub." He smiled tenderly at Ku Xuan. "I know how anxious

132

you are to get to Monterey, and I'm really sorry that we'll be losing so much time."

Shrugging her shoulders—an Americanism she had recently adopted—Ku Xuan assured him, "All that happens is meant to happen. Do not fret, Mike."

Mike had the horses pull the stagecoach a bit off the road, and the travelers made camp. They had to content themselves with eating jerky and beans once more. Since the weather was good, the two young women decided against pitching their small tent. Instead, they would sleep out in the open, next to the coach.

After they had eaten and laid out their bedrolls, Ku Xuan walked a short distance away from her companions to sit on a large rock and look up at the stars.

The long ride that day had been a time of solitude and meditation for Ku Xuan, and Lai Song, no doubt sensing her mistress's need for privacy, had kept silent during the entire ride. Ku Xuan had used this time to still the ache in her heart and the doubts in her mind about who and what she was—and where she belonged. And now, as she enjoyed the evening air, she continued to ponder her new life in California, for it was her home now.

There was much beauty in this new, rugged country, and Ku Xuan, whose training at Shan Tal had taught her to use all her senses to their fullest capacity, delighted in all that was around her. Although the bright colors of the myriad flowers dotting the landscape were now muted by the darkness, she could picture their vividness in her mind. Looking up at the diamond brilliance of the stars, then over toward the moon-silvered rocky hills, and then down to the beach below and the shimmering iridescence of the sea, she felt her heart quicken. This was a truly magical land, and she felt at peace here. Closing her eyes, she was serenaded by the wind blowing through the tall trees, the pulsing rhythm of the surf, and the delicate songs of the night birds. And all around her floated the fragrance of the flowers' perfume as silken breezes caressed her skin. There was a spiritual and physical contentment to this place that satisfied her soul.

Yet something was missing. Far down in the most secret recesses of her heart, there was a longing, an unfulfilled need that tugged at the edge of her being and increasingly called to her.

And so Ku Xuan meditated. She turned her powers of concentration inward, examining all that was within her, to find the seed of discontent that was growing there. What was it she wanted?

The answer came. At first the voice calling to her was small and quiet, no more than a timid cry from somewhere deep inside her.

Love.

It grew louder, reaching the forefront of her mind, though at first she tried to reject it.

Yet it came to her again. Love was what was missing.

The notion held no real meaning for Ku Xuan. Love had always signified something physical; making love meant the art of sexual fulfillment and physical gratification. It was a skill she had learned at Shan Tal, although that skill had thus far not been put into practice. Any other kind of love was not—she had been told—the destiny of a Shan Tal priestess.

But it was that special love she longed for now. The love one person feels for another; the love a woman can know for a man when thought and reason are set aside and pure, unrestrained truth abide between them. And she longed for this love with Mike Wakefield. She could not deny her feelings for him any longer—but she also could not act upon them, for any relationship might interfere with the mission at hand . . . finding her father.

She recalled again what Mata Lee had told her: *"The final and most exquisite way for a man and woman to share in the river of pleasure is to know love. . . ."* For one fleeting instant, Ku Xuan felt a powerful tugging at her heart to enter that river with Mike, but she could not and would not do so until she had fulfilled her promise to the abbess.

Besides, she was sure that Mike was just as reluctant to join with her, if not more so. She knew that the incident in the mine shaft had delivered quite a blow to his self-esteem, and he did not now consider himself adequate. It would be some time before he felt ready to meet Ku Xuan in midstream as her equal in love.

After spreading out his bedroll about twenty yards from the

coach—the better to be on guard—Mike flung himself down onto it and lay on his back, looking up at the stars. He was keenly aware of Ku Xuan's close proximity, and he had the feeling that if he went to her, she would not turn him away. He also inherently knew that if he did go to her, he would realize the greatest pleasure imaginable.

But he remained where he was, occupying his mind by studying the night sky and thinking back to the days of his voyage to China on board the clipper ship *Thunderbolt.*

"Look to the stars, lad," Cap had told him one night as they stared upward from the deck of the ship. "They are the one constant thing in this universe. Everything else changes—men, animals, the sea, even the mountains over eons of time. But the stars? They never change. See the North Star? Magellan used it to sail the globe, and it was in the same position four hundred years ago as it is now."

Gazing first at one quadrant of the sky and then at another, Mike had declared, "There are so many I get dizzy looking at them."

Cap put his hand on the boy's shoulder. "Sure, there are a lot of them, and that's a fact." Then he added reassuringly, "But if a body makes friends with the stars, he'll never be alone. And I'll tell you this, lad. They'll never desert you like human friends will."

Mike Wakefield had deserted Cap. It had been a difficult voyage back home on the *Thunderbolt:* the captain, grieving over the death of his sweetheart, drunk in his cabin; the crew overly lax; the cargo spoiling and ultimately lost. When the sheriff came aboard in San Francisco and plastered the mainmast with his foreclosure papers, Mike was away; and when he came back, the captain was gone.

He had tried to find Cap several times; then, as his life turned away from the sea, locating the man had become less and less important. It was only lately, since meeting Ku Xuan, that Cap had begun dominating his thoughts again.

Ironically, now he and Cap had something else they shared, something beyond that one voyage, that locked them together forever: They shared a sense of heartache over a

Chinese woman. Cap's heart had been broken by event
beyond his control. . . . Mike's was troubled by events tha
were even at that moment unfolding.

A meteor flashed across the sky, and he watched it. Some
times he felt like a meteor himself—a star with no fixe
place, blazing through life. . . .

Mike Wakefield kept alert even while asleep, and when
small pebble was rolled out of place by someone advancin
on foot, the driver opened his eyes, instantly awake. Accord
ing to the position of the stars, it was well past midnigh
although it was still quite a while until morning. Whoeve
was approaching had no good intention in mind, for he wa
definitely taking advantage of the darkness.

Sitting up cautiously, Mike looked around slowly, not con
centrating on any one spot. Using this sweeping gaze, h
detected movement . . . two silent shadows slipping throug
the darkness. He slipped his pistol from its holster and the
rolled away from his blankets toward the coach, moving a
quietly as he could. Reaching out, Mike touched Ku Xuan o
the shoulder, immediately silencing her when he felt he
move.

"Quiet. We have company," he whispered.

"Who?"

"I don't know."

The two figures crept toward the blankets where a momen
before Mike had been sleeping. One of them pulled out hi
pistol, aimed it toward the bedroll, and fired two shots, th
flash from the muzzle lighting up the night.

Standing up and running from the coach to keep it out o
the line of fire, Mike yelled at the two would-be assassins
"I'm over here!"

Both intruders turned in his direction. They blasted away
one with his pistol and the other with a shotgun, the heav
boom reverberating through the night, just as Mike dive
into a stand of scrub trees. He heard the pellets flying al
around him and felt a slight stinging sensation in his leg. On
of the pellets must have just grazed him, but he was certainl
not hit badly.

The intruders fired a second time, but now Mike was o
the ground, on his belly, out of their line of fire. Preparing t

shoot back, he used the twelve-inch-wide muzzle blast of the shotgun as his target. He fired two shots just over the shotgun's flame pattern, then two more just to the right of it, where he knew the other gunman was. He heard two muted grunts, and then both men crumpled and fell.

Pulling himself out of the brush, Mike ran toward them. He stood over them, holding his pistol at the ready just for insurance. One of the men had been hit in the head and was already dead, the other was lying on his back, groaning softly. His eyes had adjusted to the dark, and Mike could see the man's wounds clearly . . . one in the stomach and the other in the chest. He saw, too, that they were Chinese, and that surprised him.

Turning toward the stagecoach, he shouted, "Ku Xuan! Are you two all right?"

"Yes," Ku Xuan's voice answered from her place beneath the coach.

"Come here and see if you know these men. They're Chinese."

Ku Xuan and Lai Song crawled out from under the coach, rose to their feet, and walked toward Mike. Standing beside him, looking down at the two men—one dead and one dying—both women shook their heads.

"I do not know these men," Ku Xuan said. "Perhaps this one will tell us before he dies why he wished to harm us."

Kneeling down beside the dying man, Mike asked, "Why did you try to kill us?"

"I failed," the man gasped. "I have failed." He coughed and then gasped again, whispering, "Water. Please, some water."

Mike knew about the terrible dryness in the throat just before a man died, and he walked back to the coach and drew a cup of water from the water barrel they hauled with them. Carrying the cup in both hands, he hurried back and found Ku Xuan on her knees beside the man, one hand resting on his forehead. They were speaking softly in Chinese, in a dialect Mike could not understand.

"Here," Mike said, handing the cup to Ku Xuan. She raised the wounded man's head and he took several desperate swallows, making gurgling sounds as he drank.

"Thank you," the man said, speaking in English this time. He erupted into a fit of coughing; then the coughing stopped. When it stopped, so did the breathing.

"Did he tell you who they were and why they were after us?"

"They were tong warriors," Ku Xuan said, "working for Wo Hamm."

"Wo Hamm? Wo Hamm sent them? Why?"

"This I do not know," Ku Xuan told Mike, looking up at him. "But I am grateful to you for saving our lives."

"Yeah," Mike said offhandedly. "I just wish I knew why these men were trying to kill us—and I wonder if there are any more."

"I suppose we must assume that there are," Ku Xuan stated, her voice sounding somewhat tentative.

"I'd better be a little more careful from now on. Well, come on, let's get some more sleep. I doubt we'll have any more visitors . . . leastways, not tonight."

Monterey was quiet and peaceful when the stagecoach, its broken wheel repaired, rolled into town.

Until 1847 the town had alternated with Los Angeles as the capital of the Mexican province of California. It was still Spanish in atmosphere, and many of the people Mike saw along the street were Mexicans. But Americans had moved into town in increasing numbers, and Mike saw an American shopkeeper come through the front door of his dry-goods store to sweep his wooden porch.

At the far end of the main street they found the Lyons' Den, an American-style building with large windows in front and a hand-painted sign that dangled above the porch from the overhanging roof. On the blue background of the sign was painted a gold shield flanked by silver lions rampant, and the shield bore the name of the saloon.

Ku Xuan, who had chosen to ride with Mike on the driver's seat, put her hand on his wrist. "See how he uses lions to depict his name," she pointed out, her voice hopeful. "Mike, perhaps this man is my father."

"We'll soon find out." Parking the coach in front of the saloon, Mike suggested, "Let's go in and have a look around." He helped Ku Xuan down from the seat and then opened the door of the coach and offered his hand to Lai Song. Escorting the two women, the driver pushed open the batwing doors, and the three of them went inside, their expectations running high.

The Lyons' Den was more a sailors' bar than a Western saloon, so it differed from other establishments. There was no piano, for example, and the art on the walls depicted ships and foreign ports, rather than Western and mountain scenes. But like all saloons everywhere, the Lyons' Den existed to serve liquor, so it had a drinking bar, a wall full of whiskey bottles, and a dozen or more tables for the customers.

Mike led Ku Xuan and Lai Song to a table near the back of the place. Then he stepped up to the bar and asked the bartender where Daniel Lyons could be found.

"The cap'n ain't here right now," the barkeep said, wiping a glass.

"Do you know where he might be?" Mike inquired. "It's very important that we find him."

The barkeep looked at Mike and then at the two beautiful Chinese women who were seated at the table. "Who are they?" he asked as he kept wiping glasses.

"They're my employers."

The barkeep looked surprised. "*You're* workin' for *them*?"

"That's right. Now, could you tell me where Captain Lyons is?"

"You might find him down at the ship's chandler's. He don't go to sea no more, but he still feels the need to talk with his own."

Thanking the man, Mike turned and looked at Ku Xuan. "Would you like to wait here?"

Ku Xuan looked past Mike to the bartender. Smiling at him, she said, "If you don't mind."

"Mind? Miss, I figure you two girls will give the place a little class. And you'll sure make it look a lot prettier."

"Thank you."

Mike walked over to the table. "Well, I'll go see if I can find Captain Lyons, and I'll be back as soon as I can." Nodding to the bartender, the driver left the saloon.

"Would you like anything to drink?" the barkeep asked the two women.

"May we have some tea?" Ku Xuan replied.

"Tea, sure." The bartender's face took on a quizzical expression. "It's funny you should ask for that. You know, the cap'n, that's about all he drinks."

"Maybe Daniel Lyons is your father," Lai Song suggested to her friend in Chinese. "It is said that the habit of the parents is appreciated by the children."

Ku Xuan laughed, and responded, "Millions of Chinese drink tea. Since it is also your drink of choice, perhaps he is your father as well."

"Then we would be sisters," Lai Song replied, and the delicate laughter of the two women filled the tavern like the tinkling of wind chimes.

The bartender brought over the pot of tea and two cups, setting everything carefully on the table. Thanking him, Ku Xuan poured the tea, and as she sat sipping the welcome brew, she looked around the saloon. She noticed some photographs on the walls that had obviously been taken in China. Curious, she got up from the table and went to examine them.

"Well, lookie here," a brutish male voice suddenly said.

Ku Xuan turned around to see two men who had just come in standing beside the table, leering at Lai Song. The young woman was staring at her cup of tea, and Ku Xuan could tell that she was frightened.

"You ever had yourself a China girl?" one of the men asked the other. "Course, they ain't curved up nothin' like a white woman . . . more like havin' a little girl. But some of 'em's real good at pleasurin' a man." He reached out and put his hand on Lai Song's shoulder. "How 'bout it, honey? You know how to pleasure a man?"

Ku Xuan hurried back to the table. "Please," she said quietly. "We want no trouble."

"Well, honey, you just be real friendlylike, and you won't have no trouble." He laughed a brittle, ugly laugh. "No, missy, we won't have no trouble a'tall." He faced his friend. "Which one you reckon you want, Pike?"

"It sure don't matter to me; they both look fine."

"Come along, honey, and we'll find us a place and have a real good time," the first man declared, stretching out a rough hand toward Ku Xuan.

"Get your filthy hand away from her!" Mike shouted from the open doorway. In two quick strides, he reached the table and grabbed the man's hand, clamping down hard and squeezing so tightly that the brute let out a whimper of pain and sank to the floor.

"Pike!" the man yelled. "Pike, help me!"

Pike started to draw his gun, but the twin barrels of a double-barreled shotgun were suddenly shoved under his chin. The bartender had come to the women's rescue himself, reacting at the same time that Mike had returned.

"Unbuckle your gun belt," the bartender said quietly.

"Sure, mister, sure," Pike said. "I'm doin' just like you say." Pike opened the buckle and let his gun belt fall.

Releasing his grip, Mike then stepped back from the other man and ordered, "Now you drop yours."

Slowly, the man dropped his gun belt.

"Now get out of here," Mike said. "And don't come back until we're gone."

"Belay that order," a man called, and Ku Xuan looked over to see a stocky, gray-haired man wearing a dark jacket and captain's hat. "I don't want the two of you coming back into my place *ever*."

"What about our guns?" one of the men asked.

"You come by tomorrow morning at about eight bells . . . you'll find your guns and belts lying on my front porch."

"Ladies," Mike said, indicating the newcomer. "This is Captain Lyons."

Captain Lyons tipped his hat to Ku Xuan and Lai Song and then pointed to a chair. "May I join you?" he asked.

"Yes, please," Ku Xuan replied anxiously.

"I want to apologize for those two galoots. I run a proper place here, but sometimes a wharf rat will find his way in."

"We were not injured," she assured him. Then she looked up at the bartender. "Thank you for your help."

"My pleasure, ma'am."

"I shouldn't have left you," Mike declared.

Daniel Lyons shook his head. "Don't be silly, lad. How else would I have known you were here?" Turning to Ku Xuan, he smiled warmly at her, although he looked somewhat puzzled. "Now, Miss, the lad here said you wanted to talk to me . . . and I'm wondering why such a beautiful young lady would be interested in an old sea dog like me."

Ku Xuan felt excitement surge through her, and her face betrayed her eagerness as she examined the captain. There was a kindliness about him, and she sensed that he was a good man. She took a deep breath.

"Captain Lyons, I want to ask you if you are my father."

Lyon's face reflected first shock, then curiosity, and finally—Ku Xuan clearly noted—hope.

"Girl, I truly don't know," he admitted. "But I must confess that I hope it's true, for though I never saw my Chinese child, he or she would be about your age now. And if it was a girl child and her mama was any indication, she'd be as beautiful as you. Tell me about your mother."

"I do not remember my mother," Ku Xuan informed him.

Daniel Lyons sighed. "Then we're going to have a difficult time finding out, aren't we?"

"Maybe not. I have three questions to ask. If you know the answers to these questions, then you are my father. I hope you can answer them," Ku Xuan breathed.

Lyons folded his hands on the table and sighed deeply. "You don't hope it any more than I do, girl. Ask away."

"What lies beyond the inner door of the golden pagoda?"

He blinked. "I don't know."

"What secret did the garden jasmines hide?"

The expression of hope on Lyon's face was replaced by one of despair. "I'm afraid I don't know the answer to that one, either."

"Who is Tsu?"

Now the man was totally crestfallen. He shook his head sadly. "I'm sorry, girl, but I don't know the answer to any of your questions."

Ku Xuan smiled wanly, and her eyes glistened with tears. She had thought . . . hoped . . . that this man was her father, and her search would be over. Now she would have to start anew.

"Is your father supposed to know the answers to these questions?"

"Yes," Ku Xuan replied.

"What led you to me?"

Ku Xuan explained that because his name was Lyons, she thought he might be the one meant by the Chinese ideogram for Big Cat.

"Big Cat?"

"That is all I know of my father."

"Cougar!" Lyons exclaimed, snapping his fingers.

"Cougar?" Mike asked, pulling up a chair and sitting down next to him.

Daniel Lyons nodded. "Cougar Jones," he said. "He was my bos'n, and as big as a mountain, he was. When he was a young fellow, he killed a cougar by squeezing it to death. Folks took to calling him Cougar after that."

Looking excitedly at Ku Xuan, Mike explained, "A cougar is a big cat." He turned back to Captain Lyons and asked, "You think this Cougar Jones might be her father?"

"Well, he made many a trip to China. Now that I recall, seems like he did have a young woman he was especially fond of."

"Where might we find Mr. Cougar Jones?" Ku Xuan asked.

"Last I heard from him, he was somewhere south of the Santa Clara Valley, looking for gold. Just a minute . . . I got a letter from him a year or so ago. It's somewhere in my office." He stood up and walked toward a door, calling over his shoulder, "I won't be a minute. Sit tight."

As the three travelers waited, Mike reached across the table and put his hand on Ku Xuan's. "I'm sorry he wasn't the one," he told her, his eyes filled with compassion.

"I would have been pleased to call him father," Ku Xuan replied. "He seems like a good man."

"We'll find him," Mike promised.

Captain Lyons returned a moment later, carrying an envelope with him.

"Here it is. This letter's return address is Paicines. That's a good forty miles due east of Salinas."

"Thanks for all your help," Mike told him as the three of them stood up. He looked at the two young women. "I suggest we get a nice meal in a restaurant and even take a hot bath before we get started again. How does that sound?"

Ku Xuan's face beamed. She translated for Lai Song, and her friend's face lit up as well. "That sounds wonderful, Mike," Ku Xuan answered for both of them.

"Great. I was hoping you'd agree." He grinned.

Turning again to Daniel Lyons, Mike shook the man's hand. "Thanks again for all your help."

The former captain shook his head. "No thanks are needed, son. By the way, that's pretty bad country to go into," Lyons warned. "It's a rugged ride, and I heard some Indians have been acting up over that way."

"We'll be careful," Mike promised. "And we'll let you know if your former mate is Ku Xuan's father."

"Thanks, I'd appreciate it. *Vaya con Dios*, as they say in these parts."

*   *   *

The night creatures called to each other as Granger, Brewster, and Finley sat on their horses, looking down at the town of Monterey washed in moonlight. A couple of dozen adobe buildings, half of which had lights showing, fronted the town plaza, but the most brightly lighted building was what appeared to be a cantina at the far end of town.

"You think they're here?" Finley asked.

"Them people we talked to early this mornin' said the stagecoach they seen was most likely headin' this way," Granger replied.

"Yeah, but the padre at the mission said he hadn't seen them."

"He was lyin'. They went through there; they had to."

"Lyin'? But he was a priest! A priest wouldn't lie."

"He would if he was tryin' to protect someone."

"Hey, Granger, we gonna get somethin' to drink here or not?" Brewster called.

"Yeah," Finley agreed, putting his hand to his throat. "We been out so long, I could plant cotton in the trail dust in my mouth. I gotta get somethin' wet."

"Come on, then," Granger growled, leading the others toward the town.

A dog barked, an annoying yap that abruptly ended with a yelp, probably as the result of a kick or a thrown rock. A housewife in one of the outlying farmhouses launched into a tirade about something, sharing her anger with anyone within earshot.

Half a dozen horses stood at the hitch rail in front of a cantina on the edge of town, and Granger listened to the sounds coming from inside. The music stopped, and there was conversation only in Spanish and English. But the outlaw froze when he heard the unmistakable sound of a Chinese woman's voice.

Turning to the others, he smiled and declared, "Boys, our hunt may be over. Brewster, you go 'round back. Anyone comes bustin' out the back door, you drop 'em. Finley, you keep me covered out here."

Waiting until his men were in place, Granger looked up and down the street to make certain no one was watching the cantina door. Then he stepped up onto the boardwalk and pushed his way inside. Pulling his hat brim low, he headed for the bar, positioning himself so that his back was to the wall. He glanced around the room and saw a Chinese woman sitting at a table with a Chinese man. *Damn!* he exclaimed to himself. *It's that guy, Li Chen—the same sonofabitch that gave me the knockout drops! He beat me to her!*

"*Qué quieres?*" the bartender asked.

"Give me a shot of tequila," Granger ordered in English.

The bartender reached for a bottle and a glass and poured the drink. He slid the glass across the bar to Granger. "Ten cents, señor," he demanded.

Granger started to reach for his money. Then, out of the corner of his eye, he saw that Li Chen and the woman were going out the back door.

"Brewster, stop 'em!" Granger shouted. His shout startled everyone in the bar except for one Mexican who jumped up from his table with a pistol in his hand. Surprised by the move, the outlaw drew his own pistol out as quick as a snake, and the two men faced each other.

"This ain't your fight, Mex," Granger hissed. "You can stay out of it or you can die." He did not have to talk very loudly, because everyone in the cantina had fallen silent when the two men had drawn their guns.

"The Chinaman made it my fight, señor," the Mexican replied, grinning and showing a gold front tooth. "Fifty American dollars."

"You're a fool," Granger rasped.

Two pistols exploded, shattering the quiet, and the patrons and bartender scrambled for cover. Gun smoke billowed out in a cloud that filled the room, momentarily obscuring everything. As the smoke began to clear, the Mexican stared through the white cloud, still grinning, his gold tooth shining. He started to speak, but the only sound he made was a gagging rattle way back in his throat. Then the grin faded, his eyes glazed over, and he pitched forward, his gun clattering to the floor.

Granger ran through the back door of the cantina.

"Brewster! Brewster, are you out here?"

He saw Brewster on the ground some fifty feet behind the cantina. The Chinese woman was standing over him, looking down in horror, her hands clasped over her mouth. Running over to his fallen cohort, Granger could tell by the way Brewster's head was twisted that his neck was broken. He knelt beside the man and looked into eyes that were open but unseeing. It was not necessary to feel for a pulse to know he was dead.

"Come on, you," he said, reaching for the Chinese girl. "You're worth a lot of money to me."

"Hey, mister," a gruff, American voice yelled. "What the hell you aimin' on doin' with our laundry girl?" The question was followed by the sound of a shotgun snapping closed and then by half a dozen rifles being cocked.

Granger looked over his shoulder and saw that most of the saloon patrons he had left inside the cantina were now outside, many of them armed and with their weapons aimed at him.

"This here is your laundry girl?" Granger asked with a weak smile.

"Is, and has been for four years. Now what do you want with her?"

"I, uh, just wanted to ask her some questions," Granger replied. "The Chinaman that was with her stole my daughter. I think he's plannin' on takin' her back to China an' sellin' her to the heathens."

The girl said something in Spanish then, and the American who was holding his shotgun on the outlaw suddenly lowered it.

"I guess you're tellin' the truth, mister. The girl here says the Chinaman was askin' her about a half-American China girl. Reckon she'd have to be your daughter."

"Yes, yes, she is!" Granger declared fervently.

"But I thought you said he stole her. Liu Xi here says he's lookin' for her."

"That's right," Granger responded, thinking quickly. "She escaped and she's runnin' from him. I'm tryin' to catch up to her before he does."

One of the other Americans put in, "I knew I didn't like the looks of that there Chinaman."

"*Qué?*" a Mexican patron asked, and one of the Americans explained in Spanish what the conversation was about.

"I'm sorry about the man I killed in there," Granger said, regret dripping from his voice. "I didn't have no choice."

The shotgun-wielding American spit out a chew of tobacco and then wiped the back of his hand across his face. "Hell, you don't have to apologize for killin' Sanchez. We been hopin' someone would kill that no-account bastard for a long time." Clapping Granger on the shoulder, he offered, "Come on back in. You didn't finish your drink."

"Don't mind if I do," Granger said. "Uh, listen, would you mind if I talked to the China girl here a bit? She was talkin' with that chink kidnapper, and maybe she can tell me somethin' that would help me find my little girl."

The girl spoke only Chinese and Spanish, so Granger had to use an interpreter. Through the interpreter he learned that a few people had seen the stagecoach heading toward the center of Monterey.

"Hey!" someone pushing through the swinging doors yelled. "Does anyone know anythin' about that there body lyin' out in the street?"

Everyone in the cantina shoved through the batwings. There, sprawled with one booted foot lying on the boardwalk and the other in the dirt of the street, lay Finley. Blood pooled under his throat, which had been sliced from ear to ear.

"I've never seen this man," someone said. "Anybody know who it is?"

"Yeah," Granger answered, his voice agitated. "His name is Finley. He was with me."

"Let me get this straight," the man asked. "He was with you . . . and the fella layin' out back, he was with you, too?"

"Yeah."

"They was helpin' you look for the Chinaman?"

"Yeah."

"Mister, don't take this wrong or nothin', but we'd be real pleased if you'd finish up your drink an' go on out of here. You ain't none too healthy to be around."

Leading his horse away to find some place to bed down for the night, Granger growled, "For some folks it's gonna get a lot unhealthier."

It was barely past eight o'clock the following morning, and Daniel Lyons had arrived only a few minutes earlier, ready to tackle his bookkeeping, when the bartender leaned in through the door of the office at the back of the saloon.

"Cap'n Lyons?" the barkeep called.

"Yes?" he asked, not looking up from his ledger.

"There's a Chinaman out here wantin' to talk to you."

"Know what it's about?"

"Near's I can figure, he wants to talk about that girl who was in here yesterday. You know, the one lookin' for her pa."

Lyons laid down his pen and marked his place in the ledger; then he stood up and went out into the bar area. He nodded to the Chinese man standing there, who bowed respectfully in turn.

"You are Captain Lyons?" the man asked.

"Aye. Something I can do for you?"

"Please excuse the intrusion of this unworthy personage. I seek my sister, Ku Xuan."

Lyons's face registered his surprise. "Ku Xuan is your sister?"

The Chinese man smiled broadly. "You speak those words as if you have recently seen her."

"Well, yes . . . yes I have, as a matter of fact. She was in here just yesterday, along with a traveling companion, a young woman named Lai Song, and their driver, a man named Wakefield, Mike Wakefield."

"I am glad you know where they are. I have joyous news for my sister."

"You've found your father!" Then Lyons's eyes narrowed as he studied the man more closely. "No, wait a minute, he couldn't be your father. She said her father was American."

"Ah, yes, and now you know our family secret. Though we share the same mother, our fathers are different. Still, I feel a great joy in being able to tell my sister that her long quest is over. Would you tell me, please, where she might be staying?"

Lyons rubbed his chin. "Well, that's just it," he confided. "She's not anywhere about. She and the others left in search of Cougar Jones."

"Excuse me, please. What—or should I ask where—is Cougar Jones?"

Lyons laughed. "It's not a what or a where; it's a who. Though after you've seen the man, you'll be thinking *what* is a better word after all."

"Ah, I see. Cougar Jones is a man."

"Aye, that he is. And he's someone we thought might be the lass's father . . . or at least, someone who could give her a lead as to who her father might be."

"And where might I find Mr. Cougar Jones?"

"I'll tell you same as I told them. I got a letter from him a year or so ago that was postmarked in Paicines. That's all I know."

The Chinese stood and bowed again. "A thousand thank yous, which is all I can offer from someone as unworthy as I am who has no more value than dust blowing in the wind."

"That's enough," Lyons said. "I hope you find her."

The man bowed a few more times and left the saloon.

"Sure is a polite little fella, ain't he?" the bartender asked.

"Oh, all the Chinese are polite, I suppose," Lyons explained. For a long moment he stood studying the door through which the man had exited. Then he looked over at his bartender. "You notice the tattoo he had on his wrist?"

"Yeah, it looked like some kind of snake."

"It was a dragon."

"A dragon?"

"Seems to me like I heard something once about what it means for a Chinese to have a dragon tattooed on his arm. I can't recall exactly what it was, but I remember it was something very special."

"Couldn't be all that special," the bartender declared, returning to his glasses, " 'cause there sure ain't nothin' special about that fella. He's about as ordinary lookin' a Chinaman as I've ever seen."

"Yes, I suppose so," Lyons agreed with a sigh. "I hope I did the right thing by telling him where to find the girl," he added. Then he perked up. "But after all, he said he found her father—and what possible reason would he have to lie about that?"

Feeling mollified, Lyons walked back to his office and resumed his bookkeeping.

Chapter Nine

Mike Wakefield, Ku Xuan, and Lai Song were camped in the shadow of Fremont Peak, and the last morning star made a white pinpoint in the soft pink light over the pass. Awakening first, the air cool on his face, the driver sat up in his bedroll and watched as a pine tree was touched by the first wisp of dawn. He liked it early in the morning. Everything seemed so strange and unexpected.

The coals from their campfire of the night before were still glowing. Throwing aside the blankets, Mike got up and walked over to the fire and threw chunks of mesquite wood on it. He stirred the fire, and soon crackling flames danced against the bottom of the suspended coffeepot. A rustle of wind through feathers caused him to look to his left just in time to see a golden eagle diving on its prey, probably a mouse or a rabbit.

Mike poured himself a cup of coffee and sat down to enjoy the black and steaming brew. His movement had awakened the two young women, and he watched them as they broke camp. They had become very proficient, learning quickly what needed to be done and then doing it well and without hesitation.

As he watched Ku Xuan, Mike knew that he was in love with her. He did not know if she returned the feeling . . . or if indeed she could, not only because of her strange and wonderful skills, but because of her commitment to finding her father. But if she could love him, he intended, when this mission was completed, to ask her to marry him.

Once or twice Ku Xuan looked toward him and smiled, and the smile shot through to the core of his heart. How he wished there were only the two of them, alone in this valley. . . . Suddenly, Mike realized with a start that the morning star was gone and the rising sun was now streaming brightly down over the pass. He laughed to himself for admiring Ku Xuan and Lai Song for their work, while he was neglecting his own. Tossing out the last dregs of his coffee, he put the cup down and went to harness the horses.

"He is in love with you," Lai Song said quietly.

"Yes," Ku Xuan answered, "I know."

"Do you love him?"

"Yes."

"What will come of it?"

"Until my mission is over, nothing can come of it."

"You . . . you would deny your love?" Lai Song asked incredulously.

"I do not wish to speak of it," Ku Xuan answered, somewhat more testily than she had intended. She saw that a piece of cloth had blown away some distance from the campsite, and she hurried to retrieve it. She could have sent Lai Song after it, but she wanted to go herself, to get away from the questions her friend was asking. Lai Song could not know that the same questions had been burning in her own heart for several days now. If only she did not love Mike, how much easier it would be.

A strong arm suddenly grabbed Ku Xuan, and before she could let out a sound, a hand was clasped over her mouth. She struggled at first, but then gave in until she felt a slight relaxation of the grip around her. Then she tensed, kicking backward until her foot contacted flesh. She was rewarded with a gasp of pain. The arms around her let go; Ku Xuan squatted and then shot high up in an acrobatic leap, turning a flip over the head of her captor and landing on the ground behind him. Grunting in surprise, he spun around, and when he did, Ku Xuan hit him with a forearm smash that sent him sprawling on the ground in front of her.

Her attacker was an Indian, and there were six others standing around, watching in openmouthed surprise.

Another warrior leaped for her, brandishing his knife low before him. Ku Xuan did a pirouette, kicked his knife away, and then, spinning a second time, kicked him in the solar plexus and knocked his breath away. As two others came for her, she whirled around, smashing one in the Adam's apple and taking out the other one with a powerful kick to the side of his knee.

With four of the Indians down now, one of the remaining warriors raised his bow and aimed an arrow toward Ku Xuan. As the arrow was released, she leaped to one side and snatched it out of the air.

"Aiyee!" the archer shouted in surprise.

Another Indian, about fifty feet away and thus too far for her to reach even with her acrobatic skill, cocked his rifle and aimed at her. There being nothing she could do to protect herself, she composed herself, waiting for the bullet to tear into her flesh. Suddenly a pistol roared from behind her, and the Indian fell with a hole in his chest. Ku Xuan whirled around in time to see Mike shoot a second Indian, who was himself preparing to fire. The others picked themselves up and ran.

Crying out, she rushed to Mike, and he put his arms around her.

"It's all right," he whispered, comforting her. "I would never let anything happen to you."

With Lai Song coming up beside them, frightened for her own life, Ku Xuan and Mike stood locked in an embrace for a long moment. When they finally parted, Lai Song softly asked her friend in Chinese, "Were you really frightened—or did you merely pretend to be so, to soothe Mike's feelings?"

"There is no shame in soothing the feelings of someone you love," Ku Xuan replied. "But yes, I was very frightened. I know of no tricks to stop bullets."

"And she sure can't catch them in her teeth," Mike added in Chinese.

Ku Xuan and Lai Song gasped loudly.

"You . . . you speak our language!" Ku Xuan said.

Mike grinned. "Maybe I have a few tricks of my own."

Ku Xuan blushed then, realizing that she had spoken aloud of her feelings for Mike.

"Did you mean it?" Mike asked.

"About being frightened?"

"No." He looked into her eyes, and at that moment his own eyes were so open that Ku Xuan felt they were windows all the way to his soul. "Did you mean that you love me?"

"Yes," Ku Xuan admitted. "I love you, Mike Wakefield."

"And I you. But what are we going to do about it?"

"We . . . we can do nothing about it," she told him, trying to ignore the pain and torment she was feeling. "I have taken a vow to find my father. Until that vow is fulfilled, I am not free to love . . . or be loved."

Mike stared at her, and then suddenly and unexpectedly he grinned. "All right," he declared, rubbing his hands together as if he were a man about to tackle a particularly enjoyable task, "then we'd best get to it. The first thing we do is find your father. The next thing we do is get married."

"Mike, I cannot think about marriage until—"

He held up his hand to silence her. "You don't have to think about it. I'll think about it for both of us."

Ku Xuan laughed. She knew she could never love him more than at that moment—and she hoped he would not be hurt.

"Okay, ladies. Let's get this show on the road." When Ku Xuan and Lai Song both looked at him quizzically, he shook his head and smiled. "Never mind. I'll explain it to you later. Let's get going."

The stagecoach pulled into the little town of Paicines, which looked no different from other towns just like it that they had already seen. Reaching the far end of the settlement, which consisted of no more than a dozen buildings laid out around a dusty plaza, baking under the hot sun, Mike Wakefield braked the coach to a halt in front of a small building displaying an American flag and a sign in faded lettering: United States Post Office.

"This is where the letter was mailed," Mike told Ku Xuan and Lai Song through the window as he climbed down from the driver's box. "If Cougar Jones is still around, they'll know where he is."

Ku Xuan opened the door and climbed out, stepping up onto the covered boardwalk to catch a breath of fresh air. It was very hot . . . especially inside the coach. There were a few Indians on the boardwalk, leaning against the wall of the post office or sitting on the edge of the boardwalk with their legs dangling.

"Ku Xuan, they are Indians," Lai Song warned, clearly frightened by them.

"I don't think these Indians mean us harm," Ku Xuan replied as she studied them closely. Though in some ways they resembled the Indians who had attacked her, there was a vast difference. At first she did not know what; then as she looked at them more closely, she realized what it was. The Indians who had attacked her had been fierce and proud. These men were meek, and they wore their meekness on their faces and in their eyes. They seemed to have forgotten their past and had no present and no future.

Mike came out of the post office building, smiling broadly. "They know him," he said.

"Is he here, in this town?" Ku Xuan asked hopefully.

"No, he lives out on the reservation with his Indian wife."

"Reservation? I am not familiar with the use of that word."

"An Indian reservation," Mike explained. "It's a place where the government makes the Indians live."

"Is the reservation like a prison?" Ku Xuan wondered.

"A prison? No, it's more like a village, for Indians only."

"Then Cougar Jones is Indian?"

"No, he's white. But he's married to an Indian, and she can't live with the whites, so he must live with the Indians."

"I see," Ku Xuan declared, troubled. "Mike, are there such places for Chinese?"

"No," Mike said quickly. It was obvious that Ku Xuan was bothered with the concept of a reservation, and he put his hand on hers. "It's not a very good system, I'll admit, but there was a time when nearly all Indians were like the ones who jumped us today. The government had no choice and rounded them up and put them on reservations. I know it's not right. After all, the land belonged to the Indians in the first place. . . . It's a complicated story, Ku Xuan—I can't explain it all. Some things are just the way they are, and we have to live with them."

"I am sorry if I make you uncomfortable with my questions," Ku Xuan apologized. "I am still learning much about America."

"I think I have a lot to learn myself," Mike confessed. Then, as if to change an awkward subject, he asked, "Say, you've been riding with me on the driver's seat, Ku Xuan. . . . D'you suppose Lai Song would like to join us?"

Ku Xuan glanced at her friend, who nodded shyly. "Yes, Mike," Ku Xuan answered for her. "We would both like that very much, if it is not too crowded for you."

Mike helped them climb onto the driver's box, and then he sat next to Ku Xuan. Releasing the brake, he flicked the whip lightly over the horses' heads, and the stagecoach was soon once again in the country, bounding toward the Indian reservation.

When they found Cougar Jones, they saw that the descriptions of him were accurate: He was a mountain of a man with broad shoulders and a barrel chest. He was six feet six inches tall, and when he moved among the Indians, he stood out like a tree in grass. But he turned out not to be Ku Xuan's father, which was evident not only because he could not answer any of Ku Xuan's questions, but also because he knew the results of every one of his China liaisons.

"I got me two sons somewhere over there," he told them. "I think about the boys often and hope I live long enough to see 'em again. But I got no daughters, though I'd be pleased to count you as one, girl."

Ku Xuan tried but failed to hide her disappointment.

Mike then asked, "Cougar, I'm told you know a lot about China and the Americans who were over there in the eighteen-sixties. Is that true?"

"Reckon I do," Cougar declared. "I was there more'n a year."

"You know a man named Beckett? James Beckett?"

"Oh, yeah, Captain Beckett of the *Thunderbolt*. I remember him. He was a fine man. A good officer to sail under, the word was. Then he went sour, and he lost his ship. Last I heard he was workin' as a sheriff or somethin' like that."

"He quit that," Mike informed him, "and went into the hills prospecting for gold. But I don't have any later information than that."

"Why're you lookin' for him? You think he might be the girl's pa?"

"He couldn't be," Mike said. "The girl he loved was . . ."

"Executed." Cougar finished the sentence for him. "I remember now. It was quite a sad tale."

"I was on the *Thunderbolt*," Mike murmured.

"You? You were just a kid then."

"I was cabin boy. I've looked for Captain Beckett off and on since he lost his ship, but I've never found him."

"Could be that he don't want to be found. Whenever a man falls as far and as hard as your captain did, it's a long time before he's in a mood to see folks that knew him when he was ridin' high. You want my advice, you'll leave the man be."

Mike laughed wryly. "I've had no other choice all these years."

Cougar's wife spoke to him in her native tongue. Cougar listened and then smiled and shook his head.

"The wife tells me that news of your little run-in with the renegades has already reached her tribe. Them renegades have been givin' the people around here trouble long enough, and they're happy about the ones you took care of, Mr. Wakefield—and even happier that a young unarmed girl humiliated the others."

Cougar's wife spoke again, and again her husband translated. "Ku Xuan, the wife says her people are wantin' to initiate you as a shaman. Would you be willin' to go along with that?"

Ku Xuan looked at Mike. "What is a shaman?" she asked.

"You are a priestess of Shan Tal," Mike explained. "I didn't know what that meant when I first heard it, but now I do. I tell you truly, Ku Xuan, being initiated as a shaman is a great honor, one that befits a priestess of Shan Tal."

"Should I accept?"

"Not to accept would insult them, though to accept without feeling the honor would insult them even more."

Ku Xuan smiled, looking at the Indian woman. "Please tell your wife that I would be very happy to accept this initiation."

"Great, great!" Cougar declared. "That means we'll be celebratin' all day. All the women'll cook, and we'll have dances and shows. . . . It'll be a fine time."

The setting sun smeared the western sky with red and gold, and the beat of the drums and the singing of the dancers rose up from the village. It was a hauntingly beautiful sound, a rhythmic chant that caught the rattle of the dry

mesquite and the moan of the wind. The air was scented with
a rich and succulent smell as spitted meat browned and
sizzled over a dozen fires in preparation for the great feast.

Cougar's wife reached out and beckoned to Ku Xuan.

"She wants you to go with her," Cougar explained. "Your
initiation ceremony must be completed before the sun has
set."

Ku Xuan followed the woman to a circle in the center of
the village. Here, using sand of red, yellow, and white, and
various shades of gray from nearly white to black, an elaborate sand painting had been constructed.

"The painting depicts the universe," Cougar told the three
travelers. "The sand possesses much medicine, for it was
gathered only from places where strong medicine has occurred."

One of the Indians pointed to a geometric design of yellow
sand and in English said, "My grandfather lay dying for
water, and as he lay there, an eagle swooped down, landed
on a cactus, and began drinking water from a hole. My
grandfather found the hole and he drank his fill of water that
was cool and sweet. Then he gathered sand from around the
cactus because that was a place of great medicine, and this is
that sand."

Other Indians described the significance of the other colors
of sand, and each story involved some strange and wonderful
event. Finally, the gay chatter and the boasting and the
storytelling stopped, to be replaced by a loud, hissing noise.

"What is that?" Ku Xuan asked.

"It's the dance of the serpent," Cougar Jones replied.
"See? On the rocks above?" He pointed.

Ku Xuan looked up, and there, poised on a rock outcrop-
ping approximately fifty feet above them, she saw a young
man. Finely muscled and wearing jewelry of beaten silver, on
his head he wore a crown of silver shaped like a coiled snake.
Half crouched with his knees bent and pointing to his left, he
held his hands together, as in prayer, with his arms raised
over his head. He was looking to the right so that the illusion
created was one of serpentine coils.

The hissing of the villagers grew louder, accompanied by a
low humming noise. Soon the humming was joined by drums
and rattles. The man on the rock began undulating his body
to the pulsating rhythm, first crouching all the way to the
ground and then stretching up on tiptoe. His thighs, stom-

ach, and pelvis jerked from side to side and forward and back.

Suddenly the dancer leaped backward, disappearing from view. A moment later he reappeared on a rock fifteen feet below the first. He continued his dance and again leaped backward only to reappear several feet below.

The dancer finally stood on a level with the others. The rhythm of the music had become more insistent, and the dancer writhed and slithered his way along the ground until he was only inches away from Ku Xuan, and she could see every muscle of the man's body working under his skin. Then, strangely and mysteriously, it seemed to Ku Xuan as if the dancer were actually transformed into a serpent, so powerful was his interpretation and so enthralled with the dance was she.

The dance abruptly ended. With a shout, the dancer turned and ran back up the side of the mountain, leaping from rock to rock with the ease of a mountain goat until he disappeared.

"Now, you must go into the tent . . . there, to eat the peyote buttons and gain the magic," Cougar Jones said.

Ku Xuan walked to the tent as instructed. Crouching, she went inside through the opened flap. Blankets were spread on the ground, and a small clay bowl had been placed next to the blankets. Followed by Cougar and his wife, Ku Xuan was told to sit on the blankets and eat from the bowl.

"What shall I do then?" Ku Xuan asked.

"Nothing," Cougar told her, and then laughed. "It'll all be done for you."

She did not question him any further, but sat as directed. When Cougar's wife held the bowl out for her, she took some of the dried cactus and chewed it.

"Don't fight the feelings and visions that come to you," the old sailor warned Ku Xuan. "They'll tell you what you need to know."

As he continued to provide guidance, his face seemed to slip away from his body and float. Then his body turned into a wisp of smoke and curled up through a hole in the top of the tent, and Ku Xuan saw brilliant prisms of color all around. Everything else seemed muted and diffused, and she turned her eyes inward.

*   *   *

Standing in crisp white snow against a blue sky high on top of a mountain, a beautiful Chinese woman in a red kimono smiled and held her arms out toward Ku Xuan. She had never seen the woman before, but she knew at once who the beautiful woman was.

"Why have you come to me now, my mother?" Ku Xuan asked.

"I have not come to you suddenly, for I have never left. You see me, yet you see me not. You hear me, yet you hear me not. I am here, yet I am not here. If you reach for me, you cannot grasp me, and if you grasp me, you cannot hold me. Yet, I will never leave."

"But you are my mother," Ku Xuan declared.

"If that is your truth."

"What is *your* truth?"

"My truth is hidden in my eating set," the vision answered. "And your truth depends on your finding where my truth is hidden. Each of us must live with our own truth."

"I have always lived with my own truth."

"No, you deny your truth."

"Why do you say this?"

"Are you not denying love?"

"I deny love only until I have fulfilled the mission for which I was born."

"Do not deny the stream of your life, and it will flow as it must flow."

"Then you would have me act now on the love I feel?" Ku Xuan asked.

"I have said nothing," the woman intoned. "I am like the wild geese who do not intend to cast their reflection in the water, for water has no mind to receive their image."

"But I am not water. I have a mind."

"Yes, you have a mind," the beautiful woman declared, "and it is yours and yours alone to use."

As Ku Xuan watched, the woman began to take on a glow, shining brighter and brighter, until soon she glowed so brightly that Ku Xuan could not look at her. "Remember. Look . . . in . . . the . . . eating . . . set," a wailing voice called out to her.

*   *   *

"Here," Cougar Jones was saying to her tenderly. "Drink this."

Ku Xuan was lying on the blankets and he was holding her head up, giving her water from a gourd.

"Are you back with us now?" he asked, a lilt of humor in his voice.

"Yes," Ku Xuan replied and smiled. She saw Mike, Lai Song, and Cougar Jones's wife and children standing around the blanket, looking down at her.

"Did I cry out?"

"No," Cougar assured her.

The Indian woman said something and Cougar translated for her. "My wife saw a very beautiful woman standing in the snow on top of the mountain. She said the mountain was not a mountain we can reach, but was very far away."

"How . . . how does she know of this woman and the mountain?" Ku Xuan asked, astounded.

"She has the gift of sharing visions. But in your mind, you spoke in your own language and she could not understand, though she believes the woman was your mother."

"Yes, she was my mother. Your wife is a woman of great power," Ku Xuan proclaimed, and when Cougar translated, his wife beamed proudly. The sailor and his family then left the tent, leaving the three travelers alone.

Ku Xuan remembered then what her mother had said in the vision, and she looked over at Lai Song. "Lai Song, bring me my mother's eating set."

A few minutes later, Lai Song returned and handed Ku Xuan the ivory cylinder. Then she, too, left, knowing that it was a time for the two lovers to be by themselves.

Emptying the chopsticks, Ku Xuan then used a knife to lift the false bottom and pry out a sheet of paper that was folded and packed there. It was a letter from Mata Lee:

My dear Ku Xuan,

When you were but hours old, your mother's life drained from her body, leaving you in my care. I was grieved by your mother's passing yet overjoyed by the precious life placed in my keeping. But there were secrets that I had to keep to protect you. The time has now come for you to learn of your parentage.

Your mother was Lo Pai, daughter of the Manchu ruler, Lo Ching. When Lo Ching discovered that his daughter was in love with and pregnant by an American sea captain, the laws demanded that he have her executed. However, your mother's handmaiden managed to switch places with Lo Pai so that although all present believed they were watching Lo Pai's beheading, they were actually watching the execution of the handmaiden, Tsu Ling.

In the days that followed, Lo Pai came secretly to me at the temple of Shan Tal, where eventually she gave birth to you. Before she died on that same day, she told me that she loved your father and that he did not know that she was pregnant with his child. She had pretended not to love him because her father swore to kill him if she did not send him back to America.

You are more than a Shan Tal priestess, Ku Xuan. You are a descendant of royalty, a Manchu princess.

> Your humble servant,
> Mata Lee

Ku Xuan read the letter aloud, and when she had finished, she saw that Mike's eyes were open wide. At first Ku Xuan feared that he had distanced himself from her again, intimidated by the fact that she was royalty.

As for herself, the news meant strangely little. When she had first arrived in California, she had believed—since her father was American—that she already belonged to this country in part. Now, with Mike at her side, she belonged to it wholly. The news of her true lineage did not change that: The mantle of royalty fell lightly on her, like the brush of a falling feather that is borne away by the wind almost before it can be felt.

"Mike," she started to say, but he interrupted her.

Taking her hands in his, he told her in a quiet but resolute voice, "Ku Xuan, I know who your father is. There is no doubt in my mind."

"Who?"

"My old captain."

"Your captain?" She was startled at first, and then she smiled. "Ah, yes, this would explain my mother's admonition not to deny love and the stream of life would flow where it would flow. She was telling me that the key to my father was through you."

While seemingly puzzled by her words, Mike did not question them. Instead he told her, "There is one thing I still don't understand. We've been looking for someone named Big Cat. That name doesn't fit my captain."

"When we find your captain, perhaps he will know the answer to that riddle," Ku Xuan said.

"Perhaps so. All we can do is keep trying to find him. Tomorrow we'll go north again."

"Whatever you say, Mike." Ku Xuan was silent a moment. "You knew my mother, did you not?" she suddenly asked, looking at Mike now in the new light of someone who was a real and visible link with her own past.

"Yes," Mike told her softly, "I knew her." He suddenly smiled wryly. "Of course! Now I know why I was so haunted by you when we first met. You look much as she did then. She was the most beautiful woman I had ever seen . . . till I met you. Remember my vow to you," he whispered. "When we find your father, I intend to marry you."

"I will no longer deny the love that I feel," Ku Xuan promised. She held up her hands, and Mike helped her to her feet. Then they walked hand in hand from the tent.

It was after midnight. A night bird called, and Ku Xuan sat up and looked around. She, Lai Song, and Mike had camped in the Indian village that night, and while she and Lai Song slept in their small tent, Mike had spread his bedroll out under the coach.

Ku Xuan stepped out of the tent and looked around. The village had celebrated her initiation as a shaman with a lively celebration, and many of the villagers had overimbibed a home-brewed liquor. Those who had celebrated too much were still lying on the ground where they had passed out. The cooking fires had died down, and only the glowing of the coals and the lingering smell of roasted pork remained to recall the great feast.

Her path lighted by the full moon, Ku Xuan walked over to

the coach. Standing silently, she watched Mike sleeping, his relaxed breathing a soft sigh. She then looked away from him, toward the dark slab of distant mountains. The night breeze felt wonderful, and she had a sudden desire to feel it blowing against her naked skin, enjoying that wonderful sense of freedom that nudity imparted to her. Knowing that everyone in the village was asleep, she removed her sleeping gown and stood nude in the soft silver light.

Then there was a subtle change in awareness, and, though she heard not a sound, she realized that Mike had awakened. She also knew that he would come to her . . . and that she would not refuse him.

Something had awakened Mike, and he opened his eyes to see Ku Xuan standing at the rear of the coach, looking off toward the Diablo Range. At first, with only the soft moonglow lighting her, he could not be certain that she was nude. Then she turned slightly, her body highlighted and made all the more mysterious and intriguing by the subtle shadows and lighting of the night, and he was sure that she was naked.

He slid out from under the coach and walked softly to her. She turned quietly and without surprise to give herself to him. They returned to his bedroll under the coach, making love that was rich and fulfilling. While strongly physical and immensely satisfying, it was also much deeper. It was as if their mutual emotions, their mutual need and attainment, had been perfectly orchestrated to move in harmony. Afterward she stayed with him, and they slept locked in embrace.

Mike awoke once more in the middle of the night. The moon was still shining, but now it hung low over the horizon. Its light spilled under the coach and onto the bed, bathing the sleeping Ku Xuan in a soft, shimmering light. Mike reached over gently and put his hand on her naked hip, feeling the sharpness of her hipbone and her soft, yielding flesh. He let his hand rest there, enjoying a sense of possession, until sleep claimed him once again.

It was early in the afternoon when Captain James Beckett reached Monterey and, like the searchers before him, sought out the Lyons' Den. He gave the bartender his name, askin' him to pass it on to Daniel Lyons, hoping Lyons remembered him. Taking a seat at a table near the bar, Cap waited just a few moments before he saw Lyons coming toward him. It had been twenty years since he had seen the man, and Lyons was heavier, grayer, and more wrinkled, but Cap recognized him immediately. He stood when Lyons approached.

"Captain Lyons, do you remember me?" he asked.

"Aye, Captain Beckett, I remember you," Lyons replied. "Can I get you a drink, sir?"

Gesturing to the teapot, Cap told him, "I would rather have that." In fact, he had not taken a drink of liquor since starting his quest to find Mike Wakefield and Ku Xuan.

"Last I heard of you, you had some sort of run-in with old Lo Ching," Lyons reminisced, squinting his eyes.

"Aye," Cap replied, adding candidly, "and you may also have heard that I became a drunkard and lost my ship because of it."

Lyons cleared his throat uncomfortably. "Aye, but I wasn't going to speak of that."

"Sorry," the prospector apologized, holding his hand up. "I didn't mean to embarrass you, I just brought it up by way of letting you know that I've come to terms with it. I'm a different man now, Captain Lyons. Sometimes I can hardly recall what it felt like to have a deck underfoot."

"Well, you sure look prosperous enough," Lyons told him, smiling.

Cap laughed. "Aye, well, I must confess that's a late enough development. I've spent years combing the mountains and creeks for gold, barely finding enough to keep body and soul together. Then, just this past month or two, I had a great run of luck. Seems like nearly every rock I turned over showed color."

"Good heavens, man, don't tell me you've struck it rich?"

"No, not rich in the way of mansions and the like. But I did manage to find enough gold to make me comfortable for what days I might have left to me."

Lyons laughed heartily. "Then what in tarnation are you doing in Monterey? If I was you, I'd be in San Francisco enjoyin' the good life."

"I'm trying to find the man who was my cabin boy," Cap

old him. "His name is Mike Wakefield, and he's driving a
coach, taking a young Chinese girl in search of her father."

"The girl's name would be Ku Xuan?"

"Aye. You've seen them then?"

Nodding, Lyons said, "I did indeed. They were here just a
couple days back."

"Do you know where they went?"

"I sent them to Paicines in search of Cougar Jones."

"Cougar Jones? Oh, yes, I remember him. He was a big
man; petty officer for the *Cassandra*, wasn't he? I heard he
left his shoes under a lot of Chinese beds. Is he the girl's
father?"

"I thought he might be. But then a Chinese man came in
early yesterday morning. Said he was her brother and he'd
found their father." Lyons scratched his head and studied
Cap. "I'm not sure I believe him, though," he added.

"Why not? Why would someone lie about such a thing?"

"That's exactly what I've been asking myself. And I couldn't
come up with any good reason. But I do know that I've got a
pretty good eye for people," Lyons explained, "as I'm sure
you do. You say you can't remember what it's like to have a
deck under your feet, but I'm sure you can remember what
it's like to command . . . how you can take the measure of a
man just by looking at him."

"Aye, that's something that stays with you."

"Then you'll understand me when I say there's something
about this Chinaman that didn't ring true. I've been sorry I
gave him a lead on her. I can't help but feel I may have put
the lass in danger."

"Why do you think that?"

"It's just a feeling I had—and there was something about
the tattoo he had on his wrist that stirred some old memory.
Actually, about the only thing keeps me from being too
worried about the girl's safety is that she's with Mike
Wakefield."

"Mike always was a good man—" he paused and laughed,
"even when he was a boy."

Pouring a cup of tea for himself, Lyons asked, "So you've
not seen Wakefield grown? He's a fine man now, true enough."
Lyons chuckled and told how Mike had dealt with the two
men who had bothered Ku Xuan and Lai Song.

"I'm that anxious to see him again that I've taken this trip to find him," Cap explained. "It'll be good to renew old acquaintances." Then he looked curiously at Lyons and asked, "You say that the man claiming to be the girl's brother had a tattoo?"

"Yes, on his wrist. It was a dragon. I told the other fellow about it, too."

"Other fellow?"

"Yeah, a fellow named Granger. He came in here late yesterday afternoon, looking for Mike Wakefield. He was sent by Wakefield's boss, Walter St. John, to catch up with the stagecoach. Seems St. John needs him back in San Francisco."

Cap grew quiet, sipping his tea thoughtfully. Then, anxious to be on his way, he stood up to leave. "So whereabouts can I find Cougar?" he asked.

Lyons told the old China hand about the letter postmarked Paicines. "I sure hope he's up for company," the tavern keeper chuckled, " 'cause he's getting a lot of it."

After the two men shook hands, Cap made his way outside to his horse. As he headed east out of Monterey, the prospector speculated about the two men Lyons had sent after the stagecoach. He briefly wondered about this fellow Granger's showing up; he thought it odd, since Walter St. John seemed to want Mike to take all the time he needed to find the girl's father. Then he decided that something must have happened after his visit with St. John that necessitated Mike's returning. Sending Granger after the coach made more sense than sending telegrams because St. John could not know where the travelers were heading next—which a man following them could learn as he went along.

That cleared up in his mind, Cap focused on the Chinese man. From the description of the tattoo, he knew that the man had to be a priest from one of the warrior disciplines. He had said nothing about it to Lyons, because he knew Lyons would not understand. Actually, he had never told anyone what he knew about the warrior priests, but he had once witnessed firsthand their awesome fighting skills, and even now as he recalled the event, it made him shiver.

Before Cap had fallen into disfavor with Lo Ching, the

Manchu prince had arranged for him to go into the village of
Tsingyan to conduct some business. Lo Ching had provided
him with a translator, a quiet man named Pin Chu. What Cap
did not know was that Pin Chu was more than a translator; he
was also a priest of Shan Tal.

While in the tiny village of Pehshan, Cap was at the well in
the village square, filling goatskins with water, and Pin Chu
was watching over their horses, which were loaded with
goods for trade. Suddenly a commotion was heard, coming
from the north end of the village, and Cap looked up to see
six bandits on horseback, riding at full gallop and brandishing
broadswords. Some of the male villagers rushed out to try to
stop them, and they were immediately cut down by the
slashing swords.

"Pin Chu!" Cap shouted in warning.

Instead of getting out of their path, Pin Chu positioned
himself between the horsemen and the caravan. The riders
advanced, screaming like the demons of hell and swinging
their swords in the midday sun, their blades red with the
blood of the slain villagers.

"You can't fight them!" Cap yelled. "Get out of their way!
Let them have the cargo!"

The horsemen moved closer together, intending to run Pin
Chu down. That was their mistake. As the two lead riders
passed, Pin Chu grabbed the halters of both animals and
jerked sharply, and the horses tumbled head over heels,
throwing the riders. The next two horsemen managed to
swing away to avoid collision, but they did not escape Pin
Chu. He let out a shout and leaped onto the back of one of
the horses, right behind the startled rider. A quick chop to
the rider's neck sent him tumbling to the ground, but not
before Pin Chu grabbed his sword. He then wheeled around
to face the remaining bandits. It was still three to one
as the bandits ringed around him, engaging him with their
swords.

The weapons clanged loudly, ringing like bells as the blades
crossed. Then Pin Chu suddenly leaped off his horse just as
the bandits on either side of him lunged. Their blades found
flesh—each other's—and they gasped in pain and surprise.
With a deft flip of his hand, Pin Chu unseated the last bandit
and dispatched him with a chop to the neck.

Cap, in complete shock, had watched the entire episode which had taken less than a minute. After it was over, Pin Chu calmly walked over to the well and took a drink of water from the dipper.

The villagers—every man, woman, and child—sank to their knees and kowtowed before him. Then one of them shouted a warning, pointing. The first two bandits, who had merely been unseated, were recovered now and had drawn their swords and started toward the well, brandishing them menacingly. Cap had a pistol in one of the saddlebags, and although he had not had time to get it out before, he started for it now.

Pin Chu continued to drink his water, allowing some of it to run down his chin, and took absolutely no notice of the bandits.

"Pin Chu!" Cap warned, digging frantically in the saddle bag for his pistol.

Just before the bandits reached the well, Pin Chu held his left arm out toward them, exposing the inside of his wrist. With his right hand, he held the dipper to his mouth, continuing to drink.

One of the bandits let out a shout, not of challenge but of terror. Throwing his sword down, he pointed to Pin Chu's wrist. Then he sank to his knees, crying and kowtowing. The other bandit threw away his sword as well.

Cap looked at the wrist and saw only a small blue chrysanthemum. Later he learned that it was the symbol of a priest who had been trained at Shan Tal. Curious about the order he questioned Pin Chu about it.

"What would happen if two priests from Shan Tal fought each other?" he asked.

"Two priests from Shan Tal would never fight each other."

"But surely there are other orders?"

"There is Shal Minh."

"Would a priest from Shan Tal fight one from Shal Minh?"

"Yes, for evil and good cannot occupy the same space," Pin Chu had explained.

"You mean Shal Minh is evil?"

"Yes."

"You have a chrysanthemum. What does a priest from Shal Minh have?"

"A dragon."

"What would happen if a dragon and a chrysanthemum had a fight?" Cap asked.

"One would live . . . one would die," Pin Chu said simply.

Riding through the twilight, Captain James Beckett spurred his horse. If the man seeking Mike Wakefield and Ku Xuan was indeed a Shal Minh priest, they would need all the help they could get.

Chapter Ten

It was nearing dusk the following day when Captain James Beckett reached the Indian reservation beyond the town of Paicines. As he walked toward Cougar Jones's adobe home, he looked forward to meeting with the former seaman—not just for the information Cougar might be able to give him about Mike Wakefield's whereabouts, but also to talk about old times. Having been good friends with the captain of the *Cassandra*, Cap knew Cougar from the days when the big man had sailed on that ship.

After a few minutes of raucous reunion, the two old salts sat at Cougar's table, and over a cup of coffee, Cap told him why he had come.

"So you see," he concluded, "now that I've had a run of good luck, I'm feeling better about the way things have turned out. I've had this desire to see my old cabin boy and let him know it's all worked out for me—and to see how things are going for him."

Happy to have someone visit him from his seafaring days, Cougar insisted that Cap stay and get a good meal—even stay the night—and reminisce awhile before he continued his search. "Fact is," Cougar told the former captain, "Mike and the girl believe you're her father. It turns out they've started lookin' for you as hard as you're lookin' for them. So you're bound to find them real soon."

"They believe I'm what?" Cap gasped. "What makes them think such a crazy thing?"

"Well, sir, I reckon they just put a few things together," Cougar offered. "First there was the vision, where the girl talked to her mama . . ."

"To her what?" His surprise was even greater.

Cougar explained about the peyote-induced vision Ku Xuan had had, during which time she had met and talked with her mother. Coming out of the vision, she had known to look in the bottom of a case she was carrying for a letter.

"Vision or no, letter or no, I absolutely cannot be that girl's father," Cap insisted, "and I'm surprised at Mike for letting her think such a thing. He knows what happened. He was there."

"You're talkin' about the execution?" Cougar asked softly.

Cap sighed, and a shadow seemed to come over him. "Yes," he finally agreed.

"Aye, I remember the execution, for it was the talk on all the ships," Cougar said. "But this letter that the girl found said your woman wasn't really executed."

"Dammit, man, that can't be true! I saw the execution with my own eyes."

"No, sir, you didn't," Cougar told him. "Truth is, I ain't real sure what did happen, but near as I can figure, you and everyone else saw just what Lo Ching wanted you to see. Your woman managed to get away; then she went up to the Shan Tal temple and had her baby up there. Accordin' to the letter, she died right after the girl was born. That girl's not only your daughter and a princess, she's also a Shan Tal priestess."

The prospector just sat motionless, a bemused grin on his face, letting everything sink in. Shaking his head repeatedly, he kept murmuring "I'll be damned" over and over. Suddenly he bolted up out of his chair and stared down at Cougar. "There's a Shal Minh priest after her!" he declared, his tone extremely agitated. "I've got to catch up with them and help them!"

Cougar put his hand on the man's arm. "Take it easy, Cap. Fact is, that guy showed up here earlier today, givin' me some cock-'n'-bull story about bein' Ku Xuan's brother." A sly grin split the old sailor's face. "Seein' as how he didn't know that I knew he couldn't be"—the grin faded—"not to mention I spotted that dragon tattoo on his wrist and remembered what it stood for, I sent 'im on a wild-goose chase." He paused and squinted at Cap.

"What is it?" the prospector asked.

"Well, I'm just wonderin' if I did the right thing when that other guy showed up."

"Other guy? You mean some guy named Granger?"

"Yeah! How'd you know that?"

Cap related everything that had transpired with Daniel
Lyons and then asked, "What exactly did you do with this
Granger fellow?"

Frowning, Cougar replied, "I didn't like his looks. He said
he was from Walter St. John's company, but I dunno . . . somethin' about 'im didn't ring true." Grinning again, he added,
"So I sent 'im after the Chinaman."

Cap roared with laughter. "I like your solution, Cougar. If
Granger's on the up-and-up, he'll be able to keep an eye on
the Chinaman—and if he's not, throwing him off the trail
gives me a chance to catch up with the stagecoach and tip the
odds a bit." Sobering, the former seaman peered at his fellow
China hand and said, "I trust your judgment, Cougar. If you
didn't like the cut of Granger's cloth, it's probably a good idea
to assume he's up to no good."

That night, as Cap lay in his blankets, still stunned by the
thought that he might have a daughter—a very beautiful,
intelligent daughter who was here in California—he searched
his mind for memories of the time in Canton, of the days with
Lo Pai. Odd, he realized. For years he had used liquor and
the solitude of the hills to help him avoid the memories, and
now he was consciously calling them up. And he discovered,
to his surprise, that the memories were no longer painful,
though they were somewhat bittersweet.

He turned over on his bedroll, putting everything into
perspective. Apparently there was a good chance that it had
not been Lo Pai who had been beheaded. How that could be
he did not know, but his former cabin boy had been witness
to the same terrible tragedy that day, and if the evidence was
powerful enough to convince Mike, then he was very interested in meeting this young woman.

Late the following afternoon, the Shal Minh priest sat on
his horse on a rise overlooking the road, just above a stagecoach station, and smiled. Heading his way, perhaps two
miles off, was a bright red stagecoach.

Up until this moment, Li Chen had been berating himself

for his stupidity. On the way to the town of Paicines, his carelessness had caused him to lose almost a full day's lead when, because he had not been watching, he had allowed his horse to step into a prairie dog hole. The animal had broken its leg, and Li Chen had had to walk for hours before arriving at a town. Then no one would sell him another horse, so he had had to kill a man and take his mount from him—and that had forced him to throw his pursuers off his trail by riding a circuitous route. And he should have known that the man named Cougar had not been truthful and had led him far off the trail of Ku Xuan. Fortunately, he had finally realized it, and he had decided that to continue trying to locate the stagecoach would be folly. Instead, he would return to San Francisco, and with the patience instilled by his Shal Minh training, he would await the inevitable return of Ku Xuan to that city, her only home in America.

Having therefore taken a shortcut to the road north, Li Chen found that his luck had changed. He had providentially intercepted the coach and was, even now, watching it move north with such speed and determination that he wondered whether the travelers might have identified, if not located, Ku Xuan's American father.

The Shal Minh priest had known all the circumstances surrounding Ku Xuan's birth, and from the beginning had known who her father was. He also knew that her father would not be aware of Ku Xuan's existence, because he, like everyone in Lo Ching's court and his subjects, believed that Lo Pai had been executed. Li Chen was probably the only man alive who knew all the events surrounding that fateful day in the courtyard over twenty years ago.

On the day Lo Pai had confessed to her maidservant that she was pregnant, a palace servant named Ho Fong had overheard the conversation between the two young women. He had learned in that same conversation that Lo Pai planned to leave Canton and go to California with her American captain. To a palace politician like Ho Fong, such news offered a golden opportunity, and intending to curry favor with Lo Ching, he hurried to carry the news to his prince.

What Ho Fong did not realize was that his information was Lo Pai's death warrant—and his own. Far from being rewarded, Ho Fong was put to death as the bearer of unwelcome news. Yet despite the man's execution, Lo Ching's problem with his daughter remained, for her disgrace was now public knowledge, and the prince would have to deal with it in such a way that the public would be satisfied.

Though not an official in Lo Ching's court, Li Chen, as a Shal Minh priest, had enjoyed a position of much power and respect. That had given him access to the innermost chambers, and using that access, he had moved stealthily and unobserved through the halls of the palace. He had been hiding outside Lo Pai's chambers while she and her maid had made preparations for the princess to join her American captain, and the priest became an eyewitness to what happened next.

"My lady, you cannot take so many things," Tsu Ling had whispered.

"So many things?" Lo Pai rejoined in exasperation. "How can you say I am taking many things? Look what is being left behind!" She waved her arms around her room. "I'm taking only these four trunks."

"But how will we get these trunks out to the pagoda?" Tsu Ling asked. "And how will your captain get the trunks from the pagoda to his ship? My lady, if you are going to do this thing, then you must realize that you are turning your back on what you are."

"But my dresses. And my jewelry."

"Are they more important than your love for Bic-kett?"

"No," Lo Pai agreed, shaking her head emphatically. "No, they are not more important. You are right—I am being foolish. I need none of this. I will leave it behind. I will leave it all behind, for it means nothing to me."

"And what about your responsibility as a princess of the Manchu?" a familiar man's voice suddenly asked. "Does that mean nothing as well?"

Turning around, Lo Pai and Tsu Ling let out a gasp, for standing in the door was Lo Pai's father. The two women fell to their knees and bowed low, touching their foreheads to the floor.

"So," Lo Ching said flatly, stepping into the room, "you would be leaving tonight with the *fan kuei?*"

"Yes, my father," Lo Pai said quietly. "I carry his child."

"I see." Lo Ching did not raise his voice or shout, but the

igns of great anger were visible. His dark eyes shone with an
nner fire, a blood vessel on his temple throbbed, and his
oice was as cold as ice.

Lo Ching walked over to gaze through the bedroom win-
ow toward the *fan kuei* captain's ship, riding majestically at
nchor. Undoubtedly at this very moment, Lo Pai's captain
vas aboard his vessel preparing for the long voyage back
cross the Pacific, unaware of the drama unfolding in the
alace.

"How is it you were able to see the *fan kuei* often enough
o come to this condition?" Lo Ching asked quietly.

"A matter of chance, father."

"No, you had to have help. Who helped you?"

"It was I who made the arrangements, Your Excellency,"
su Ling confessed. "I am a most unworthy wretch to have
inned against you so."

"So you are. And you will die for your sins," Lo Ching told
er, "as will Lo Pai and the *fan kuei* who has betrayed me."

"Father, I am willing to die, but spare the others. It was
ny crime, not theirs."

"You will not die alone," Lo Ching announced.

"Please, Excellency, allow me a word with you," Tsu Ling
egged.

"Why?" Lo Ching asked. "Do you wish to plead for your
niserable life? For if you do, I will save you the time. I will
rant no such plea."

"Then grant but a moment of time for one who has so little
ime left," the handmaiden asked.

Lo Ching sighed. "You may speak."

Out in the hallway, Li Chen slipped closer to the doorway,
he better to see and hear all that was occurring. He watched
s Tsu Ling reached up and took an amulet from around her
eck. Holding it in her hand, she extended it toward Lo
Ching, asking, "Do you remember, Excellency, when you
ave me this amulet? It was for breathing life into your
aughter, for when she was born, the spirit of life was not
elivered with her."

"I remember," Lo Ching murmured.

"You told me that I should keep it, that one day I would
ave a request, and if I made the request in the name of this
mulet, you would grant it, no matter what the request might
e."

"Yes, yes, I remember," Lo Ching declared impatiently. "And so now, you will ask that I spare you. Very well, I spare you your miserable life."

"Thank you, Father," Lo Pai said quickly, bowing to him.

"Yes, thank you, Excellency," Tsu Ling said. "And now trade my life for the life of my lady and her American captain."

"No!" Lo Pai gasped, and she put her arms around Tsu Ling. "Father, please, do not make such a bargain with her."

"You do not have to worry, for I cannot make such a bargain," Lo Ching assured her. "Such a thing as you have done cannot be kept quiet. Soon, all the people will know that my daughter betrayed me. I cannot let you go free. The people expect your execution. To do any less would be to betray their trust."

"Excellency, I know a way to save your daughter and satisfy the people," Tsu Ling suggested.

Lo Ching stroked his chin and looked at Tsu Ling for a long moment. "Tell me this way," he finally commanded.

"Say that you are going to execute her," Tsu Ling explained, "and lead a woman to the chopping block with a veil over her head. After the execution, personally claim the body for a royal burial so that no one will realize that it was not Lo Pai, but someone else."

"This someone else," Lo Ching asked, "will it be you?"

"Yes, Your Excellency."

"Tsu Ling, no!" Lo Pai cried.

"Daughter, do not interfere!" Lo Ching ordered harshly.

Tsu Ling looked at Lo Pai with a sweet smile on her face. "My lady, do not stop me from doing this glorious thing. For my one, insignificant life, I can prolong the lives of three others. Yours, Bic-kett's, and that of the baby yet unborn."

"But I cannot let you do that," Lo Pai insisted.

"Do you wish the baby and your *fan kuei* to live?" Lo Ching challenged.

"Yes, Father," Lo Pai said, weeping now, "but I don't wish Tsu Ling to die."

"She must die. I have no other choice. The laws of the land must be obeyed."

"But what will become of me afterward?" Lo Pai asked.

"You will go to the Shan Tal Temple," Lo Ching told her. "There you will stay for the remainder of your life, never to reveal your identity to anyone, never to contact me or be contacted by me again. The child, when it is born, will be taught by the priests of Shan Tal, and it will become a priest . . . never to be made aware of its noble heritage."

Lo Pai put her arms around Tsu Ling and sobbed. "I don't want you to die."

"She must. And you will write a letter to your *fan kuei*," Lo Ching ordered. "Explain to him that you have a responsibility to your class and to your people. Tell him you will not meet him and that you never wish to see him again."

"That won't stop him from coming to see me."

"That is too bad," Lo Ching said coldly, "because if he does come, I shall have to have him killed."

"Perhaps I can stop him," Tsu Ling suggested. "He trusts me. I can deliver the letter and assure him that the letter is genuine. You can spirit away Lo Pai to the Shan Tal cloister, and I will then dress in a royal gown and, as Lo Pai, go to my execution."

"Very well," Lo Ching agreed. "It will be done."

The Shal Minh priest had never shared his knowledge of the events of that day with anyone, until the time seemed opportune to inform the warlord who had overthrown and killed Lo Ching that the prince had a living descendant. He knew that the warlord—plagued by revolutionaries who would use the existence of a princess as a rallying point—would offer Li Chen a fortune, even by the standards of a Shal Minh priest, if he would find and kill the only person who could threaten his rule.

Li Chen had accepted the job; now he would complete it.

As he guided the stagecoach north, Mike Wakefield could barely suppress his excitement in anticipation of finding James Beckett. He was careful, though, to spare the horses, and when he pulled over to give them a chance to rest briefly, he called down to Ku Xuan, who, with Lai Song, was riding inside the coach for this part of the journey.

"After we reach the next swing station and change teams," Mike said, "we could go on and make it as far as San Jose by nine tonight. We could eat and take lodging in a hotel there, then start out again for San Francisco first thing in the morning."

"I *would* like another bath," Ku Xuan admitted, "although I am anxious to find my father, now that we know who he is."

"I have to warn you. I've been looking for him off and on for several years without success, so even though we at least know now who we're looking for, it still may not be easy to find your father."

"Oh, Mike, do you think we *will* find him?" Ku Xuan asked anxiously.

"Oh, yes, we'll find him all right," Mike promised. "We'll find him if I have to personally walk up every river, stream, and creek bed and climb every mountain in California. I'm absolutely certain he's prospecting in these parts, and I've heard several reports about a man who fits his description." He looked at her and grinned. "Besides, I have a lot more reason to find him now. I'm going to tell him to come out of the hills and get cleaned up, because he has to give his daughter away in marriage."

"Mike, are you happy?" Ku Xuan asked.

Grinning, he shouted, "I've never been happier in my life!" With a loud whoop and a flick of his whip, Mike started the horses onward.

Riding hard, Captain James Beckett saw the cloud of dust some five miles off in the distance and hoped it was the stagecoach bearing Mike Wakefield, Ku Xuan, and Lai Song. He estimated that they would be reaching a swing station soon, which meant they would be stopping to change horses—as would he. Perhaps they would stop long enough to eat as well, which would give him the chance to catch up with them.

Spurring his mount, he rushed to close the distance between the travelers and himself.

"Well, I'll be damned!" Granger exclaimed when he saw the stagecoach.

Feeling frustrated and angry over being led on a wild-goose chase by the seaman back at the reservation, Granger had decided he had no choice but to go back to San Francisco, to try to pick up his intended victims' trail there. Having ridden over rough terrain to the main road, he had come up over a hill and suddenly seen the stagecoach just a few miles away, heading north. He could catch up with it, pick off the driver, and then take the Chinese girl that Wo Hamm wanted. He spurred his horse, hurrying the animal on. It had been a long, hard chase, and by God, Wo Hamm had better make it worth his while . . . or he might just decide to see what some of Wo Hamm's possessions were worth.

Leaving his horse tied to a tree, Li Chen made his way down the rise and entered the swing station. He had long since learned that the stagecoaches always stopped to change teams, so all he had to do was wait a few minutes, and Ku Xuan would be delivered into his hands.

The Shal Minh priest pushed his way through the door, taking the unarmed young station manager by surprise and felling him with one swift blow.

Li Chen believed he had killed the young man, so he wasted no time in checking to be sure. Positioning himself by the door, he closed it almost all the way, leaving an opening just wide enough to peer through, and waited. With every passing minute, the drumming of horses' hooves and the clacking of the wheels became louder. Then the coach pulled in front of the station, and he heard the driver calling for his team to halt.

Peering through the doorway, Li Chen watched as the driver climbed down from the coach and started walking toward the station building. Timing his move perfectly, he flung open the door and shot out his foot, kicking the driver in the head just as he stepped onto the porch, knocking him unconscious. Then he ran over to the coach.

He assessed the two young women, both of whom were dozing. One looked so much like Lo Pai that it was a simple matter to determine that she was the Manchu princess.

"Please get out, Ku Xuan," he called inside.

The young women inside the coach sleepily opened their eyes. When they stepped out, they seemed surprised to see the Chinese man. Looking toward the small adobe building, they cried out at the sight of the driver's crumpled form.

"He cannot help you," Li Chen informed them, deliberately holding his arms up in front of him. Ku Xuan gasped when she saw the dragon on his wrist, and Li Chen smiled. "Yes, I am a priest of Shal Minh."

The handmaiden cried out, her fear showing clearly on her face.

"It will be all right, Lai Song," Ku Xuan told her soothingly. Then she started to go to the driver.

"Stop!" Li Chen ordered.

The young woman obeyed. "I am concerned about my driver," Ku Xuan told him. "May I see to him?"

"You may send your handmaiden if you wish, Your Highness."

Ku Xuan was obviously surprised by his address. "You know about me?"

"Oh, yes, I know about you. That's why I have come to kill you."

Suddenly Lai Song lunged at Li Chen, a small knife in her hand, and the priest knew that had her intended victim been anyone other than him, her attack might have been successful. As it was, however, he dropped her with one sharp blow to the neck.

Moving so quickly that she caught Li Chen by surprise, Ku Xuan launched herself into a forward cartwheel, catching him in the chin with the bottom of her foot. She lashed out with all her strength with a blow that would have broken the neck of most men. But Li Chen was not like other men, and although the blow stunned him, he recovered quickly.

With a shout, he aimed a blow toward Ku Xuan, but with an acrobatic leap, she managed to avoid most of the force of it. Li Chen's thrust left him somewhat off-balance, though, and Ku Xuan managed to hit him in the side of the head with the heel of her palm. Again it was a good, telling blow—but again Li Chen took it with no reaction.

There was no element of surprise left now for either one of them, and like participants in a macabre dance, the two Chinese fighters circled each other. With a shout, Li Chen suddenly thrust forward, slashing out with the edge of his right hand, but Ku Xuan leaped up and did a flip over the top of his head, landing on the ground behind him. The blow from his hand, the one meant for Ku Xuan's neck, went through a panel of the stagecoach, cutting through it as though it were soft butter.

Spinning like a ballerina on one foot, Ku Xuan kicked out with her other, catching Li Chen in the middle of the chest, and he smashed through the hitch rail. When the woman leaped toward him to follow through, the priest managed to grab her foot and flip it up. But Ku Xuan obviously knew to go with the energy to keep from having her leg broken, and she did a complete back flip from his throw.

Ku Xuan wound up on the ground and Li Chen tried to follow up on his advantage, but she rolled to one side and kicked out at him again, striking him in the knee. The priest stoically accepted the pain, refusing to acknowledge that it was the most telling blow of the fight thus far and the first time she had managed to injure him.

Obviously hoping to capitalize on his injury, she jumped to her feet and moved in quickly, swinging at him. But he easily parried her swing and lashed back. For a moment the air was filled with the swishing sound of their arms and hands as they thrust, parried, and counterthrust.

An onlooker would have thought that the man would make quick work of the woman, but while Li Chen had the advantage in strength, Ku Xuan was quicker and more graceful, and she managed to hit him often. One of his eyes was swelling shut, his nose trickled blood, and the bottom half of one of his ears was torn loose. But the priest could tell that he was growing tired of parrying and avoiding his blows, and if he connected just once, it would be the end.

Suddenly the handmaiden moaned, and Ku Xuan's concentration was broken for an instant. That instant was all Li Chen needed, and with a shout of triumph, he sent his flat palm smashing toward her head. She managed to move so as to catch the blow with her shoulder, but the shock obviously passed all through her fatigued body, for she went down. Leaping beside her, Li Chen put his foot on her neck and looked down at her.

"Now," Li Chen declared in Chinese, "all I have to do is twist my foot and your neck is broken. Good-bye, Your Highness."

"No! Good-bye to you, worthless dog!" a man's voice suddenly shouted in Chinese.

Startled, Li Chen looked to his right and saw that the driver had regained consciousness and was standing with a revolver in his hand. The priest dodged just as Mike squeezed the trigger. The shot missed Li Chen, but it distracted him from Ku Xuan.

The Shal Minh priest suddenly had a throwing star in his

hand. With a flick of his wrist, Li Chen sent it spinning toward the driver, but the young man knew from experience that a gunfighter never should stand in the same spot after his first shot, and he was already dropping and rolling as the star hurtled through the air. The weapon buried itself in the station porch railing as the driver fired a second time. This time he did not miss, and the bullet caught Li Chen in the chest.

Throwing his hands to his wound, he sank to his knees with blood spilling from between his fingers. He looked up at Ku Xuan, who was just now regaining her feet, and rasped, "It was a good fight. My sister taught you well."

"Your sister?" Ku Xuan cried. "Do you mean Mata Lee was your *sister*?"

"Yes."

"But the men who killed her . . . you knew them?"

"I sent them," Li Chen said flatly.

"But how? How could you do that?"

"She was Shan Tal. I am Shal Minh," Li Chen told her, as if no other explanation was needed. He took a few more raspy breaths and then fell forward on his face.

Watching carefully, Mike held his pistol ready for another shot if necessary. Suddenly he noticed the stationmaster staggering groggily toward him and Ku Xuan.

"Wakefield, it's you—what happened . . . someone must have hit me. . . ."

Mike could see that the manager had indeed been struck hard, though he seemed to be recovering. He was about to holster his weapon and assist the young man when he heard a new voice off to one side.

"Drop the gun, Wakefield!"

He turned to see Cole Granger walking toward them, his pistol aimed at Mike's chest. He was grinning wickedly.

"Well, now, I'm glad to see you took that chink out of the picture," the outlaw said. "He's been causin' me more trouble than I wanted to handle. And this way, all the money will be mine."

"All what money?" the driver asked.

"Why, the reward," Granger informed him. "Seems someone in China's willing to pay a lot of money for this little girl's hide, and I aim to collect it."

"Mike, who is that man coming up behind this one?" Ku Xuan asked in Chinese.

A graying, bearded man was moving stealthily toward Granger. Answering her in her language, Mike told Ku Xuan, "It's been a long time, and his hair color's changed and the beard's been added, but I'd recognize Jim Beckett anywhere. That's the man we've been looking for."

"My father?"

"Yes."

"What's all the jabberin' about?" Granger demanded. "You think talkin' chink is goin' to let you get somethin' over on me?"

"We were just discussing the man who's sneaking up on you," Mike informed him levelly.

Cap was holding an ax handle and raising it over his head.

"Haw!" Granger exclaimed, laughing loudly. "You think I'm goin' to fall for that old trick?"

"Maybe you should have," Cap declared from behind him, bringing the handle crashing down on the outlaw's head.

Ku Xuan rushed over to Lai Song and found that her friend was coming to, and Mike and Cap ran toward each other and hugged each other.

"Ku Xuan, come here," Mike called. "I want to introduce you two."

As she walked toward them, Cap's eyes widened and his face twisted in confusion.

"Lo Pai? My God . . . it can't be!"

"Lo Pai was my mother," Ku Xuan told him softly.

Cap ran his hand through his hair. "Yes . . . yes, of course she was. When Cougar told me that you thought I was your father, I didn't see how it could be. I still don't know how it can be, but when I look at you and see Lo Pai, I have absolutely no doubt." Grinning with delight, he then said, "I understand you have a few questions you want answered before you can be sure."

"What lies beyond the inner door of the golden pagoda?" Ku Xuan asked.

"Beyond the inner door of the golden pagoda, there is a little room, a private prayer room for the princess—and it was where I sometimes met Lo Pai."

"What did the garden jasmines hide?" Ku Xuan asked next.

"A secret passageway," Cap answered. "It was to be used

as an escape route for the royal family should there ever be a revolution. Not even the palace guard knew of it. It was also the passageway I used to sneak in and out of the grounds to meet with your mother."

"Who is Tsu Ling?"

"Tsu Ling was Lo Pai's handmaiden." Cap smiled. "Have I answered all your questions?" he asked.

Tears welled in Ku Xuan's eyes. "Yes, my father."

"Now *I* have a question," Mike announced. "Do you have any idea why we were looking for a man named Big Cat?"

"That's all you had to go on? That's how you started this search? Looking for a man named Big Cat?" Cap asked, astonished. Then he burst out laughing.

"You're awfully amused," Mike noted wryly. "Does that mean you know something about it? Who Big Cat is?"

"I am," Cap confessed. "You see, whenever Lo Pai or Tsu Ling said my name, Beckett, it came out Bic-kett. That sounds a lot like Big Cat, so that was the Chinese ideogram they chose for my name."

"Well, you certainly led us on a merry chase," Mike said with a laugh, putting his arm around Ku Xuan and pulling her close to him.

"Now just a minute; just a minute, here," Cap declared in mock seriousness. "Young man, that's my daughter you're fondling, and I would like to know exactly what your intentions are."

"My intentions, sir?" Mike tilted Ku Xuan's face up to his and kissed her. When their lips finally parted, Mike looked at his former captain with a big smile on his face. "That's an easy question to answer. My intention, Cap, is to become your son-in-law. I plan to marry this girl."

"Is that true, daughter? You're going to marry this man?"

Ku Xuan looked deep into Mike's eyes, her mouth curled into a satisfied smile. "Yep," she answered, giving her best imitation of Western American, "I reckon I am."

STAGECOACH

STATION 41:

RED BUFFALO
by Hank Mitchum

It is July 1886, and the Reverend Del Harrigan is riding a stagecoach to a small town in southern Dakota Territory called Red Buffalo. Wishing to live simply and peaceably, the former army captain has left Philadelphia to become the pastor of a small church. He quickly learns that the West is still wild as he and his fellow stage travelers are threatened by hired gunmen wanting to kidnap one of the passengers. Harrigan wards off the gunmen, only to become the object of a female passenger's affections. The lady is a card dealer who takes him for a gambler.

But his greatest challenges await him in Red Buffalo. Harrigan falls in love with the newly widowed local schoolteacher and campaigns to win her trust and her heart. However, his newfound happiness is jeopardized when the lady card dealer, feeling spurned, plots to destroy not only Harrigan's budding love but his reputation.

When a Sioux chief threatens to wipe out the whole town of Red Buffalo to avenge the murder of an aged Indian, it falls on Harrigan's shoulders to prevent the slaughter. In the midst of a blazing prairie fire, he must reclaim the trust of the woman he loves and fulfill the promise of a new life—for himself and for his town.

Read **RED BUFFALO**, on sale May 1989 wherever Bantam paperbacks are sold.